A Howling *in* Brooklyn

Luciano Di Giallonardo

NEWMAN SPRINGS PUBLISHING
320 Broad Street
Red Bank, NJ 07701

First originally published by Newman Springs Publishing 2023

ISBN 978-1-63692-538-7 (Paperback)
ISBN 978-1-63692-539-4 (Digital)

Printed in the United States of America

To my late parents, who died before the book was published.
Mom, Dad, I hope I made you proud.

PROLOGUE

In a dark room, someone spoke. "Where do I begin?" Darkness turned to light. A man sat in a room, both hands handcuffed to a black table. Coffee cups sat on the table, some finished and some not. He looked straight at them. His eyes were bloodshot from a lack of sleep, his dark hair messy and out of place. He had not shaved for days. He was exhausted and drained. He was wearing a dark T-shirt and jeans. The room was lit by a single light above him. The walls were dark-red brick with a single barred window to the left. He kept looking at the window and back.

A voice in front of him spoke. "What are you looking at?"

The man, looking ahead, said, "Is it midday? What time is it?"

A male voice replied, "Why? Do you have to be somewhere tonight?"

The man yelled, "Just tell me the time!"

A second voice spoke. "Calm down. It's twelve thirty in the afternoon. Are you okay with that?"

The man dropped his head and took a gulp of air. "Thank God. I hate to have this conversation at night."

A second voice spoke. "Why are you afraid of the dark?" He giggled.

The man glared at the second man.

The first man said, "Okay, okay. Both of you, relax. Do you know why you are here?"

"I should know. I used to be the one sitting where you guys are and did the interrogating myself."

The first man replied, "Very good, detective. One more question. What day is it?"

"It's November 1."

"Very good, detective. Now that we have cleared that up, let's begin. Tell us what happened last night."

"I honestly don't remember," the man answered.

The first man said, "You don't remember any of the events from last month. Are you kidding me? This is a very serious situation. Your career and pension are on the line! If you don't tell us something, you will lose it all, and that I guarantee you, detective!"

"I've already lost so much. What's the point now?"

The second man said, "The point is that only we can decide your fate, depending on whether you tell us the truthful events of last month or not. My god, the entire neighborhood wants to pin a medal on you. They even started a GoFundMe to bail you out. They think you're a hero."

"I'm not a hero."

"Okay, so you're not. But you have been under the radar since all this got started, so I ask you again, what happened and why? Don't leave out any details because I promise, if you do, this will be a very long night for you."

The man looked up, eyes wide open. "We can't do this all night. I'll talk. We have to get this done before nightfall. The moon will be out tonight, and I cannot have that!"

The first man said, "There is no full moon tonight. It will be cloudy with a chance rain."

"Cloudy? But my charts—"

"For the love of God, are you going to give us the weather report now?" the second man interrupted.

"Hey, calm down," the first man said. "Sorry, he gets a bit agitated when he hasn't eaten. Okay, detective. So what's it going to be?"

With his head down, he again took a deep breath. The he looked up and said, "From the beginning?"

"Let's hear it, then."

"From the beginning." The first man turned on the digital recorder and leaned over to turn the DVD recorder.

Satisfied, he took a deep breath, looked at them both, and began. He closed his eyes, and his mind went back, way back to another time in his life before this hell started.

*****

My name is Detective Daniel Marco. My friends call me Danny. I was born on June 16, 1985, and raised in Brooklyn, New York. I'm thirty-three years old. I'm six foot four inches and weigh 247 pounds. I was raised in Dyker Heights, Brooklyn.

My girlfriend's name is Marie Marconi. My parents are Peter and Ellen. They own a family pizzeria, which my grandfather opened, called Marco's Pizza. I have two sisters, Mrs. Gina Marco-Dolori, and my younger sister is Theresa Marco.

As far back as I can remember, I've always wanted to be a cop. My childhood friend Paul Corillo and I, at thirteen years old, made a promise to become police officers for the NYPD. It all started one day on our way home from school. We stopped by the local store near where we lived on Seventy-Second Street and Thirteenth Avenue.

I was in the mood for a candy bar. We walked into the store. There was no one up front, and we didn't know what to think. Then at the end by the coolers, we heard people talking.

"I don't think we should be here," said Paul.

"Wait," I replied. "Listen."

The voices grew louder and louder. Then we heard, "You knew I was coming today, and you don't have anything for me? I take that as an insult."

I slowly walked around the shelf and saw the store owner. It was Mr. Chin Lei. He was the friendliest guy ever. This was his store, and he was proud of it, but the two guys, one in front of him and one behind, were not so friendly.

"When we come, you pay. You don't pay, then there is a serious problem. Do you understand?"

The second guy behind Mr. Chin gave him a punch in his lower back.

Mr. Chin was in pain by the sound of his voice. He was sixty years old, and these guys looked like they were in their thirties.

"Come on," whispered Paul. "We can't be here."

But I refused to leave. I wanted to help. Paul was scared, and so was I. But we couldn't move. Then I heard, "Next time we come, you better have something for us. Understand? No more excuses."

"I understand," said Mr. Chin.

"That's good. We understand each other, Lei. That's very good. Now we can move on. Let's go up front."

As they turned from the cooler, the three of them saw us. Mr. Chin turned white.

One of the two guys with him said something in his ear, and Mr. Chin smiled at us as they came to the front.

"You boys should not be here. Please go home to your family."

The guy next to him said, "Yeah, kid. You both go home before your parents start to worry." He smiled at me and Paul. Paul was speechless and scared.

I looked up at the guy and said, "Why were you hitting Mr. Chin? What did he do to you?"

Mr. Chin's eyes just looked me, and his expression said, *Shut up!*

The second guy said, "Beat it, kids, and now."

The other guy responded, "Easy, Vince. Is that the way you talk to your kids? I'll handle this." Addressing us, he continued, "Don't worry about him. He's not such a pleasant guy."

This giant of a man walked closer to me, knelt down, and looked at us. "So what're your names?"

Paul quickly spoke. "Don't tell him, Danny." Paul was so nervous that he just told them my name.

The guys started laughing. The man looked at me and said, "That is friendship." Then he said, "Listen, Danny, what you saw was not what you think. I will just be straight with you. You and your buddy didn't see a thing. Forget what you saw and forget us. Move on, and everyone is happy. Okay?"

"Okay," said Paul.

He laughed again, and so did his buddy. Then he looked at me with a serious look and said, "Do you understand, Danny?"

I looked at him, then at Mr. Chin and the other guy. I looked at Paul and then back at the guy and said, "Yeah, I understand. I didn't see a thing."

The guy smiled. "Good. I like it when people understand." He stood up, reached into his pocket, took out two twenty-dollar bills, and gave them to us. "Put it in your piggy bank," said the tall man. "Now, boys, please go home and remember what I said."

Paul grabbed me by the arm and said, "Let's go, Danny." He pulled me back. "Let's go!"

I never took my eyes off the tall man as I walked backward. When we were outside, walking past the store window, I kept my eyes on the tall guy until he was gone.

As we walked closer to my house, I looked at Paul and said, "Can you believe this? He gave us twenty dollars to be quiet and not say anything."

Paul looked at me and said, "I think we should listen and move on."

I looked at Paul. "This is our neighborhood. We can't live like this. What if they hit my grandfather's pizzeria? Then what? Maybe we can't do anything now, but we can when we grow up."

"What did you have in mind?" asked Paul. "Beat them up when they're old?"

"Paul, when we grow up, we will be cops. And we will protect our neighborhood from guys like them. Let's make a pact, Paul." I extended my hand to see if Paul would agree.

He smiled and said, "Well, the chicks do love guys in a uniform." We both giggled. "I'm with you."

We made a pact and shook hands.

As the years passed, Paul and I graduated from the police academy. As a police officer, I've seen so much garbage and the worst low-lifes during my days on patrol. I've made arrests, raided drug havens, and cleared traffic accidents. I tried to settle disputes and sometimes over parking.

On the job, I gave it 100 percent. I didn't back away from anyone, no matter the situation. I did my job. All the hard work promoted me to detective along with my childhood friend, Detective

Paul Corillo. We were like brothers, and we were always there for each other.

I lived in a good neighborhood, on Thirteenth Avenue and Bay Ridge, with good people who looked out for one another. And they loved the fact that a cop lived in the same neighborhood.

The stores were nearby, and there were trains and buses for easy transportation. The locals were good, hardworking people supporting their families. Then you had the nonlocals who preyed on these people and the store owners, making collections, the same type of guys Paul and I saw when we were kids.

If you didn't make a payment, they hurt you, and if you still didn't make a payment, they hurt a family member. You know who these guys are. They never worked a day in their life, and they think they own you by fear. They were the wise guys, mob men with no care for human life.

I've crossed paths with them on the job, but nothing serious until now. They all worked for Don Ginetti. The guy was a ruthless animal with so many people in his pockets. No one spoke against him. If you did, no one would ever see you again. He had beaten every charge against him and walked away with a sick smile. He was always two steps ahead of us, and we couldn't figure out why. Maybe he had a source in the NYPD who was feeding him information, but the only problem was we never found out who it was or if we were wrong.

His nickname was "the Untouchable Don." But soon everything changed the day these bags of garbage walked into my dad's pizzeria. What happened to me in Pennsylvania would change my life forever, and nothing would ever be the same again.

CHAPTER 1

It's October, my favorite month. I love October because at the end of the month, it's Halloween. I loved trick-or-treating with my sisters and Paul. And now I get to see these little kids trick-or-treating in new costumes that would make a nun faint. I also love watching horror movies. Marie thinks I need to grow up. But hey, it's only once a year, and I love to scare her when I get a chance.

*****

It was 9:00 p.m., and playing on the TV was an old black-and-white movie. "Prepared to be scared as we present *Frankenstein Meets the Wolfman*, starring Bela Lugosi and Lon Chaney Jr."

A figure walked away from the TV and toward the bathroom. Someone was taking a shower. A hand reached for the doorknob and slowly opened the door.

A woman was taking a shower. She heard the door open. "Danny? Is that you?" Smiling, she said, "Well, if you are going to come in, remember it's my shift tonight at the hospital."

A hand pulled back the shower curtain. To her shock, she saw a man wearing a werewolf mask. She screamed, and the man took off the mask. It was her fiancé, Danny Marco, scaring her to death. He started laughing. Frustrated, she got angry and said, "How many times have I told you to cut that shit out? And yet you still do it. Are you trying to give me a heart attack?"

Laughing, Daniel Marco tried to console her. "Baby, I'm sorry. I just could not resist. The look in your eyes was priceless." He continued laughing.

Marie gave him a cold look that could kill. "Get the hell out of here before I pull off a Norman Bates!"

"Come on, honey. I'm sorry."

Marie looked at him. "Get the hell out of here now!"

"Okay, you don't have to tell me twice." Danny was still laughing before he closed the door. Turning, he said, "Can I leave Wolfie with you?"

"Danny!"

He shut the door. He walked back to the couch, wiping tears of laughter from his eyes, and sat down to finish watching the movie. The phone rang, and he answered. "Danny?" It was Paul Corillo, his longtime friend since childhood. "Well, did you do it?"

"Yeah, and she is not talking to me, again."

"I told you not to, but you never listen. You insist on doing things that you think you have to do."

"Yeah, I know," said Danny.

"Well, did she get scared?"

Smiling, Danny replied, "She screamed bloody murder." They both laughed.

"You are one sick bastard." Both were still laughing. "Well, just keep away from her, or she will pull off a Norman Bates on you."

"What? She said the same thing. Are you both talking behind my back?" They were both laughing again.

"Listen, buddy, your big day is coming soon. I'm getting everything ready for you."

"Now wait, Paul. You don't have to throw me a bachelor party. We talked about this."

"Yes, we did. And we agreed to have this party for you."

"We?"

"Yes, we, friends from the precinct, our guys from the neighborhood. A nice going-away party."

"Very funny," said Danny.

"Hey, it was Marie's idea too."

"What?" exclaimed Danny.

"She practically begged us to do this for you."

"I think she might be trying to get me out of the house," Danny said, laughing. "Hey, she may be having a party of her own."

"Look, Danny, we've been friends forever. Let me do this for you. You had my back so many times. It's the least I could do for you."

"Okay, you win."

"Great! We will pick you up Saturday morning at nine o'clock."

"Saturday morning?" asked Danny. "Where the hell are you taking me?"

"That is for me to know and you to find out, which you won't, detective. Pack up and get plenty of sleep tonight. We have a long road trip."

"Road trip?" echoed Danny.

"Come on, Danny!"

"Okay, fine."

"We'll see you Saturday morning."

"Just don't forget the beer," Danny added, laughing.

"And do me a favor. Leave that stupid mask home."

"Fine. Anything else, Dad?"

"Yeah, I can hear the TV. What are you watching?"

"Oh, it's a classic, *Frankenstein Meets the Wolfman*."

"I had to ask. I just hope you don't watch this shit when you are married."

"It will be a short one if I do," said Danny.

"See you Saturday 9:00 a.m. sharp. Night, buddy."

The door opened from the bedroom, and Marie walked out, ready to go to work at Maimonides Medical Center. Danny got up. "Are you still mad at me?" he asked, arms wide open.

With a smirk, Marie replied, "How can I be mad at a jerk?" They both started laughing. Then they hugged and kissed.

"I really wish you didn't have to do this night shift."

"Danny," said Marie, "weddings are not cheap. We need the money."

"Babe, we don't need to have a huge wedding."

3

"Hold it right there! My sister Patricia had a big wedding, and I think I deserve one too. Your mom wants to see a big wedding for us. Do I have to tell Gina?"

"No no no! Don't you dare say anything to my sister, especially this. Her voice can wake the dead, and I won't hear the end of it."

"Then it's settled. Our wedding will be magical."

"I just love magical things," said Danny.

"You jerk," replied Marie, laughing. "Come here." She gave him a kiss. "Will see you tomorrow, and please watch something other than this."

He got the remote and gave it to her. "Okay, find another channel."

She changed the channel. "There, this is perfect. *Law & Order*."

"What are you trying to say, Marie?"

"See you in the morning." She got her coat and car keys and left.

He looked at the TV and thought, *Law & Order? Like I don't see enough of this.* He changed the channel back to what he was watching. Before he sat down, he looked out his window and noticed a dark figure across the street. It seemed to be looking at him. He turned away from the window, waited a second, looked back, and saw the dark figure again. He pulled back. Concerned, he went to his desk and took out his badge, a mini flashlight, and his Glock 19. He checked to see if it was loaded and put it in his waist pocket.

He went to the front door. He slowly looked out the front-door window and saw that the dark figure was still there, looking into his window. He decided to go out the back and surprise this mystery person. He slowly opened the back door, pulled out his gun, and looked around. Seeing that it was clear, he slowly walked up toward the front. He took out the mini flashlight as he got closer. He stopped toward the edge and pulled out his gun. In one quick motion, he stepped out, pointing both flashlight and gun.

The dark figure was gone. He looked up and down the street and behind every vehicle. Nothing. He put his gun back in his side pocket, turned off the flashlight, and went back inside.

A mysterious figure was watching him, but Danny didn't notice it. This mysterious figure was breathing hard, almost like a growl. With a pair of glowing eyes, this figure focused on Danny until he went to the back and closed the door.

Danny returned to his window again. The dark figure was gone. He made sure the front door was locked and let it go.

Danny sat down in his recliner and watched the horror movie. Halfway into the old black-and-white film, a scene came up where the wolfman was walking in a foggy dark night, looking for his prey, when suddenly he stopped and looked directly at Danny. Confused, Danny thought it might be part of the scene. Then the wolfman pointed his finger at Danny and started to talk in a growling voice: "Danny!" Danny was startled. He looked around to see if maybe Marie was playing a joke on him, but he didn't see her. He looked back at the TV.

"Danny," the growling voice said again. "Listen to me very carefully. You have been chosen. Soon you will be given a gift that has been passed down for generations, and you will be one of us!"

Danny spoke back. "What gift? What are you talking about?"

"Silence! Accept this gift! Embrace it! Use it! Don't fight it! It will be part of you, and you will be part of it. Tell me you will accept it."

Danny was confused and scared. He didn't know what to do.

"Tell me you will accept it!"

Danny stared at this wolfman talking to him from his TV. He rubbed his eyes, sweat running down his forehead. His heart was racing. "Oh God, Marie was right. Why do I watch this crap?"

"Crap? This your destiny! Danny, you will experience power and hunger like you never felt before. Accept it!"

Danny was frozen.

"Accept it! Accept it! *Grawwwww.*"

Danny woke up and jumped out of his recliner. Looking around and rubbing his head, he took a deep breath and started to giggle. "A dream. Oh boy, it was a dream. Ha!"

He looked down at the TV to see that very same scene again. Danny quickly turned off the TV.

*****

Saturday morning, October 6

Paul arrived with other officers: Lt. Frank Mano, Sgt. Tony Messina, and police officer Raymond Amato. Danny waited outside and watched as they pulled up to the curb of his house. Danny started laughing.

"What are you laughing at?" said Tony Messina as he opened the window.

Danny looked at them and said, "I never thought I would be picked up by the Sopranos."

"Very funny." Paul got out of the driver's seat and walked toward Danny. "Why do you always have to be a wiseass?"

"'Cause I'm from Brooklyn."

They all laughed.

"Come on. Let's go."

Danny grabbed his overnight bag, put it in the trunk, and got in the front seat. "Hey, Paul. Before we go, we need to make a stop."

"Here we go," remarked Frank Mano.

"Danny, we need to get moving before traffic builds up."

"Guys, let's just stop by my parents' pizzeria."

"Why?" asked Raymond Amato. "Do you need to tell your mom where you're going?"

"Nah," said Paul. "He wants to tell his dad he is not getting cold feet and not skipping town."

"Are you guys done? Seriously, are you guys done?"

"We're just busting your chops, Danny. Relax," Paul replied.

"Okay, I just wanted to stop by there 'cause my dad made us six pizza pies and hot Italian heroes. But if you guys prefer Chinese—"

"You heard the man. Let's go!" Raymond Amato interrupted.

Paul shook his head and drove off in his black Dodge Charger.

*****

It was a sunny day at Marco's Pizzeria. Danny's father, Peter Marco, was making the delicious fresh pizza while his mother was attending to the customers. His younger sister, Theresa, was helping her parents while attending Brooklyn College. His older sister would usually come by later in the day while her kids were at school.

"I've never seen it this busy, Mom," Theresa exclaimed.

"Hey, I'm not complaining, and neither is your dad."

"Are you both gonna talk or work?" Peter asked.

"So grouchy you are," Ellen replied.

"I'm Calabrese. What did you expect?"

"Yeah, and I'm Sicilian, so what's your point?"

They laughed and kissed each other.

"A marriage made in heaven," said Theresa.

Their laughter turned to shock when the door opened and three men walked in.

"How you doin', *paisans*?" said Nicky Ginetti, nephew of mob boss Salvatore "the Don" Ginetti. Nicky stood there in his dark-blue tracksuit, white T-shirt, gold chains, and slicked-back hair. His two friends had the same look.

Theresa went to stand by her mother as Nicky walked up to the counter to talk to Peter Marco. He leaned on the counter and said, "Well? How you doin'?" No response. "Well, I usually get the same thing back!"

Some of the customers got up and left. Peter looked at him and said, "What do you want?"

"Hey, that's no way to speak to a fellow *paisan*."

"You are not a *paisan*. You're a fucking insult to our community," replied Peter Marco. "I will ask you again, what do you want?"

Looking at his two friends and smiling, Nicky said, "We just came in to get something to eat. This is a pizzeria, right? You serve customers, and we are three paying customers."

Theresa said, "Sorry, but we don't have dog biscuits. Try the pet shop next door."

"Theresa!" her father yelled out.

Nicky put both hands to his chest. "Oh god, that hurts." He turned to his friends. "Guys, didn't that hurt?" Then he looked back at Theresa. "That's funny. I gotta remember that one. Really very funny." He laughed. "You got a smart mouth on you. What else can your mouth do?"

Ellen was shocked, and Theresa was ready to tell him off the Brooklyn way. Peter leaned into Nicky from the counter, but Nicky's boys stepped in.

Nicky spoke. "Relax. Everyone, relax. Nothing bad. It's all in good fun."

Peter looked at him and said, "Will you get the hell out of here?"

Nicky looked at him. "I just wanted to get some pizza for me and my friends. Pizza and three drinks."

"And then will you guys leave?" said Peter.

"Cross my heart and hope to die, stick a needle in my eye," said Nicky. He and his friends all laughed. Peter got three slices from the tray and put them in a box while his wife got three drinks. Theresa went into the back kitchen.

"That's $7.50, please."

"What? You didn't warm them up," Nicky remarked.

"It tastes better cold since you have a cold heart!"

Nicky looked at him, took out ten dollars, and said, "Keep the change." He gave the pizza box and drinks to his friends. He leaned into Peter, smiled, and said, "Peter, *paisan*, did you get a chance to think about my business proposal? It would benefit us and benefit you more."

Peter's face turned red. His wife, Ellen, was standing behind him, scared and shaking. Peter leaned in from behind the counter, face-to-face with Nicky. "Listen to me, little boy, 'cause that's what you are, a little boy living in a man's body trying to impress his uncle. You come into my business, which my father built with blood and sweat, while you guys never worked a day in your life and expect me to go into business with a jerk like you? And then you run your

8

mouth with these two pieces of garbage thinking they got your back 'cause little boy Nicky can't fight his own battles. You're pathetic! Why don't you get out of here before your mom wonders where you are!"

Nicky's face turned red as he clenched his fists. His two friends knew what was coming. Nicky looked at Peter dead in the eyes and said, "You got some balls talking to me like that!"

Peter responded, "At least my balls are not in my uncle's mouth!"

Nicky's eyes widened. He grabbed Peter by the shirt, but his boys tried pulling him back. Ellen yelled, "Stop it!"

That was when the door opened, and Danny Marco walked in, along with his fellow officers. "Take your hands off my dad, now!"

Nicky let go, put his hands up to his chest, and said, "Easy, Mr. Police Officer." Smiling, he added, "It's all a misunderstanding. Right, guys?" His two friends agreed, laughing. "I was talking to your dad when he looked like he was about to fall. Maybe something on the floor made him slip, and I stopped him from falling."

Danny looked at his dad and his terrified mother, who was shaking. Paul and the other three officers told the two guys to step outside, escorted them out the door, and asked for their IDs. Paul came back in to stay with Danny.

Nicky looked at them. "Well, I got my pizza. You police have a doughnut day, okay?" he said with a smirk.

Danny grabbed his arm and took him to the men's room. Paul followed. When Danny saw his sister come out of the kitchen, he instructed, "Go stand with Mom and Dad, now!"

Danny, Nicky, and Paul walked into the men's room while the other customers left. Paul locked the door. Danny was livid.

"Hey," said Nicky, "I said it was a misunderstanding. No need to get rough." He looked behind him, at the toilet bowl. "What? You gonna watch me take a shit?"

"Shut your mouth and sit down!"

Nicky looked at the toilet. "You want me to sit on that?"

Danny forced him to sit down. Looking down at Nicky, he said, "You don't talk. Just listen to me very carefully." He pointed at Nicky. "Don't you ever, *ever* touch my dad again! Don't you ever come back here again. Don't you ever disrespect my family, and don't you ever disrespect Marco's Pizzeria. This is my grandfather's legacy. He worked very hard to make his dream come true for his family, not for you. Do you understand?"

Nicky turned away, saying, "Yeah, whatever."

But Danny grabbed him by the chin and forced him to look at him. Paul said, "Danny?"

"I got this, Paul!"

"Hey, will you get your friend off me?" Nicky asked.

Danny slapped his face. Paul could not believe what he just saw. Nicky's face turned a deep red.

With his other hand, Danny took out his badge and held it up to Nicky's face. "See this, Nicky?"

"Yeah, it's your badge!"

"Very good. Then we understand each other. Don't you ever come back here again. I will arrest and lock you up for harassment, and you will be taking a piss with Bubba up your ass! So what's it going to be?"

"Fine. You won't see me here again."

Danny stood next to Paul, looked down at Nicky, and started to laugh. Paul started laughing with him. Nicky was confused. "What's so funny?"

Danny looked down at Nicky. "Tell me, Nicky, you ever get those bad stomachaches that's so bad that you have to go to the bathroom and take a shit?"

"Well, yeah, so what's your point?"

"I'm getting there, so shut up and let me finish. After you take your dump and all that horseshit comes out of you, Nicky, you get up and flush all that lard down the toilet. But not all of it goes down. There is that one little crust of shit that will not go down but instead floats by itself, hoping to get out before it drowns and goes down the drain."

Nicky's face turned red. Danny looked at Paul. "Paul, you know what I'm talking about?"

"Yeah, I know." Paul was smiling.

Danny turned back to Nicky. "You see, Nicky, that piece that didn't go down is you, trying not to drown before you sink in. And that's what you are, a piece of shit!"

Nicky turned dark red, but he knew he couldn't do a thing. Paul and Danny were laughing. Nicky gave a smirk and said, "Ha. That's funny."

Paul looked at Danny and said, "Oh no, there's no toilet paper."

Danny responded, "No worries. This asswipe doesn't need toilet paper."

At the front, Peter was with Ellen and Theresa and the three other officers. They looked to the left and saw Danny with his arm around Nicky's shoulder, followed by Paul. Paul was trying to keep a straight face. Lt. Frank Mano looked at the other officers and said, "I can't wait to hear how this turned out."

As they got closer, Danny looked at Nicky and said, "You see, Nicky, open communication is so important, don't you agree?"

"Yeah, I guess."

"I knew you would agree." He took his arm off Nicky's shoulder. "Bye, Nicky." As Nicky started to walk out, Danny said, "One more thing, Nicky. Wait."

Nicky looked up and turned around. "What?"

"When was the last time you took a shower?" Danny's mother put her hand to her mouth and turned away, along with her daughter. His father, Paul, and the other officers were smiling.

"What's that supposed to mean?" asked Nicky.

Danny started rubbing his hands and smelled his shirt. He looked at Nicky and asked, "How much cologne did you put on? What? You just opened a bottle of Stetson and poured it all over you? You smell like a bad onion."

Paul and the others were trying to hold it in.

Nicky looked at them. "Yeah, sure," he replied with a smirk. "Can I go now?"

"This is a free country, Nicky. You could have left anytime you wanted."

Nicky looked at him and went out the door, where he bumped into Danny's older sister, Gina. Nicky looked at her and stepped to the side.

Gina said, "Next time, say 'excuse me,' you fucking little shit!"

Nicky stopped, eyes wide open and ready to explode, until his friends came up and grabbed him. They left.

Gina walked in, and they looked at her and started laughing. "What the fuck was that all about?" Everyone started laughing hard. Theresa came around to explain to Gina what had happened.

"Danny, you crazy bastard," said Paul. "You pissed him off."

Tony Messina laughed. "He's probably jumping up and down going home."

Danny's family came around the counter and gave everyone hugs. While Danny was hugging his mother, he caught someone from across the street staring at them. Then he realized it looked like the dark figure from last night. He turned away to hug his father, but when he looked back, the figure was gone.

*****

Walking with his two friends, Nicky was steaming mad. "I am going to shove my foot up his ass." He tried to turn back, but his two friends stopped him.

"No, Nicky. Let it go. He's a cop, and we don't touch cops or their families."

"These fucking rules suck!" said Nicky. "Things need to change!"

"Nicky, you want change? Then speak with your uncle."

"You make a move on that cop without his approval, and it will come back to bite your ass."

"All right, I know where my uncle is. Let's go."

They looked at each other, worried, but they went along.

*****

Driving on the Verrazano-Narrows Bridge that connected Brooklyn to Staten Island in a black Dodge Charger, five men were laughing hysterically over what had just happened at Marco's Pizzeria. Paul was driving, Danny was on the passenger side, and the other three were in the back.

"Oh Christ, that was just insane funny," said Tony Messina. "You told him he was that piece of shit that would not go down? That has to be a classic!" They all laughed.

"But the best part was when Gina walked in, and they bumped into each other, and she called him a piece of shit," said Paul Corillo from behind the wheel. Laughter erupted again. "Yeah, but I'm not too comfortable going away after what just happened."

"I hope he doesn't bother them again," said Danny.

"Don't worry," replied Lt. Frank Mano. "I've called the district and explained what happened. They will keep eyes on the pizzeria."

Danny turned around. "I hope there is no daily police presence. That will really make my mom nervous."

"Don't worry," assured Frank Mano. "All plainclothesmen. They won't even know they are cops."

"Yeah, just one thing," added Raymond Amato. They looked at him. "Just make sure the men's room has toilet paper." They all started laughing again.

On the Staten Island Expressway, Danny saw signs for the 440 going to the Outerbridge Crossing to New Jersey. "We're going to Jersey? Atlantic City! You guys are great! Gambling and beer, what's better than that? Plus, we got pizza and heroes we can eat at the hotel before we go gambling," said Danny with a smile. He looked at Paul and looked behind at the other three. They were not speaking. Paul had a smile on his face. "We are going to Atlantic City, right?" asked Danny.

"You didn't tell him?" asked Ray Amato. The three in the back started shaking their heads.

"If I told him, he never would have come, and then we would have had to tie him up," answered Paul.

"Where the fuck are we going?" asked Danny.

"Marie made it very clear, no Atlantic City. You're both saving for your wedding, and that's all she needs for you to blow your money away at the poker table," Paul explained.

Shaking his head, Danny said, "So did Marie plan everything for us? You know, a Tupperware party?"

All the men laughed, except for Danny.

"Relax," said Raymond Amato. "Just sit back and enjoy the ride."

Danny sat back and said, "Okay. We have come this far, so might as well."

Then Frank Mano declared, "I really have to go to the bathroom."

They all started laughing as the car drove over the Outerbridge Crossing.

*****

Sitting in the back of a parked black BMW 6 Series was Nicky Ginetti. He was neither laughing nor smiling. He was entirely in anger after what had happened at Marco's Pizzeria. He replayed in his mind how he was insulted and disrespected by Detective Danny Marco, how he had called Nicky a piece of shit. The anger was building up when there was a knock on the side window. Nicky was startled and opened the back window.

One of the men who was with him, Lenny G, said, "Come on, Nicky. We've been here for twenty minutes. He's been waiting for you."

Nicky opened the door and stepped out. It was twelve o'clock in the afternoon. They were parked outside the Il Colosseo restaurant in Bensonhurst, Brooklyn. The men walked in. It was still early in the day, and the restaurant was not yet busy with customers looking to dine out. They walked in. Toward the left, two well-dressed men were enjoying a meal and drinking wine. One of them got up as Nicky and his men walked toward them. He gestured for them to stop and backed up to another man sitting behind him. This man was well-dressed in the finest suit money could buy. He was wearing a well-tailored suit and was clean-shaven. He had thinning hair and dark features with a cold look. Nicky was waiting impatiently to talk to him, but he knew better. He had to wait until this man was ready.

The man was sitting in his chair reading the sports section of the newspaper. He was holding a small spoon in a cup of hot espresso, his eyes focused on one section of the sports page. He put down the newspaper and said, "Fucking Red Sox! I had five grand on this game." He took a sip of the espresso and put the cup down, then looked up and saw Nicky. He said, shaking his head, "Well, nice of you to finally come in! It's not like I had anything better to do than waste my fucking time waiting for your fucking presence!" This man, sixty-nine years old, was Salvatore "the Don" Ginetti, the Untouchable Don.

He signaled for his guard to let Nicky pass. "Sit down," said the don. "As for you two, go to the bar and get a drink." They looked at Nicky. "Did you two not hear what I said?"

"Go," said Nicky to his friends. They went to the bar. The other man sat back down to finish eating. "Uncle Ginetti," said Nicky, "we have a problem."

"We have a problem?" repeated the don. "Not we, you. You have a problem with following my authority!"

"What? You know?" asked Nicky.

Slamming his hands on the table, the don said, "What the fuck is that supposed to mean?" Nicky was shaken and nervous. "I know everything that goes down. I have eyes and ears everywhere! Whatever is going down, I know. Anywhere, anytime, anyplace, I know! I know for a fact you went to Marco's Pizzeria when I specifically told you not to! The owner's son is a detective for the NYPD. I told you to stay away. We don't screw with anybody related to any cop. It's not good for us and not good for business. Why don't you ever fuckin' listen to me? Talking to you is like talking to a corpse." The don sat back in his chair. "So I guess things didn't go well, did it?"

Nicky started telling him what had happened, including after he had left. The don brought a finger to his forehead, rubbed his eyes, and started to laugh.

Confused, Nicky asked, "What the fuck is so funny?"

The don looked at Nicky. "What's so funny? Detective Marco called you a piece of shit! That's what's so funny." Nicky's face turned white, and his mouth hung open. "Serves you right! A little humiliation goes a long way, my nephew."

Nicky tried to say something, but Don Ginetti raised his hand to stop him. "I am going to say this once again and for the last time, Nicky. You are never to go back there again. You break my rules again, and for the love of God, I will forget you are my sister's son, and I will beat the fucking shit out of you. Capisce?"

"Yeah, capisce," replied Nicky.

"Good. Now get the fuck out of here and go home so I can finish my espresso in peace."

Nicky got up to leave but turned around and slammed his hands on the table, startling the don. "Uncle Ginetti, this is pure fucking bullshit. These old rules have got to go. We need to set new standards! People need to fucking respect us and be taught a lesson regardless of who they are! If you are not going to change this, then it's time for new blood to step in!"

Don Ginetti got up and shouted, "Who the fuck are you to talk to me like that? What are you telling me?"

Hands up, Nicky said, "No disrespect, Uncle Ginetti, but I think you should step down."

The men at the bar started choking on their drinks. "You guys, outside now!"

They left. Nicky started to speak.

"Look, Uncle, I know I am wrong, but—"

Don Ginetti grabbed him and pushed him against the wall. "You disrespectful fuck! How dare you! Take a step down? You have been watching too many reruns of *The Sopranos*. It doesn't work like that. I didn't become Don Ginetti 'cause of my good looks, you ass. If word gets out about the way you spoke to me, I wouldn't be able to show face anywhere. All the other bosses would think I'm a pussy, and then they will start to question me. And if that happens, then the real problem begins, and worrying about a fuckin' pizzeria will be the last thing on your mind. We have rules to follow! Breaking these rules will be our downfall. Am I getting through to you?"

"Yes, Uncle, yes. I was just pissed off. I won't say it again. I promise."

"And what else?"

"And I promise I won't go back to Marco's."

The don let him go and straightened out his suit. He looked at Nicky and smiled. Then he gave him a kiss on the forehead. "Listen, Nicky, you are my sister's son, and I love you. Please do not disrespect me again, and don't ever challenge my authority again."

"Okay, Uncle. I'll get out of here."

He turned to leave, but the don stopped him. "No, Nicky. Wait. Can you do me a favor, please?"

Smiling, Nicky replied, "Anything, Uncle. What is it?"

"In the men's room, someone flushed the toilet after taking a crap, but all that shit didn't go down. Go get the plunger and clean it out, and then you can leave."

Shocked, Nicky asked, "You're joking, right?"

"Do I look like I'm joking? Go clean the fucking toilet now!"

Red faced, Nicky turned toward the men's room and went in. He was not happy.

Don Ginetti, satisfied, sat down and resumed drinking his espresso before he slammed the cup down. "Fucking cold!" He turned to the waiter in the kitchen. "Hey, *un espresso caldo!*"

*****

Raymond Amato drove the black Dodge Charger through the Garden State Parkway to New Jersey; he replaced Paul Corillo as the driver after their last stop so Paul could rest his eyes. In the passenger seat, Danny Marco had fallen asleep and was dreaming. But in his dream, strange things were happening beyond what should happen in dreams. It was almost as if he were being contacted telepathically, as if someone or something was trying to tell him something that was about to happen.

In his dream, he saw a fire in the middle of the ground. It was dark, surrounded by a thick cover of trees. In his dream, he looked up at a vibrant full moon. No stars, no dark clouds, just a full moon. He saw dark figures around the fire, and suddenly he was the fire! He felt no burning pain, yet he saw these dark figures around him.

He couldn't make out how many there were, but they were there, standing with their arms raised and chanting words he could not understand.

In the car, his closed eyes were moving from left to right, something called rapid eye movement (REM). It was as if he were following things that he was seeing in his dream. Then suddenly one dark figure approached him, and the dark figure spoke. It had a woman's voice.

Speaking in a ghostly manner, she said to him, "Danny Marco, you are the chosen one. Our visions have shown us that someone with great strength and courage will come and join us. We are reaching out to you to let you know we are waiting for you, and the gift you will receive will give you power and strength like you've never experienced. This gift has been passed down from generation to generation. And now it is your time. Join us, Danny Marco. Join us, and we will grow stronger, and soon, very soon, you will see that we are to mate. It is written that we must. It is our destiny to mate, and we will grow. I await you. Come to me. Come to me."

As the dark figure approached him for the first time in his dream, he saw the red color of her eyes and heard howling! He woke up, startled and confused. His heart was beating so fast it felt like his chest was about to explode.

"Easy, Danny. Easy," said Raymond Amato. "What did hell were you dreaming?"

In the back seat, Paul Corillo answered, "Guys, it's obvious. He knows he's getting married, and Marie has him on a tight leash."

They started laughing.

"You guys are a barrel of laughs." Danny looked to see where they were. He saw a sign up ahead. Exit 20 to I-476 Allentown, Pennsylvania. Danny said, "Pennsylvania? What the hell? I demand to know where the hell we are going, and don't tell me to relax! Enough with the bullshit already!"

"Danny, calm down," said Sergeant Messina. "That's an order! Just take a deep breath and relax."

Paul Corillo added, "Danny, sorry for all the secrecy, but would you have come if we told you?"

"I guess not," said Danny. "Sorry, guys."

"We are just about at our destination," said Frank Mano.

Raymond Amato turned onto a bumpy dirt road that shook the car. Danny held on until he saw dark trees on both sides of the dirt road. No light posts, nothing. Danny started to think of his dream until they reached a lone dark cabin, well-built, with a large garage and surrounded by more trees. He saw a satellite dish, a power generator on the side, and floodlights that were still turned off. He saw pieces of thick-cut logs and a huge outdoor kegerator.

"So this is the surprise? You took me out here to Pennsylvania in the middle of nowhere instead of gambling?"

"Danny, this was my grandfather's getaway retreat when he needed peace of mind away from the city," said Lieutenant Mano.

"It's peaceful and relaxing. And with the dish, you can watch all the porn you want. And Marie said—"

"Oh, enough with what Marie said," said Danny. They all laughed.

"With all the bullshit we deal with at the district, we need this, brother."

Danny laughed. "Sorry, guys. I appreciate this. It sucks we came all this way for a weekend."

"Who said it was for a weekend? Danny, being a lieutenant has its privileges," said Lieutenant Mano. "We will be here for a couple of days until we get tired of looking at one another's asses. I have everything squared away with the district."

"You guys are the best," said Danny.

They stepped out of the car, got their belongings from the trunk, and entered the cabin, not realizing that they were being watched from a distance by two dark figures.

A female voice came from one of the dark figures, saying to the other in a ghostly fashion, "Now it begins."

Danny looked out the window and could not shake the feeling that he was being watched.

They settled in.

CHAPTER 2

October 7, Sunday, 8:00 p.m.

The men were relaxing, watching sports on TV and eating the pizza and heroes provided by Danny's father at Marco's.

"The food is so delicious," said Paul Corillo. "The sauce and cheese, everything is so delicious and filling."

"Marco's is the best," said Danny Marco. "And we appreciate our customers." They all started laughing.

"One thing," said Paul Corillo. "What do we eat tomorrow?" They looked at one another.

"Well, we can always hunt," suggested Frank Mano. They all laughed again. "Don't worry, guys. We won't go hungry. The freezer is filled with steaks, bread, and anything else you like. I made sure of it, and the kegerator is filled with beer and anything else you want. We will be fine."

"You thought of everything," said Tony Messina.

"Well, we want to have a good time and relax. Right, Danny?"

Danny did not respond. He was in another world, thinking of the dream he'd had of that woman with the red eyes and the sound of howling. It felt so real to him, but he could not understand if there was a connection with the first dream of the talking werewolf. Both dreams were telling him that he was the chosen one. And then there was the dark figure watching from his home and at the pizzeria. Since yesterday, he felt like he was being watched. Was there a connection? Or was his mind playing tricks on him?

And then there was the woman in his dream telling him they were to mate and that she was waiting for him. There was so much going through his mind when he felt a punch on his left arm. Startled, he came out of his deep thoughts and looked up to see Paul Corillo.

Paul had punched him on the arm to wake him up. "What the hell is wrong with you?"

Danny looked to see the others looking at him with concern. "Why did you hit me?"

"Danny, we were trying to get your attention, but you were in another world," answered Frank Mano. "We said your name several times, but you were gone. That's why Paul hit you so you could snap out of it. Where did your mind drift to? You were really gone."

"I'm sorry, guys, but I'm just not myself," Danny responded. "Something has been bothering me since we left."

"If it's your parents, don't worry about them," assured Ray Amato.

"Yeah, Danny, try to enjoy yourself," added Paul. "Penny for your thoughts." He started to laugh to get the rest laughing, and it worked.

"Say goodbye to your single life, Danny boy," joked Frank Mano. They all laughed together, and Danny joined in.

Paul laughed, but he knew something was wrong. "Danny, come with me into the kitchen please. Let's have a chat."

"Paul, I'm all right. Seriously, I am," replied Danny.

"Danny, in the kitchen, now," demanded Paul.

"Well, someone is in the doghouse," said Ray Amato. And they laughed.

Danny got up and walked with Paul into the kitchen while the others resumed watching sports.

Paul looked at Danny. "Listen, Danny, don't bullshit me. We've known each other since childhood, and I can read you like a book. I know something is wrong with you, so please don't insult my intelligence by telling me nothing is wrong. Please tell me what the fuck is wrong. You were so gone tonight I was thinking of shooting my revolver just to wake the fuck out of you! Now what's wrong? Are you really getting cold feet and having second thoughts? What is it?"

"Okay, okay, Paul, but after I tell you what's going on, you will think I am totally nuts."

"I knew you were nuts the first day I met you," said Paul, laughing. "Okay, then, I'm all ears. So what's bothering you?"

Danny took a very deep breath, looked at Paul, and started from the beginning. He shared the night in his apartment when he saw a strange figure watching him from his window, and how when he went to go check, it was gone. Then while watching an old horror movie about Frankenstein and the wolfman, he told Paul he fell asleep and dreamed that one scene where the wolfman looked at him and told him he would be given a gift that had been passed down from generation to generation.

He then told Paul about the day at his father's pizzeria with Nicky Ginetti. After Nicky left, he mentioned seeing the strange dark figure from across the street, and then it was gone. Finally, when they were driving to the cabin, he had the dream of standing in a firepit and a female voice from a dark shadow telling him he was the chosen one, that soon he would have great power, and that they were to mate. Then the female came up to him, and he saw her red eyes and heard a howling that startled him awake. And now, when they arrived at the cabin, he had the feeling that he was being watched.

"Well?" said Danny. "Paul, this is what's been bothering me all day. Now I told you everything. So, Paul, what do you have to say to that?"

Paul leaned on the kitchen counter, arms folded, and stared at Danny with a confused look.

"Paul?" said Danny. "I know it sounds insane—trust me, I do—but it feels so real. And please don't tell me I watch too many horror movies, Paul. I'm telling you, for some reason I feel like something bad is going to happen to me!"

Paul was speechless and confused. Trying to fully understand and make sense of what Danny had just told him, he was at a loss for words. His longtime childhood friend actually believed everything that had happened to him, that something was really going to happen to him. Finally, his mind cleared up everything he had just heard, and he said, "Are you out of your fucking mind? Really? Do you honestly expect me to believe this bullshit?"

The guys in the living room heard Paul yelling and looked toward them. Danny looked at them and at Paul. He shook his head and raised his hands. "Paul, you just don't get it. There are just too many coincidences going on, and I know it sounds crazy."

Paul raised his hand to stop Danny. "Enough. Please, enough!" Danny shook his head. "Danny, I love you like a brother. We have been through so much, and we fought back. We have seen some strange crap on the streets of Brooklyn, and we were able to make sense of what was going on. But, Danny, what you just said to me makes no sense at all! If people find out what you just said to me, it would ruin you and your career, and worse. Now I don't know if it's the wedding jitters or if, yes, you are watching too many horror movies, which I think you are. Whatever the case is, you need to get over it and fast. Your wedding is coming up soon. Marie is the best thing that has ever happened to you. For the love of God, man, don't blow it. You will regret it. Am I getting through to you, Danny?"

"Yes, Paul. Yes, I understand," said Danny. But in the back of his mind, he was still convinced something bad was going to happen to him.

"We need to forget this conversation ever happened and move on. But you need to work this out and clear your mind. Please, Danny!"

"Okay, Paul. Okay. You don't have to tell me twice. I get it."

They both took a deep breath, turned around, and went back to the living room.

"Everything okay?" asked Ray Amato.

"Yes," answered Paul. "He just didn't know if he should use Viagra on his wedding night."

They all started laughing. Danny smirked and looked at Paul. "You asshole."

Paul slapped him on the back. "Come on, Danny. Sit down and let's finishing watching the game."

They sat, but Danny's focus was on the window. He still could not shake the feeling he was being watched. Paul noticed Danny staring out the window. From outside, a pair of strange ghostly eyes were looking at Danny, accompanied by heavy breathing.

*****

Meanwhile, back in Brooklyn at Marco's Pizzeria, it was almost closing time. The last of the customers were leaving, saying good night to Peter and Ellen. "What a busy night," said Peter Marco, wiping the sweat from his forehead.

"Yes, it has been busy," replied his wife, Ellen. Behind the counter, Peter was cleaning up. Ellen walked up to him. "Peter," she said.

Peter looked up, still wiping the pizza counter. "Yes? Are you okay?"

"I'm fine, but I wanted to ask you. How much longer will you be doing this?"

"This?" Peter asked, confused.

"Peter, you are here from morning till closing. I never see you take a break, nor have I seen you take a day off."

"Where is this coming from? What are you trying to tell me? Is it because of what happened this morning?"

"Yes and no. This morning with Nicky Ginetti was scary. Thank God Danny and Paul arrived just in time. But it's the other things. We haven't taken a good long vacation for a while. You are working yourself so hard, and I feel you are going to burn out just like your father."

Peter looked at her, then walked around the counter with a smile and his arms out to her. Smiling, Ellen went to him, and they hugged. "Listen, honey," Peter began. "I will not burn out. I promise you. And yes, we are long overdue for a vacation, and I promise you we will take that trip to Italy and visit family. We have a lot to prepare before we go on vacation. Danny and Marie are getting married soon. After they are married, we will make plans for our vacation."

"You promise?" said Ellen.

"I do."

They kissed and hugged again. Ellen felt a bit relieved, and they continued to clean up before going home.

*****

Walking out of the Bay Club in Brooklyn, New York, Nicky Ginetti got in the back seat of his black BMW with two ladies he had picked up. His two goons were in the front seats. His dark hair was slicked back. He was wearing the best Italian clothes, a dark silk shirt, dark pants, and gold watch. His arms were around the two ladies.

"Well, ladies, the night is still young and energetic," said Nicky. "Are you ladies interested in a private party?"

One of the two gorgeous ladies replied, "Depends what type of party and who else will be there."

"Just us three," said Nicky, smiling and laughing. He was intoxicated from all the alcohol he drank. Both women laughed. "Ralph," said Nicky, "let's go to my special place." The driver smiled, and so did the other man as they drove off.

On the road, one lady said that she was hungry and wanted to know if they could stop to pick up some food. Nicky replied, "I don't know if any place is open now. There should be food at my place." He was smiling at both ladies.

The other lady responded, "We are not too far from Marco's. Let's go there."

Nicky's smile turned to anger. "Stop the car!" The women were startled and moved away from him. "I said stop the fucking car now!" Ralph parked the car, confused. "Both of you bitches, out and go home!"

"What?" said one of the ladies. "What's wrong? You ran out of Viagra?"

"Get out of my car and go home, bitches!"

Disgusted and upset, they got out and started walking away while calling Nicky a prick dick.

"What the hell is wrong?" asked Ralph.

Nicky pointed right. "The next block is Marco's. Let's go there now!"

"No!" protested Ralph. "Your uncle said to stay away." But before Ralph could finish, Nicky jumped out of the car and started running toward the pizzeria. "Come on," said Ralph to Bobby. "This is not good!"

"Don Ginetti will explode if he finds out."

Nicky Ginetti was fueled with alcohol and complete rage. The events at Marco's, the humiliation by Danny Marco and his family, and his uncle Don Ginetti ordering him to stay away had reached a boiling point. His face was red, his skin pulled back from his nerves, sweat going down his forehead, as he made his way to Marco's Pizzeria. He was in such a rage that he did not hear his two bodyguards yelling for him to stop until he reached Marco's.

Inside Marco's Pizzeria, Ellen Marco was cleaning up before they closed for the night. She was startled as the door opened wide and in came Nicky Ginetti, breathing hard, sweating, and beet red, his fists clenched. Ellen screamed, "What the hell are you doing here? Get out!"

From the kitchen came Peter Marco, hearing his wife scream. He rushed to his wife and stood in front of her while Nicky's goons came in, also breathing hard and in shock. "Get the hell out of here, Nicky, now!" screamed Peter Marco.

"I'm not going anywhere, old man, until you learn to respect me," said Nicky. Ralph grabbed Nicky by the arm, but he pulled back. "Don't touch me," said Nicky.

Ellen was scared and shaking. "Peter, I'm sorry. I didn't lock the door."

"Don't worry about it," replied Peter. "Go to the kitchen and call 911 now!"

"Nobody is calling no cops," said Nicky as he pulled out a gun. Ellen screamed.

"What the fuck do you want, you...you little prick?" said Peter.

"You are going to learn to respect and to watch your mouth when you talk to me because I am new blood here. I am the new school. The old school is dead, and you will be too, so watch yourself, old man! Your son is not here to save your ass now! As of tonight, this is my pizzeria!"

Peter was scared for his wife, not knowing what was going to happen. "Nicky, get the hell out of here now, you little shit!"

"You're fuckin' drunk!" Ralph tried again to calm Nicky down. "Nicky, let's get out of here now before things go south. Your uncle warned you not to come back here, remember?"

"We are not going anywhere," said Nicky, "until this prick learns to show respect." He pointed his gun at Peter. Ralph tried to grab Nicky's arm again, but Nicky turned and said, "You guys wait outside now!"

Peter saw the opportunity and lunged for Nicky's gun, and they both struggled to beat the other. Ellen was screaming. Bobby and Ralph were frozen until they both tried to pull Nicky and Peter away, which seemed like forever, until they heard a single gunfire.

"Oh God! Oh God!" screamed Ellen. As the men pulled away from each other, Nicky looked down at his bloodied silk shirt and then at Peter. Peter's shirt was soaked with blood too, and then more blood started coming out of his mouth. He looked down and fell to the floor hard. Ellen was screaming, "Peter! Peter! Oh God, no, Peter. You shot my husband, you bastard!"

Nicky looked down, blood on his shirt and gun in his hand. Ralph grabbed the gun, and Bobby grabbed Nicky. "Let's get the hell out of here now," said Ralph. They pulled Nicky out of the pizzeria and into the car. Ellen was still screaming for help, kneeling beside her husband, Peter Marco. Blood flowed out of him and onto her, his face pale and sad. Ellen got up and called 911.

"Nine-one-one, what's your emergency?"

"This is Ellen Marco of Marco's Pizzeria. My husband has been shot! Please help! Please help."

Speeding away in his black BMW, Nicky Ginetti, shirt covered in the blood of Peter Marco, was in shock at what had happened. He was unable to speak as he looked behind him at the pizzeria.

"Nicky? Nicky? Nicky!" said Ralph.

But Nicky Ginetti was in a state of shock and inebriation. He stared at the blood on his shirt.

"He's in another world," commented Bobby as he drove the car. "Call Don Ginetti now!"

"Oh, dear God, this is a nightmare," said Ralph. "And it's going to get worse." He stared at his cell phone nervously, and then called Don Ginetti.

At his home in Bensonhurst, Brooklyn, the Untouchable Don Ginetti was relaxing in the family room drinking a glass of wine, when his phone rang. He looked at his cell and answered, "Hello. Who is this?"

"It's Ralph, Don Ginetti. We have a serious problem." Ralph started to tell Don Ginetti the events of that night.

Don Ginetti's face turned red. He was shocked. "Where is he? Good. Get him over to the warehouse and stay out of sight! I will meet you there in an hour." He threw his cell phone on the floor. "That little fuck never listens!"

"Salvatore?" asked his wife, Josephine, coming from the bedroom. "What's wrong?"

"What's wrong?" retorted Don Ginetti. "Your fucking nephew is an idiot. That's what's wrong! I'll be back later." Don Ginetti went to change his clothes while thinking of the mess his nephew had just caused the family. "God fuckin' help us." Knowing that his nephew had disobeyed his order to stay away from Marco's Pizzeria, his face was angry as he looked into the mirror.

At the same time as these events were happening in Brooklyn, it was close to midnight in Allentown, Pennsylvania. In the cabin in the woods, five men were relaxing on the two sofas and watching the sporting events on the satellite dish. Danny Marco was sitting on the recliner with his feet up and shoes off, looking at his watch and back at the TV.

"Does someone need their beauty rest?" asked Paul Corillo, smiling at Danny while the other three laughed.

"You guys are a barrel of laughs," retorted Danny Marco.

"Danny?" said Paul. "We need more beer."

"Okay," replied Danny. "Why are you telling me? Just go out to the kegerator and get some more."

"No," said Frank Mano. "It's your last days as a free man, so get used to being ordered around. Go get more beer."

The men started laughing, but not Danny as he sat up in the recliner. "You can't be serious?" he said.

"I'm very serious, plus I outrank you, detective." He smiled at Danny.

Paul, Tony, and Raymond could not hold it in and started to laugh. "Fine," said Danny, shaking his head and smiling. "I will go get more beer for you ladies." He was laughing at them as he got up and put on his shoes.

"Enjoy your surprise," said Raymond.

"What surprise?" asked Danny. But before he could go outside, there was a knock on the door. Danny was surprised that someone would be knocking at this hour. He turned to them and said, "Okay, what are you guys up to now?"

They all looked at each other with no answer. There was a knock on the door again. All four men stood up, looking at the door.

Danny went to the door and said, "Yes, who is this?"

"Hello," said a male voice from outside. "My name Sebastian Jacobson. Sorry to wake you up at this hour, but we seem to have taken a wrong turn, and we are looking for directions."

"Directions?" said Tony Messina. "There shouldn't be anyone near for miles."

Frank Mano looked out the window, and all he could see was a dark figure at the door.

"One minute," said Danny.

"Put on the floodlights as soon as he opens the door," said Sgt. Tony Messina to Ray. He then signaled the men to prepare to draw their firearms just in case. They responded and were ready. They all stood looking at Danny. Danny's hand was on his firearm, while the other hand prepared to open the door. He counted to three and opened the door.

The floodlights went on. There was a blinding brightness. Danny covered his eyes for a moment until the stranger spoke.

"And the Lord said, 'Let there be light.'" He covered his eyes. "Is this how you treat people who knock on your door?" asked the strange man.

"Turn off the floodlights," Danny said to Ray.

Ray turned off the lights, and the brightness was gone, leaving the moonlight and the soft light from within the cabin. The men stared at the stranger standing outside the door. It was a man in his seventies, with thinning long gray hair, a full beard, and a wrinkled face. He was wearing a long black coat and boots with a round black hat. He smiled at Danny. "I'm so sorry to interrupt you at this hour of the evening. As I said, my name is Sebastian Jacobson." He extended his hand to Danny.

Danny, not knowing what to make of this, extended his hand to Mr. Jacobson. "Hello. My name is Danny Marco."

"Pleasure to meet you, Mr. Marco." As the others watched, he continued. "As I said, we seem to be lost after making a wrong turn and came upon your cabin. We saw lights and knew someone who could help us was home."

"We?" said Danny.

Mr. Jacobson looked down and shook his head. Looking at Danny again, he said, "Oh, please forgive this old man. I'm not as sharp as I was when I was a young man like you." His arm extended out to his left. "This is my daughter, Lisa Jacobson."

She stepped next to her father. She was a very beautiful and attractive woman, with long curly black hair, deep dark eyes, full lips, large breasts sticking out from her dark dress, and an incredible full body that would make any man hungry for her. Her dark eyes looked lustful and commanding as if she had set her sights on Danny.

Danny was speechless for just a second, while the other four men could not believe what they were looking at. How could something this incredible be out here? Then Danny came back to reality. "Please do come in. I am so sorry." They entered, and Danny closed the door. "You are not disturbing us at all. Right, guys?" The others were still in a bit of a shock at the sight of this gorgeous woman in the cabin. It was almost as if she were controlling them with her seductive smile and those eyes. "Guys?" asked Danny.

Paul Corillo finally spoke. "Welcome. My name is Paul Corillo." He walked to Mr. Jacobson and shook his hand, still looking at Lisa. The others came forward. "This is Frank Mano, Tony Messina,

Raymond Amato, and the blushing bride you met at the door is Danny Marco."

"Blushing bride?" said Sebastian Jacobson.

Danny shook his head with a smile. "Don't listen to them," he said as they laughed. "I'm getting married, and they took me here for a guys' getaway."

"Well then," said Mr. Jacobson, "congratulations." He shook his hand again. "Marriage is quite a wonderful thing and brings families together."

"And lots of children," added Lisa Jacobson. "That is the fun part." She smiled at Danny. The others knew what she was thinking.

Danny quickly said, "So you said you were lost?"

"Yes," answered Mr. Jacobson. "We were on our way to Lehigh County to visit my son Jacob Jr. But we left too late, and as evening came, it became evident that we were lost. Then Lisa noticed the dirt road. We took a chance, and here we are."

"Well, it's a good thing you did," replied Danny. "Please sit down." The other four made room for them to sit on the couch. Lisa sat, her legs folded, showing off her beautiful legs. Ray Amato tried not to stare as they all sat. Tony Messina checked on MapQuest for their destination to Lehigh County.

"Let me make a pot of hot coffee," offered Paul.

"Very kind of you," said Mr. Jacobson. "Please forgive me for asking, but I noticed you all have guns?"

"Please do not be alarmed," said Danny. "We are New York City Police officers." They all showed their IDs.

"Well," said Mr. Jacobson, "at least Lisa and I are in good hands this evening." He smiled at everyone.

"Indeed," agreed Lisa with her seductive smile.

"Well, the coffee is brewing," said Paul.

"I believe I found the route you can take," said Tony Messina to Mr. Jacobson.

"Wonderful," replied Mr. Jacobson. "I knew you men could help us."

Danny looked at everyone and caught the eye of Lisa Jacobson. Her eyes were so intense yet so beautiful, staring at Danny as if she were talking to him with her eyes.

"Well," said Danny, "if you will all excuse me, I need to get out and bring in some more beer."

Danny put on his jacket, and as he was about to go outside, Lisa Jacobson stood up and said, "Please let me join you." She walked closer to Danny, her eyes focused on him.

"Wait," interrupted Raymond Amato. "I'll come with you."

"It's all right," said Danny. "We won't be out long."

"Besides," added Lisa, "two is company, and three's a crowd." She laughed. Danny looked at the guys, and they laughed.

"My daughter the comedian, she is," said Mr. Jacobson.

As Danny and Lisa walked out, Paul set down the coffee, and Tony Messina gave the driving directions to Mr. Jacobson. Frank, Raymond, and Paul looked at one another as if saying, *Oh yes, she wants him.*

Paul walked over to Ray. "So that's the surprise?"

"No," replied Ray.

"Are you kidding?"

"I put a werewolf mask in the kegerator."

"What?" exclaimed Paul. Then he looked out the window and saw Danny and Lisa walking toward the kegerator.

"So how long have you lived here?" asked Frank.

"Well," answered Mr. Jacobson, "my family has lived here for generations. They came here early from Europe. But here is the interesting part."

Suddenly Paul looked away from the window, and all four men were listening to Sebastian Jacobson while Danny and Lisa Jacobson were outside.

Walking out the front door of the cabin, Danny Marco walked with the mysterious and beautiful Lisa Jacobson. Her seductive smile and eyes just stared at Danny as if putting him in a trance. Danny was taken by her eyes and incredible body and then came to realize Marie would kill him if she knew what was going on. He started to walk quickly so as not to make eye contact with Lisa Jacobson. He reached the kegerator, but before he could open it, Lisa stood right next to him. "So you are getting married?"

"Yes," replied Danny. "I can't wait. We have been planning our wedding for some time, and soon it will be here. I love her so much." Danny was hoping Lisa would get it and back off.

"Tell me, Danny, are you happy?"

Danny had a confused look on his face. "Am I happy? Well, yes, I am going to marry the woman I love, and I hope to have children with her."

"Really," said Lisa with the seductive smile. "Do you think your fiancée will be happy with you?"

"What? What's that supposed to mean? How dare you even say that? She loves me, and I love her. That's all that matters."

She stayed calm, still smiling. "Danny, she cannot give you all that you want, but I can."

Danny was shocked at what Lisa just said, and he was getting upset and trying to keep his cool. "You don't know anything about me. You just met me and already you know what's good for me?" He laughed. "I think you have been living out here way too long. You need to go out more into the city and be part of life." After that, he suddenly realized something. "Wait just one second. I should have known. This was all a setup by Ray."

"I'm sorry, but I don't understand," said Lisa, gazing at Danny.

"Just drop the act, will you? He said there was a surprise waiting for me, and it was you and your father. If he really is your father. How much did Ray pay you?"

"I have no idea what you are talking about," replied Lisa. "All I know is we were destined for each other. I can excite you in ways you've never experienced and more. It's our destiny."

Danny was shocked. "Destiny? Who told you that?" Danny remembered the dream he had, where the voice had told him the same thing. He shook it off. "Nice, but I'm not biting." He looked toward the cabin and yelled, "Nice try, Ray," but got no response. He started to wonder what was going on inside.

"Danny," said Lisa Jacobson, "look at me."

"No! Enough with the games. You and your dad can go home. This game is over." He leaned down to open the kegerator and found a werewolf mask inside. He jumped back, startled for a bit, and then smiled. "Oh great, that's real funny, but enough already."

He turned around toward Lisa, and she lunged forward to him, grabbing his groin. "Do I look like I'm playing? I want this inside me so we can mate."

Danny was taken by surprise. He tried to remove her hand and looked at her eyes, which seemed to have just turned red. She finally let go, and he backed away. "You are fucking crazy! Go take a dip in the cold lake and leave here now. You and your father. Enough of this bullshit!"

Angry and embarrassed, he walked past Lisa, swung open the front door, and saw the men sitting next to Sebastian Jacobson. They looked up at Danny, startled, and he walked toward Ray Amato. "Nice try, but your plan didn't work. Who else was in on it?"

"Calm down, Danny!" said Paul. "What the hell is wrong with you?"

"With me? I don't think any of this is funny, and oh yeah, nice job on the werewolf mask. Real funny!"

Mr. Jacobson got up and said, "I think it's time for us to leave. It's getting too late, and we have taken up enough of your time. Thank you so much for the directions and the coffee, gentlemen. Is my daughter outside?"

"Yes, she is," answered Danny. "Tell her I said nice try."

"Yes, well," Mr. Jacobson said, putting on his hat. "Thank you again and have a good night." He turned to walk toward the door but stopped and looked at Danny. "Good luck on your wedding, son." Danny just looked at him. Mr. Jacobson smiled and walked out, and Paul closed the door after him.

Outside, he came up to his daughter Lisa. "Well," said Jacob, "I take it things didn't go as planned?"

"He will come to understand his destiny," replied Lisa. "It's just a matter of time." They looked at each other and then back at the front door to the sound of Danny Marco yelling. They looked at each other again, smiled, and walked away.

Inside the cabin, Danny was yelling. "What the hell were you guys thinking? I let you guys get away with so much, but this is the last straw. It really is enough!"

"Danny, what the hell is wrong with you?" asked Paul Corillo.

"Yeah," said Ray Amato. "You stepped outside with that hot ass and you come back in all pissed off. What? She didn't like your manhood?"

Danny went for Ray. Quicky Paul and the others rushed in to break them up. "Enough," shouted Joe Mano. "That's an order! Both of you, back away now."

"What the hell happened outside?" asked Tony Messina. Danny told them what had happened when he was outside with Lisa Jacobson before he stormed into the cabin.

"Danny, we had nothing to do with them two showing up tonight," Paul confessed. "I swear to God we didn't. I just don't get it. There should be no one living around this area."

"Then explain this to me," said Danny. "Why didn't you guys come outside when you noticed we never came back in?"

They looked at each other, confused. "Well, Danny, you were only gone a minute," Paul answered.

Danny turned white and yelled, "A minute? Are you guys that drunk? How about thirty minutes?"

"That can't be right," said Tony Messina. "You had just stepped outside with Lisa for a minute, and her father was telling us about his family, and that's when you came storming in like the Marines."

Danny grabbed his head and shut his eyes. "Has the whole world gone insane? We were outside for thirty minutes. Oh yeah, and thanks for the werewolf mask."

Paul looked at Ray and then spoke to Danny. "Danny, please clam down. I think we had enough excitement for one night. Guys, let's go to bed and try to get some sleep."

"Damn right," remarked Danny. "We are leaving tomorrow. I don't want to stay another night in this place."

"Fine," replied Frank Mano. "We will talk about it first thing in the morning, but let's get some sleep."

"Wait," said Danny. "My nerves are shot to hell. I need a drink to calm down. Beer. It's still in the keg. I'll go get it."

"Wait," replied Paul. "Let me."

"No," Danny insisted. "It's my last dance being single, right? I will go."

Paul gave in. "Fine."

Danny looked at him and the other three and walked outside to the kegerator. He opened the door and took out a six-pack. He took one can, opened it, and took a large gulp. "What a fucking night." As he was set to go back in, he suddenly heard the voice of Lisa Jacobson behind him saying, "Danny?" He closed his eyes, laughing. He said with a smile, "Oh God, you just don't give up, do you?" He turned around, and his smile turned into fear when he saw something coming toward him fast.

Inside the cabin, the men were startled by his scream and firing gunshots. "Danny!" said Paul Corillo. They drew their weapons and moved quickly outside toward Danny, who was in horrible pain, blood coming out of his shoulder as he lay on the ground.

"Holy shit," exclaimed Paul. "Danny!" The floodlights came on, and all men stood by Danny, pointing their guns into the darkness. "Something bit him. We have got to get him out of here, now!"

Suddenly they heard loud howling in front of them in the dense night.

"What the fuck?" exclaimed Ray Amato. The howling grew louder and stronger and sounded like whatever attacked Danny was now coming back for them.

"Stand your ground, men," said Lt. Frank Mano. "Prepare to fire on my command!" As the howling got closer and closer, each man had his gun pointed into the darkness.

"Come on, Lieutenant. Danny doesn't have much time," urged Paul.

"Quiet!" said Lt. Frank Mano. "Steady! Fire at will! Fire at will!" The four men started firing their guns straight into the darkness.

Gunshot after gunshot, they continued shooting. When their guns ran out of bullets, they reloaded and kept firing into the darkness, while Danny lay on the ground, losing blood.

"Cease fire," ordered Lieutenant Mano.

Whatever was out there, it was gone for now, so they quickly turned their attention to Danny Marco.

"Let's get him to a hospital and fast!" said the lieutenant.

Paul looked down at Danny, who was barely conscious but could hear Paul's voice. "Danny, stay with us. We are going to get you help. Can you hear me?"

He blacked out and then came to for a minute and felt his body moving faster. He saw lights and a doctor and nurses. He heard their voices. "Prep him now. He has lost a lot of blood."

"Please save him, doctor." He saw Paul Corillo.

The doctor looked at Danny. "Can you hear me, Detective Marco? Can you hear me?"

Again, Danny blacked out.

Danny opened his eyes and found himself outside the cabin. He was lying on the ground and in pain. He didn't understand how he got there. He called out for Paul and the guys, but no one answered. He was alone in the darkness, or so he thought. He then heard a female voice. "We are together. It is our destiny to be together." He saw a dark shadow coming toward him. Closer and closer, the shadow came until he knew who it was, Lisa Jacobson. She was smiling and looking at Danny. He saw that she was fully naked. Her beautiful body shone in the moonlight, and her large breasts were full and big. Danny was getting aroused. She came to him and said, "My love, we are together, and we will mate. It's our time, and it's now." Smiling, she sat on top of him, and right away, Danny felt himself inside her. She took him in and went to town on him, holding her breasts and licking her lips. Her eyes were closed in the moonlight, just him and her. Danny was getting aroused, feeling himself inside her.

More and more, he wanted more, and then he heard a voice. "Danny?" He turned and saw his fiancée, Marie, looking at him and in tears. "How could you? I love you! How could you do this to me? We are getting married. How could you do this to me?" She turned and ran away in tears.

"Marie!" said Danny.

"Ignore her," urged Lisa Jacobson. "She is not worthy of you. You belong to me."

He looked at her, and she looked up to the moon. He felt himself getting more aroused. Then when she opened her eyes, she looked down at him, and he saw the red of her eyes. It had been her in his other dream. Now it was making sense to him. But why? Why did he dream of her? He had never met her until now. He looked up at her, at her incredible body and her red eyes; she was smiling at Danny. Suddenly she looked up and howled at the moon.

Startled, he woke up in the hospital room. "Danny, you woke up," said his mother, Ellen Marco; with her daughters; his fiancée, Marie; and his childhood friend, Paul Corillo.

Danny was breathing hard, trying to calm down after the dream. "Danny, my baby." His mother hugged him, crying. "Welcome back, my love."

His fiancée, Marie, was also crying. Then she hugged him and kissed his forehead. "We were so worried about you. We didn't think you were going to come back to us."

"He's a fighter, my pal Danny," said Paul Corillo, shaking his hand. Both his sisters hugged him.

"How do you feel, baby?" asked Marie.

Danny yawned and looked at everyone. "I'm hungry. No, I'm starving."

"That is a good sign," said his mother, smiling.

Danny looked at them. "Well, didn't anyone bring me some pizza at least? Or did you all eat it?"

The smiles on their faces turned to sadness, and Danny suspected something was wrong. A good detective knows when something is wrong, and the look on their faces made him realize someone was missing—his father, Peter Marco.

"Where's Dad? I guess the pizzeria is more important than me." He laughed, but no one was laughing. Again, he sensed that something was wrong until his mother started to cry.

"Danny," said Marie, "we need to tell you something."

Now Danny Marco knew something was very wrong. He saw sadness in the people in his room and now wanted answers. He yelled, "What the hell is going on? Where is Dad? Why do you all look so sad? I need to know what is going on!"

"Danny, please calm down," pleaded Ellen Marco, holding his hand.

But Danny was angry and demanded answers.

"Danny, please, this is very hard on all of us," said Paul Corillo.

At that time, a nurse came in to check what was going on. But his sisters quickly went out with the nurse so it was just Danny, his mother, Marie, and Paul.

"What the hell is going on?" asked Danny.

"Danny," said Ellen Marco, "your father is gone."

Danny was in shock and disbelief. "What do you mean he's gone? What happened?"

With Marie and Paul, Ellen started to tell Danny what happened on the night of October 7 when Nicky Ginetti entered Marco's Pizzeria.

"Oh my God! No, no. Dad," said Danny. With tears in his eyes, he said, "My father is dead? Dad!" Danny was crying, along with his mom and Marie. "I hope that little shit Nicky Ginetti is getting it good in the bathroom. That little piece of shit."

"Danny," said Paul, "he didn't go to jail. He is out and a free man."

"What the hell do you mean he is out?"

"Danny, please listen to me. This is hard on all of us." Paul then told Danny the chain of events that happened after the shooting at the pizzeria. "Danny, I read the report. After your father was shot, Nicky was tracked down. He was hiding in his uncle's warehouse. The warehouse was raided, and Nicky was arrested, along with his crew and Don Ginetti."

"He was there too?" asked Danny.

"Yes. It was a huge score, plus the gun and bloody shirt Nicky wore that night were found. The blood on his shirt was a match to your father's blood. We thought for sure we had him."

"If you thought that, then how is it that he is not in jail for murder?" asked Danny.

Rubbing his eyes, Paul then told Danny what happened afterward. "So Nicky, his uncle, and their crew were all arrested. The gun and bloody shirt were found and went into police evidence, and we waited for the trial to begin. But then something happened. The gun and shirt just disappeared."

Danny was in shock and disbelief.

"And because there was no gun or shirt, charges against Nicky were dropped for lack of evidence, and he was set free."

Danny was getting angry. "How could the gun and shirt just disappear? Did anyone try looking for it to see if it was filed wrong?"

"Danny," said Paul, "the entire evidence room was searched, and it was never found."

"What fucking bullshit!" exclaimed Danny. "That piece of shit killed my dad, and he walks away with that stupid smile on his face. I am going to wipe his face on the ground when I see him! I need to get out of here and now."

"Danny," said his mother, holding him down. "Please stay calm."

"Calm?" said Danny. "Mom, he killed your husband, and you are asking me to stay calm!"

"Danny, please," pleaded Marie.

"No!" said Danny. "I'm having a fucking nightmare!"

"Danny, we tried to pin harassment on Nicky, but nothing," explained Paul. "He claimed your dad attacked him that night when all he wanted was pizza."

"This cannot be happening!" exclaimed Danny. "The gun and shirt just vanishing could only mean one thing."

"Inside man," said Paul.

"That is the only answer," replied Danny. "I cannot believe all this. I need to wake up from this nightmare! Paul, we need to find out who it is and fast."

"Wait," said Paul. "Please wait."

"Wait for what? He killed my dad and walks away? No! This ends now."

"Danny, please listen to what I have to say," pleaded Paul.

Danny looked at his mom and Marie. "What else? Just fucking tell me. What else?"

"First," said Paul, "you have been suspended from active duty until further notice."

"Suspended? Suspended for what?"

"Nicky Ginetti filed harassment charges against you, claiming you tried to stuff his head into a toilet bowl at the pizzeria."

"Bullshit! You were there. I never did that!"

"I know you didn't, but the judge didn't buy it and said you had a personal grudge against Nicky."

"Bullshit! And what about you?" Danny asked Paul.

"I've been placed on desk duty till further notice."

"I can't believe this bullshit. I should have just stayed in a coma."

"No," said Marie. "I need you. We have to get married for your father."

Danny looked at Marie. "You can't be serious. Marriage? My father is dead, Nicky walks away, and all you can say is marriage?"

"What the fuck is wrong with you?" Marie, startled at his comment, stepped back in tears.

"Danny, that was wrong to say," said his mother. "Marie loves you. We all love you, and we need to move on for your father's memory. Please, Danny."

Danny rubbed his eyes and scratched his head. "Mom, there is so much to do now. Marie, I'm sorry for snapping at you, but now is not the time to talk about marriage. We have a funeral to arrange, and the pizzeria needs to keep running for Dad's memory. It's my job to step in and take over the business. And I promise you, Nicky Ginetti will not be making any more visits while I'm there."

They looked at each other again, as if preparing Danny for another shock. Danny saw this, and he knew how to read people from his experience as an NYC detective. "Well? Spit it out. Just say what's on your mind now. It's not like I'm going anywhere soon."

His mother spoke. "Danny, we lost the pizzeria."

"What do you mean you lost the pizzeria? Is this a fucking joke? How much more can I take?"

"Danny," said his mother, in tears. "After your father was killed, we tried so hard to keep it going in his memory. People came to pay their respects, and we all worked hard. Even Paul came in to help. But the stress was too much. With you in the hospital and trying to keep the business going, it was getting harder and harder. And with people knowing that Nicky Ginetti was there that night, very few customers would come. The bills started piling up until we couldn't do it anymore. We had to close it down. I'm sorry, Danny."

Danny was in a world of confusion and sadness. Ever since the night at the cabin, his world had been turned upside down. He wished he could wake up from this nightmare, but he couldn't. Reality was finally setting in. And it was only going to get worse before it would get any better. With his hand on his injured left shoulder, he said, "I need to get out of here."

"No," said Marie, "not until the doctor clears you."

"Fuck that. I need to see my dad one last time before he is laid to rest."

"Danny," said his mother, tears streaming down her face as she held his hand, "I'm sorry. We should have told you this first."

"Oh dear God. I'm losing my mind," he said as his cried. "What? What the hell is going on?"

"Danny!" said Paul. Danny looked at his best friend. "Peter has been laid to rest. The funeral was two weeks ago."

"Two weeks ago? Paul, what are you saying? I was attacked last night."

"No, you were attacked three weeks ago," Paul explained. "Danny, it's October 28. Three weeks have passed since the night at the cabin. I'm sorry."

Marie and Ellen were in tears.

"Are you telling me that I have been in a coma for over three fucking weeks?"

"Danny, the doctors tried everything they could, but nothing was working. It was almost as if you didn't want to come back."

"Three weeks? I was in a coma for three weeks? Oh, Christ! Why is this happening to me? Why? I never got a chance to say goodbye to my father." Danny could not hold back anymore and broke out in tears. His mother and Marie tried to console him, but he quickly brushed them away.

"Danny," said Marie, "I'm sorry. Really, I'm sorry."

"I'm just overwhelmed right now. It's too much to absorb and realize what has happened."

"You need rest," said Marie. "Let's go and let him rest for a while," she told the others.

"No," Danny protested. "Wait. Marie, you and Mom go and get some rest. Paul, I need you here. We need to talk more."

"Danny, what else do you need to know?" asked Marie. "We can stay."

"No," Danny said, startling both Marie and his mom. "I'm sorry. Please, I need to speak with my partner."

"Fine, Danny. We will leave you both alone, but you need to rest afterward," Marie instructed.

"I will." As they proceeded to leave, Danny stopped them. "Wait!"

"What?" asked Marie.

Danny shook his head, breathing hard. "That smell."

"What smell?" asked Paul.

"You don't smell it?" inquired Danny.

"Smell what?" said his mom.

Danny sniffed the air and looked toward the door. "Ammonia! I smell ammonia."

"Danny, we don't smell it," said Paul.

"Well, I do," replied Danny. "Maybe the janitors are washing the floors, but honestly, I don't know how you can't smell it. Oh, for the love of God, why are you all testing me? Mom, Marie, please go tell whoever it is to stop. That smell is killing me."

"Okay, Danny," said his mom. "We will see you tomorrow. But before we leave, there is something I have for you." She reached into her purse and took out a gold cross. "Danny, this belonged to your father. I am sure he would want you to have it." With tears in her eyes, she put it around his neck and gave him a kiss. "I am so happy you are back." She turned and left with Marie.

After they left his room, his mother went to the nurses' station to speak with the nurse on duty. "Excuse me?"

"Yes?" said the attending nurse.

"I am Ellen Marco, Danny's mother. He said he can smell a strong scent of ammonia and wanted to know where it was coming from."

"Ammonia?" The nurse looked confused.

"Is there a janitor washing the floor nearby?"

"I'm sorry, but the only floor being washed is at the end of the hallway. And the door is closed," the nurse explained.

"How could he smell it if we don't?" Marie and Ellen were both confused and didn't have an answer. They smiled at the nurse. "It's okay," said Marie. They said good night and left, wondering how Danny was able to smell it.

Inside his room, Danny and Paul tried to understand the events that got him in the hospital. "My mind is going in circles since the night at the cabin," said Danny.

"Tell me about it. All hell broke loose right after Sebastian and Lisa Jacobson left."

"I've never met anyone like them before. It's almost as if they were controlling us."

"Controlling us?" asked Paul. "How?"

"I don't have an answer to that, but that's the only thing I can think of."

While both men were talking about the events of that night, outside his hospital room a pair of ghostly eyes were watching them, but the men didn't notice until Danny looked out the window. "Paul, close the window blinds please."

Paul was confused. He looked at the window and then at Danny. "What's wrong?"

Danny shook his head. "I don't know, but I can't shake the feeling that we are being watched."

Paul smiled. "Come on, Danny. Are you going to start that again?"

Danny responded with anger. "I said close the fucking window blinds!"

Paul was shocked at Danny's latest outburst. He got up to close the blinds. "There. Are you happy now? What the hell is wrong with you?"

"I'm sorry. Please sit down. I feel like I'm having a complete nightmare. Please sit."

Paul sat down but was concerned about his childhood friend. "Danny, can you remember anything that happened to you that night at the cabin?"

Danny closed his eyes and started to remember as much as he could, and then he looked at Paul. "Paul, when I was outside with Lisa Jacobson, she came on to me."

"What?"

"She came on to me big-time, telling me I was meant for her, and she wanted to have sex with me. She even grabbed my groin."

"Holy shit! I can't believe it. I should have checked on you. What happened then?"

Danny continued. "I thought this was the surprise waiting for me that you guys planned, and I laughed at her. But she insisted she knew nothing about a joke and wanted me. I told her again I was not interested and asked her and her dad to leave. That's when I came back in so angry and pissed."

Paul was shocked at the events that had taken place outside the cabin that night. But Paul had another question for Danny. "Danny, after they left, you went back outside for beer. Can you remember what the hell attacked you?"

Danny closed his eyes again as he tried to remember that night. Then he looked at Paul. "I remember I was really pissed at you guys. I didn't believe you guys hadn't planned any of it. But I remember getting the beer from the kegerator. I opened a can for a drink, and that's when I heard Lisa."

"Wait. She came back?"

"Well, I thought she did."

"What do you mean you thought she did?"

"Paul, I thought I heard her voice behind me saying my name."

Paul was confused. "Then what?"

"Well, I thought she did not want to give up with the joke or whatever was going on. That's when I turned around, and all I remember seeing were those red eyes coming at me."

"Red eyes? Wait a minute. I thought you said Lisa. It was Lisa?"

"I thought it was Lisa. Damn it. I recognized her voice, but when I turned around, I saw red eyes coming straight toward me. That's when I drew my gun and started firing. Then I felt teeth, sharp teeth, biting into my left shoulder, and after that, everything went blank. Didn't you guys hear me?"

"Danny, we heard you scream and then shots. We ran outside and found you barely conscious. There was so much blood coming from your shoulder. We thought for sure a wild animal attacked you. But then we heard howling."

"Howling? You mean wolves?"

"I don't know. But that's what we heard, though we couldn't see them."

"Jesus Christ! What happened then?"

"We knew we had to get you out of there and fast, but the howling was getting louder, and it sounded like they were coming back. We drew our guns and just started firing straight into the darkness. It didn't seem to work, so we reloaded and started firing again, and this time, it looked like whatever was out there ran away, maybe in fear or maybe to regroup. Whatever it was, we had to get you out of there. But there's something else…"

"What?"

"You mentioned red eyes coming at you."

"Yes."

"I saw red eyes, Danny. I didn't tell anyone this." Paul started to remember the one thing he saw and didn't tell anyone about until now. "When we heard the howling and started shooting, I could have sworn I saw red eyes moving fast, and then they were gone. I don't know what to make of it. But when it stopped, we were able to rush you to the hospital and get you help before it was too late. You had lost so much blood, and we thought for sure you weren't going to make it."

Danny was shaking his head in disbelief, thinking he was still dreaming, but he was not. His whole world had been turned upside down, and it kept getting worse. "What happened after?" he asked.

"We contacted Pennsylvania State Police and informed them of the attack by possible wolves in the area."

"Did they find the wolves?" asked Danny.

"No," answered Paul. "In fact, they stated there had not been a wolf sighting in years."

"That can't be right! Then what attacked me?"

"They have no clue, buddy, none whatsoever."

"What about the Jacobsons?" asked Danny.

"Danny, we informed them of Sebastian and Lisa Jacobson and gave them a good description. Pennsylvania State Police started searching but found no one even close to the description we gave them. If the Jacobsons are there, they are probably living off the grid. When the police searched the cabin, they found the beer in the kegerator, so they assumed we were drunk. They did find the shell casings from our guns, but no signs of wolves anywhere."

"Right. We were all drunk and imagined the same people. What bullshit! Then what about whatever attacked me? Did I do it to myself?"

"Easy, partner," said Paul. "Wildlife experts are still searching for whatever attacked you, but for now, there is nothing. As for the Jacobsons, if that's their real name, they are hiding well enough not to be found."

"But why would they be hiding?"

"Again, buddy, I just don't have the answers. You are just very lucky to be alive. It could have been worse."

Danny looked at his shoulder and then at Paul. "Paul, I don't feel anything. No pain, nothing."

"Maybe it's the pain meds."

"No. I just don't feel anything except the stitches." Danny reached for his left shoulder and started to remove the stitches.

"Danny, what are you doing? You could start bleeding again. Stop it!"

But Danny was determined and ripped off the stitches. Instead of blood spewing out, there was nothing. His skin had healed as if it had just been a minor cut.

"Oh, Christ," exclaimed Paul. "You had a huge hole in your shoulder, and now it's not there. I don't understand."

Danny rubbed his shoulder and looked at Paul. "Paul, I need to get out of here and now."

"What? You are in no condition to leave. Please wait for the doctor to release you."

"No. I need to get out of here now. I'm feeling better. Don't ask why, but I do feel better. Fuck these doctors. They just want to milk my insurance, but it's not going to happen. Plus, that smell of ammonia is making me nauseous."

"How do you smell ammonia?" asked Paul. "I don't smell a thing."

"Paul, I smell it! Damn it! Let's get the hell out of here. Call my mom and Marie. Tell them we're leaving Pennsylvania tonight. I've had enough."

"Buddy, we're not in Pennsylvania anymore. We are back in Brooklyn, at Maimonides Hospital. We had you transferred here so it would be easy for your mom and all of us to come see you."

Danny was laughing and shaking his head. "Anything else you want to tell me?"

"Well, there was the time you needed a sponge bath."

"Get out of here and let me get dressed," said Danny, laughing at Paul.

"Okay." Paul was laughing as he left the room. He walked to the nurses' station.

"Yes," said the nurse on duty.

Paul took out his badge and ID. "I'm Detective Paul Corillo. Detective Danny Marco will be leaving tonight, and I accept full responsibility."

"I'm sorry," said the nurse, "but without the doctor's release, I cannot allow it. I will not sign him out. I could lose my job for this."

At that moment, Danny came out of his room dressed and ready to leave.

"Danny," said Paul, "we have a problem. She will not release you without your doctor's approval. Let's wait another night, buddy, and see what happens tomorrow."

"Tomorrow?" said Danny. "There is no tomorrow." He leaned over the counter to the nurse and looked at her. "I understand your policy, but you need to understand I will not stay here another night. I'm an NYC detective, and my partner will sign me out on my behalf. Now, where do I sign out?"

"Maybe I didn't make myself clear to you, Detective Marco," replied the nurse. "I cannot and will not sign you out."

Danny leaned over again, but this time with a firm, strong, and determined voice, he said, "I'm leaving tonight."

Shocked by his approach and scared to death, the nurse took out the release form. Paul and Danny signed out.

Paul looked at Danny. "Dude, you didn't have to make a scene. What the hell is wrong with you?"

"Sometimes you just can't be nice, Paul," replied Danny. They got on the elevator and left.

Shaken, the nurse was approached by another nurse from behind her.

"What's wrong, Kelly?" asked the second nurse.

"Detective Marco. He insisted on leaving, but I told him no and that he had to wait for the doctor to approve his release. But then he got mad and shouted at me to release him. I looked into his eyes and decided to let him go."

"Don't let it bother you, Kelly. We get shouted at by people all the time."

"I know, but he was different."

"How so?" asked the second nurse.

"His eyes. I looked into his eyes, and I could have sworn they were red."

The other nurse laughed. "Honey, you've been working too hard. Go on break, and I will cover for you."

"Thanks so much. I think a break will do me good."

Nurse Kelly got up from her station and left for her break. The other nurse walked around the station and sat down, and from there, only the name on her nameplate could be seen: Jacobson.

CHAPTER 3

"Finally, we are out," said Danny. "I really hope this does not come back to bite me in the ass."

"I'm taking a big risk here, Danny," replied Paul. "You are still not 100 percent despite what you are saying."

"Paul, please, enough."

"Okay, so let's go home."

"No!" protested Danny.

"Why not, Danny?"

"I'm starving. I need food. What time is it, Paul?"

"It's only 7:30 p.m."

Danny looked up and toward the left. "Man, I smell burgers. Let's get some."

Paul was again confused. "Danny, how the hell do you smell burgers? I can't smell a thing. You have been acting strange since you woke up."

"What are you saying, Paul? I'm different?"

"No, it's just I've never seen you like this."

"Come on, Paul. It's still me, good ol' Danny, and I'm hungry. Let's find that diner."

"Okay," said Paul, staring at Danny as they walked to the parking lot.

As they approached Paul's car, he tripped and dropped the car keys.

"Great," said Paul. "Where are those keys?" Paul bent down and searched for his keys in the darkness. The streetlamps were on, but he still could not find his car keys.

"For the love of God, Paul, are you blind?" asked Danny. "The keys are right in front of you!"

"Where? I don't see them."

"Move please." Paul got up, and Danny bent down to retrieve the keys behind the tire. "Happy now? Come on and let's go."

"Wait a second. How did you see the keys from where you were standing?"

"What can I say, Paul? I have excellent vision. Now let's go already!"

"Fine. Jesus, you are acting weird tonight."

They got in the car, and Paul drove off to the nearest diner close to the hospital. Things were about to get even weirder tonight for Paul and Danny.

Inside the diner, the waitress, customers, and Paul were all looking at Danny as he consumed several burgers while another waitress brought a platter of burgers to their table. She looked at Paul nervously as if to ask, *What is wrong with him?*

Paul looked around at the other waitress and the customers. Smiling, he said to them, "It's okay. My friend just got out of the hospital and was in the mood for a burger or two." He was still smiling at them when he turned to Danny. "Danny, you are embarrassing yourself. What the hell is wrong with you?"

"Come on, man. I told you, I'm starving. I was in a coma for weeks. This body needs food."

"Coma?" said the waitress.

Paul quickly took out his badge to ease the waitress. "Danny, you are going to shit out like a horse later."

Danny chuckled, took a long sip of Cola, and sat back. "Man, that was good. I never knew how good burgers tasted till now. I should bring Marie here next time."

Paul shook his head. "Okay, enough. I don't think they will let you back in since you ate just about all the burgers." Danny laughed as Paul requested the check from the waitress. "Okay, Danny, now I'm taking you home. You need to be with your family. Your dad would have wanted you to go home now."

Suddenly Danny looked at Paul with shock on his face.

"What?" said Paul.

"Go home? Really, Paul? Go home after what that piece of crap Nicky Ginetti did to my father? You expect me to just go home? Bullshit! We are going to the warehouse. We have to find proof that he killed my dad."

Paul was scratching his head and looking at Danny. "Danny, in case you forgot, you have been suspended until further notice by our commanding officer. If you get caught, it will be all over for you and me. No, Danny, we are not going."

"Fine. Worry about yourself, but not me. My dad needs justice, and I am going to bring Nicky down. Don't worry, Paul. Your name will not be mentioned if I get caught." Danny got up and headed for the door.

"Wait! You fuck, wait." He got up and went after Danny.

Outside, he confronted Danny.

"Don't try to change my mind, Paul. You will have to arrest me if you want to stop me, but good luck trying."

"Danny, listen to me, please. Remember when we were kids? Remember the pact we made?"

"Yes, Paul. So what's your point?"

"The point, Danny, is that we are in this together, and as crazy as I think you are going there tonight, I'm with you. I will probably regret it, but I'm with you till the end, partner."

"Paul, you don't have to do this."

"I know I don't, but I will."

"Okay, then. It's close to 9:00 p.m. We will go in about two hours. Should be quite enough for us to find what we can."

"Danny, we just go in and leave, okay?"

"Yes, Paul. Okay."

"I hope you mean it, Danny. I really hope you do."

*****

It was 11:00 p.m., and the sky was cloudy. They arrived at the warehouse on Tenth Avenue in Brooklyn. "We have some cloud cover that will block our approach," said Danny. "Let's move in."

53

They walked slowly past some parked cars, and one of them was a black BMW belonging to Nicky Ginetti.

"Holy shit," Paul whispered to Danny. "Nicky is here, and looks like there is a meeting tonight. Danny, we are outnumbered here. We need to leave now."

"No!" protested Danny. "We need to find the bloody shirt and gun. We've come this far."

"And we will come again," said Paul. "It's too risky." Suddenly Danny stopped and stood with his hands up. "Danny? What the fuck are you doing? They will see you."

"They already have, Paul."

Paul turned to see three men with guns pointing at them. "Up slowly, and don't try anything," said one man. Paul stood with his hands up. One man searched him and took out his gun and badge.

The other man found nothing on Danny but said to him, "What a catch. Wait till Nicky Ginetti sees you both. Bring them inside." With guns pointed at their heads, they were brought inside the warehouse.

Inside, they walked toward a room where they heard voices and saw a group of men sitting around a table playing cards. They looked up at both Paul and Danny. As they approached the individual with his back to them, one man walked around him and presented him with Paul's badge and identification. With his back facing them, the man said, "Well, well, look what the kitty dragged in." It was the voice of Nicky Ginetti. He stood up, turned, and walked toward Paul and Danny. "Welcome to my humble home, Mr. Police Officers. Oh yeah, I forgot. You're not a cop anymore." He pointed to Danny.

"How the fuck did you know, you little prick?"

"Danny!" said Paul.

Nicky walked over to Danny with that smirk on his face. "You don't think I know what's going on, Danny boy?" Then he slapped Danny's face. Paul tried to move but was restrained by the other men. "Who's the piece of shit now, Danny boy? By the way, I'm so sorry for your daddy."

Danny went for Nicky but was punched in the stomach and went down. There was nothing Paul could do but watch.

Nicky grabbed him by his hair and said, "You are now in my house, Danny boy. How does it feel to be the piece of shit now?" Danny spat in his face. Nicky backed away to clean his face. Then he took out his gun and pointed it at Danny.

"No!" Ralph, his driver, screamed. "If you kill them, the cops will come down on us and hard. Let's call your uncle."

"Not this time," said Nicky. "This ass humiliated me, and now it's time to return the favor." He looked at his guys. "Take him to the back room and tune up his pretty-boy face for his soon-to-be wife to see. Bobby, go with them."

They dragged Danny into the next room while Paul pleaded with Nicky to stop before he regretted it. He was also punched in the stomach and went down. While down, he looked toward the door Danny was dragged into and was helpless to help him. Ralph tried to tell Nicky to stop before it was too late, but Nicky would not listen. Instead, he was smiling to the sound of punches and kicks as Danny was being beaten.

In the other room, four men were giving it to Danny with punches to the face and stomach. Danny went down and was kicked repeatedly. With blood coming out of his mouth and nose and the pain in his body, there was little more he could take.

"Pick him up," ordered Bobby. Danny's face was covered in blood. His nose was broken and in pain. "Stay away from Nicky Ginetti," said Bobby. "Or the next time, it will be your wake." Danny, weak and bloody, spat blood in Bobby's face. Bobby wiped the blood off and punched Danny in the face. Danny fell down hard and crawled near a window. "You little fuck," said Bobby. "Now this is the end for you."

Danny was beaten and bloodied all over. He managed to open his eyes toward a brightness coming from a window. The brightness came from the moon. The clouds had dispersed, and the moon was full. But on this night, the moon was Danny's ally. He started to feel a rage inside him. His heart started pounding faster and faster as he stared at the moonlight. He felt his body changing from within. His fingernails turned razor-sharp, and his skin grew tighter. His anger and thirst for blood grew stronger, and he felt a rage burning inside him straining to be set free. He started to growl as he felt his anger growing stronger.

Bobby looked at the others and started to laugh. "Who let the dogs out?" With a smile on his face and the others laughing, he leaned down to Danny and said, "Does Snoopy want a doggie bone?" Danny quickly turned his head to Bobby, showing his raging red eyes. Bobby's smile turned to fear.

The people in the other room heard screams and gunfire. They quickly drew their weapons and pointed it at the door. "What the fuck was that?" asked Nicky Ginetti. They heard more screams until it was silent. The men looked at one another and didn't know what to do. Nicky had his gun pointing down at Paul.

Ralph called out, "Bobby? Anybody? What's going on in there?" Guns still pointed toward the door, the men were shaking, not realizing what was about to happen. But there was still silence until they started to hear growling coming closer and closer to the door. All men had their guns drawn to the door, when suddenly the door swung open, and something came rolling out. It was the bloody head of Bobby.

"Holy fucking shit!" screamed Nicky.

The image they saw would be the very last thing they would ever see again. Rising from his hind legs, a hairy beast slowly began to stand up. With blood on its sharp teeth and sharp claws and its angry red eyes looking at the scared men, it glared at Nicky and then released a horrible screaming roar.

Danny Marco was no more. In his place was a raging beast—a werewolf.

"Kill it!" screamed Nicky.

They started shooting, but the werewolf quickly jumped away and smashed all the lights. The men were all blind in the darkness, but the werewolf had perfect night vision and attacked each man, ripping them to pieces while the others kept shooting until they were ripped to pieces too. Nicky, Ralph, and another man grabbed Paul and ran outside while shooting back at the werewolf.

Nicky was still pointing his gun at Paul's head. "You are my ticket out of hell. Don't fucking move!"

Ralph continued shooting and then looked at Nicky. "Get the fuck out of here!"

Those were the last words Nicky would hear Ralph say. The werewolf thrust his razor-sharp paw into Ralph's back and out his chest.

"Oh God!" screamed Nicky as blood came out of Ralph's mouth and he fell to the ground dead. Now it was just Nicky and his other man, but he ran away in fear. "Where the fuck are you going?" screamed Nicky. Now it was just Nicky, Paul, and the werewolf. Nicky was now frightened. For the first time in his life, he was now the victim. His men were gone. It was just him. He let go of Paul and started shooting at the werewolf, but it jumped out of the way from the bullets.

Paul was confused as to what he was seeing and looked back, wondering where Danny was. Nicky ran to his car while Paul, still confused and shocked, went over to Bobby's body, got his cell phone from his pocket, and made a call for help.

Nicky was shaking and scared. He had just seen his men killed by a beast he could not explain. He tried to start his car but was surprised by a loud thump on the roof. He screamed and started shooting up. A razor-sharp paw punched the windshield in, scattering broken glass into Nicky's face and grabbing him by the throat. He was helpless. The werewolf pulled him out as he gasped for air. The werewolf snarled at him with blood on its teeth. Nicky looked into its red eyes. He knew it was over for him. All the pain he had caused other people had now come back to him. But he still managed to speak his final words to the werewolf as he looked into its red eyes.

"You are going to be so fucking sorry when my uncle gets you, you motherfucker. You have no idea who the fuck you're dealing with," were his last words. The werewolf sunk its razor-sharp paw right into Nicky Ginetti's chest, killing him instantly, before dropping his body.

The werewolf looked up, claiming victory and howling up to the moon, but it forgot one person. Paul Corillo.

"Freeze!" said Paul. The werewolf turned around to see Paul Carrillo pointing a gun at it. "Don't move."

The werewolf did not understand. It snarled at him. "What the fuck are you?" asked Paul. It jumped off the car and walked slowly toward Paul, who had the gun still aimed at the werewolf. "I said don't move! Take off that mask!" Then as the werewolf walked closer in the moonlight, Paul noticed something around its neck, something that sparkled. As he started to focus more and more, he realized what it was. A gold cross. Then he remembered it was the gold cross Ellen Marco gave Danny, the gold cross that had belonged to Peter Marco. Suddenly Paul dropped the gun and finally started to understand what exactly had happened to Danny. The night at the cabin, the dreams he was having, and Lisa Jacobson—everything was starting to make sense for the first time. With sadness in his eyes, he looked at the werewolf who was also his childhood friend, Danny Marco.

"Danny," said Paul, "I'm so sorry. I'm sorry I didn't believe you. What did they do to you?"

The werewolf just looked at Paul and snarled more.

"Danny, can you understand me?"

Suddenly the werewolf looked up, hearing police sirens. Paul had called for help, and they were on their way. "Danny," said Paul to the werewolf, "you need to get out of here now! They will kill you. Go!" He waved his hands for the werewolf to leave. As if it understood Paul, the werewolf turned and started to run. It jumped over parked cars and then climbed a building and ran faster. Paul watched it until he couldn't see it anymore. "God help us all," said Paul as police cars arrived on scene.

The werewolf continued to run and jump as far as it could until it reached the New Utrecht Avenue train station. There was an oncoming train, but the werewolf leaped on top of the rushing train, looked up into the full moon, and howled again in victory. Onlookers waiting for their train heard the howling and saw the werewolf. The werewolf turned to the people and howled again.

*****

October 22, Tuesday, 7:00 a.m.
Danny's apartment

Danny was lying in his bed with a window open in his room. He was in a deep sleep and dreaming. He saw himself running and breathing hard as if he were chasing his prey until he saw himself in his room. He looked at the mirror and saw the face of the werewolf. He growled.

He woke up in fear. Shaking and confused, he looked around until he heard banging on the front door.

"Danny, are you in there? It's Paul Corillo. Danny, open the door now!"

Danny got up and noticed that he was naked. There were some scars on his skin that were healing. He quickly put on some clothes and called out, "Paul? Give me a minute."

Paul was in no mood to wait. "Danny? Open the fucking door now."

When the door was opened, there stood Danny Marco, confused and looking tired. Paul stepped in, and Danny closed and locked the door. Paul turned to Danny, giving him a hug. Danny was confused.

"Paul, what's going on?" asked Danny.

Paul looked at him. "What do you mean what's going on? You have no idea what happened to you last night?" They walked into the living room and sat down.

"Last night," Danny mumbled. "Yes, we were at the warehouse."

"Yes," replied Paul. "And we got caught by Nicky's crew. Remember?"

"I remember that, and I remember getting tuned up."

"And?" said Paul.

"I don't remember. Did I black out?"

"Black out? You don't remember, do you?"

"Remember what? What the fuck is going on? Why can't I remember?"

Shaking his head, Paul reached out for the remote control. The TV came on, showing the morning news.

"What's going on?" asked Danny.

"Shut up and listen." Paul pointed to the news.

As the local news came on, Danny was shocked at what the news reporter was saying regarding last night's events.

> In local news, at a local warehouse in Brooklyn owned by the Untouchable Don, Salvatore Ginetti, several men were brutally executed. From what medical examiners are saying, their bodies were just ripped apart. Among the dead was the nephew of Salvatore Ginetti, Nicky Ginetti. He was found dead outside the warehouse with a huge hole from his back to his chest. Medical examiners have never seen anything like this. The police believe this may be the work of a rival gang. No other information has been given at this time. The police are looking for anyone who witnessed anything. Several people have reported that they heard loud howling. They said it didn't sound like a dog but like a large animal.
>
> Other witnesses reported seeing a large hairy man jumping on top of a local BMT train and growling. Police are investigating if the two incidents are related. It may be possible someone is getting an early start for Halloween this month and is seeking attention.
>
> But going back to the slayings at the warehouse, I would not want to be that person once Salvatore Ginetti finds out. More on this later.
>
> This is Mike Riggs for News One.

Paul turned off the TV and looked at Danny Marco. The look said it all.

"Nicky is dead?"

"Yes," answered Paul, "and his whole crew. They were ripped to pieces by you."

"Me? I don't remember what happened last night, and you're saying it was me! What the fuck is going on, Paul?"

Paul took a deep breath and began by recounting how they both arrived at the warehouse, how they were caught, and Danny being dragged into the next room and started getting beaten up. Then Paul told him what happened after.

"Danny, after the gunfire and screams, we all heard something coming toward the door. Nicky and his crew were shitting their pants. Then one of his guys' head comes flying out the door, and that's when we saw it."

"Saw what? What the fuck did you see?"

"Danny, it wasn't you. It was a hairy beast," said Paul. "I've never seen anything like it. It stood up tall. Like a monster. It focused on us until it saw Nicky. It moved so fast, taking out his crew. Then outside, Nicky tried to get away in his car, but it grabbed him through the windshield and ripped out his chest."

"Holy Jesus!" Danny put his hands on his head, trying to understand. "Paul, where the fuck was I? Didn't you come looking for me?"

"Danny, that thing that killed Nicky and his crew, it was you!"

"What? Paul, have you lost your mind? Me? I don't remember any of this shit. How could you say it was me? I was probably knocked out from the beating."

"No!" said Paul. "Listen to me." Danny looked at Paul. "I looked at that thing and was ready to fire. I told it not to move, but it kept getting closer, and that's when I realized that it was you." Paul pointed to the gold cross. "Danny, it was wearing the cross your mom gave you. Danny, you're a fucking werewolf!"

Danny was speechless. He had no words. He was a werewolf. "How is this possible? Think."

"Your dreams you told me about, how uneasy you felt at the cabin as if you were being watched. And then the Jacobsons. It all makes sense. They were waiting for you all this time."

Danny Marco started to remember—the night in his apartment when he saw a mysterious dark figure looking at his window from across the street, the dream he had of a werewolf talking to him from a TV show, and seeing the same figure again from his father's pizzeria and at the cabin, the feeling that he was being watched, and, yes, Lisa Jacobson.

"Holy Christ!" exclaimed Danny. "Lisa attacked me? She's a fucking werewolf! She must have bitten me, and now I'm cursed. That's why she said I was to be her mate. She said she saw it. Crazy bitch. No matter what she saw, she cursed me."

Paul could not believe what was going on.

"How is this possible? How can something like this exist? It shouldn't, but it does," said Danny.

"Danny, listen to me," replied Paul. "The top brass wanted to know why I was at the warehouse. I told them I received a tip on stolen merchandise and was checking it out. They wanted to know where you were, but I told them I had taken you home. Danny, you need to be careful and alert. Don Ginetti will be out for blood."

"We need to tell my mom and Marie," said Danny.

"Are you insane?" asked Paul. "That's the last thing you want to tell them. The few people who know, the better. But one thing. When we got to the warehouse, it was already dark. Why didn't you turn into the werewolf then?"

Danny started thinking. "Paul, there was no full moon."

"What? The moon?"

"It was a cloudy and dark night. The moon's light didn't change me. But I guess when it started to clear up, then it happened." Danny quickly went to his computer and typed up, *Next moon phase.*

"See, Paul, the moon was bright afterward. There will be another moon phase tonight and the next couple of days, and then no moon phase till next week. But the weather is unpredictable. Anything can happen," said Danny.

"Then what about tonight?" said Paul.

"I will need something strong to put me out. I need strong meds that will control me."

"Danny, this is insane!" exclaimed Paul. "We have to find another alternative."

"Paul, this is the only way, and you know it." Danny turned to print copies of the next moon phase. He then turned to Paul. "Please find me some strong meds. Even from your informants. I need something to knock me out for the night. I can't go to Marie. She will not understand."

"I will see what I can do about the meds, Danny," replied Paul. "Until then, stay in and don't go out."

"Paul, you don't have to do this."

"Danny, we've known each other since we were kids. We always backed each other up no matter what the problem was. I will not walk away from you now. Please try and get some rest."

"I will," assured Danny.

"I will check back with you later and hopefully have some strong meds for you." Paul walked to the door and left.

Danny was shaken up. His whole life had changed the minute he went to the cabin. "God help me," he said. He started to walk and bumped into a night lamp. It started to fall, but Danny quickly swung and grabbed it with one hand and put it back up. Danny never knew about his quick reflexes. *Does this have something to do with the werewolf?* he wondered.

The phone rang. His fiancée, Marie, was on the phone. "Hello? Danny? What are you doing home? I went to the hospital to see you and was told you were released and that Paul took you home. You could have called, you ass!"

"Marie, I'm sorry. You're right. I should have called you, but I'm so down I needed to be alone and mourn my dad."

"Danny, you jerk! Why do I love you so much? I'll see you tonight, baby."

"No! Marie, please, not tonight."

"What's wrong with you? We're getting married, and you're acting so distant."

"Marie, please, it's not you. Please just give me some time to myself. I promise you this will pass, and we will get married. But I need to be alone for a while."

"Fine, Danny. I will give you your space. But, Danny, don't wait too long. I can only deal with this so much." She hung up.

Danny sat on his couch, wondering if he would ever wake up from this nightmare, but he knew he wasn't asleep. His phone rang again, and he answered, thinking it was Marie. "Marie, I'm sorry.

There is a lot going on that I just can't say right now. Please try to understand. Hello? Marie?"

"Danny, my love, soon we will be together." It was not Marie. It was the voice of Lisa Jacobson.

He screamed, "Lisa Jacobson? What have you done to me? You turned my life upside down! How did you find me?" There was no response. He looked at the caller ID. Unavailable. He threw the phone down. He screamed, "Why me?"

*****

It was midday at the Ginetti residence. Friends were at his home paying their condolences for the loss of his nephew Nicky. He was sitting on the couch with his wife and sister when he was approached by another man. Something was said to him privately. He got up and told his wife he would be right back. They walked down the hallway of his home to another door that took them down the basement. There, he met with several other men in another makeshift office, soundproof for specific reasons. Sitting in a chair was another man, shaking and scared. He was a total mess and drinking a strong drink to calm him down. He saw Salvatore Ginetti. He got up.

"Sit your ass down," ordered Don Ginetti. Another man brought him a chair, and he sat opposite him. "Look at me," said Don Ginetti. The man looked at him. This was the man who had gotten away that night at the warehouse. "I want to know what happened last night. Who killed my nephew? The media is saying some bullshit about a strange animal. Tell me what happened."

"Don Ginetti, you're not going to believe me."

"I said, tell me what happened," said the don.

Shaking and knowing he had no choice, he told Don Ginetti what happened last night and how the boys caught Paul Corillo and Danny Marco outside the warehouse. "Nicky wanted to make an example of them both."

"Why didn't anyone call me?" asked the don.

"We tried to, but Nicky brushed us off and said no."

"Damn Nicky. He never listened. Then what?"

"Well, the cop Danny Marco, he got wise with Nicky, so Nicky told the guys to take him to the back room and rough him up while the other cop was with us."

"You didn't go with them?"

"No, sir. I stayed behind."

"Then what?"

"We heard the guys giving it to Marco while Nicky was smiling. But then something happened afterward." He closed his eyes as the memory started playing back in his mind.

"What the fuck happened?" asked the don.

"Sir, we heard screams and then gunfire."

"Screams?"

"Yes, but not from Marco. From our boys. There was so much gunfire, and then everything went silent. We didn't know what was going on. We drew our guns out and aimed it at the door. We didn't know what to expect until it happened."

Don Ginetti and the others listened.

"Something came flying at us from the doors. When we looked down at it, it was Bobby's head."

"What the fuck do you mean Bobby's head?" said Don Ginetti.

"Something ripped his head off and threw it at us."

The other men started whispering, but the don spoke to them. "Shut the fuck up! Then what happened?"

"We heard footsteps coming closer to us. We pointed our guns at the door, waiting for what was going to come out, until it did." He started breathing hard. "Don Ginetti, it stood up staring at us."

"It? What do you mean *it?*"

"It stood up, all hair, blood on its hands and mouth. Teeth looked like shark's teeth. And those eyes. So red you could feel it going through your body. It looked at us, and then it just roared. Nicky screamed at us to kill it. We started shooting, but it moved so fast. It broke all the lights, so we were blind in the dark. But it knew exactly where we were. It started killing the guys. Ralph kept shooting, while Nicky grabbed the other cop and started going for the door. We followed. I ran across and stood by Nicky and the cop. Ralph told us to run, and then something went through his chest like a hand. Then it was just me, Nicky, and the cop. Then it went after Nicky. He let go of the cop and ran to his car. Nicky didn't have a chance. The thing busted the windshield and pulled Nicky out and did the same thing to him, put his hand right through him."

Don Ginetti's hands were shaking. Then he said, "Wait a minute. Where the fuck were you?"

"Forgive me, Don Ginetti. But when I saw that thing outside, I ran."

"You ran? You fucking left my nephew alone to die and you ran! You fucking shit." He stood up, ready to strike him, but then stopped. He walked away for a moment while the others looked on. "You're telling me a hairy guy that looked like a monster killed Nicky and the others? And you expect me to believe this?"

"Don Ginetti, it's all over the news. Other people saw it too."

"Bullshit!" exclaimed the don. "Must have been someone working with those fucking cops dressed up like a sick bastard, and you fell for it, you little prick!"

"Don Ginetti, please forgive me. I didn't know what else to do." The man was crying and scared.

Don Ginetti walked up to him, put his hand on his shoulder, and said, "It's all right. Everything will be fine. You need to disappear for a while."

He stepped back, and another man stepped in, pulled out a gun, and shot him dead. The soundproofed walls shielded the sound of the gun.

"Get rid of him," said the don. Men carried the body away. "What kind of bullshit is this? A hairy-looking guy with red eyes and sharp teeth kills Nicky and our boys, and this one expects me to believe it was an animal? No. Those cops must have had a guy waiting for them if something went sour, so he got dressed up and ready for pre-Halloween. Nicky is dead, and those fucking cops walk away!"

"Don Ginetti," another man said, "our inside source says Danny Marco was suspended after we filed charges against him for harassing Nicky."

"So the fucker is no longer a cop? I'm putting an end to this. Call our guy and find out where Marco lives. Tonight, we put an end to this once and for all, and Nicky can rest in peace, that little shit. He never listened."

"Don Ginetti, I don't know if the other families will sanction this."

He turned around. "Fuck the heads! This is my nephew who was killed, not their nephew. You guys do it, but get it done tonight. I want Marco dead tonight. Call me after you kill him. I want this over. Call me once it's done."

"Yes, Don Ginetti." The men walked out, leaving Don Ginetti thinking about Nicky and his mother and his asshole brother-in-law, whom he had no care for.

*****

Hours passed, and day turned to evening. Paul Corillo dropped off some very strong meds to help Danny sleep and not wake up to another nightmare. Danny Marco had taken several pills. He was sleeping in his bed, but he was dreaming again. He was dreaming he was the hunter searching for his prey. Growling sounds came from within him when he heard the voice of Lisa Jacobson.

"Come to me, my darling. It is our destiny."

The pills he took did not have any effect on him. He was breathing hard and moving his hands. While this was going on, a car was parked outside his home. There were three men in the car, looking at his house. These men were sent by Don Ginetti to kill Danny Marco. The driver looked at the two men. "Guys, go in, kill him, and leave. Nothing else."

The two men acknowledged him, got out of the car, and headed toward Danny's house. They managed to break into the back very quietly and went inside. Thinking that Danny was asleep, they assumed this would be an easy kill. But not everything would go according to plan. The driver waiting outside called Don Ginetti. "They are inside now, sir. Won't be too long." Don Ginetti, along with his other associates, waited to hear if Danny Marco was dead.

Inside the house, Danny was growing restless in his sleep. He grabbed the sheets from his bed, twisting his head back and forth and breathing hard. At the same time, the two hit men entered and proceeded to his bedroom to kill him. Inside the room, the light from the moon shone brightly through the window. Danny opened his eyes, and they were red and burning. The werewolf was coming again. The two hit men stood by his bedroom door and heard a growling sound.

One said to the other, "Fuck, he has a dog! Let's move." They opened the door and saw fear.

The driver sitting in his car with Don Ginetti on the phone suddenly heard screams and gunfire. "What the fuck!" said the driver.

"What's going on?" asked Don Ginetti.

Suddenly the driver heard a crash. From outside, he saw one of the men fly out to his death from the bedroom window. It was as if he was thrown out.

"Holy Christ!" said the driver. "Don Ginetti, he killed our guys!"

"What the fuck is going on?" exclaimed the Don.

Suddenly the driver looked out and saw something coming out of the window. It was tall and hairy with paws and red eyes looking right at him. "Oh my God! Don Ginetti, it's that thing!"

"You have got to be kidding me!" said the Don. "Get out of there."

The driver dropped his phone, started the car, and sped away. But the werewolf saw this and went after the driver, jumping over cars and getting closer to the driver, who was scared to death. "Sir, I can't shake this thing. It's getting closer." Don Ginetti and his men could do nothing but listen to the horror. The driver slammed into other cars as the werewolf was getting closer. Other people watched as the driver got out and started shooting. The onlookers dropped for cover. The driver knew the end was near, for standing on top of another car was the werewolf. He screamed, but the werewolf grabbed him by the throat and picked him up. The driver was in the grip of a powerful beast who looked at him with his red eyes. The other people watching couldn't believe what was happening before them.

"What the fuck is going on?" said Don Ginetti on the phone.

The driver's last words were, "Mr. Ginetti, get away before it comes for you."

The werewolf pulled back its razor-sharp paw and sunk it into the chest of the driver, killing him. Screams of fear came from the pedestrians. Some had their iPhones out, taking a video of the carnage.

The werewolf had killed another prey. And like the others, he dropped the dead body, looked up toward the moon, and howled. Don Ginetti stood up and looked at the others for an answer, but they had none. They had just heard the howling of the werewolf, and from what the driver had said, the don was next!

The werewolf looked at the people around him who were taking his picture and videotaping him. He growled at them loudly. They backed away in fear, still taking his picture as the werewolf ran like the hunter he was, jumping over cars and running up a building until he disappeared into the night. And from another spot, on top of another store, a pair of ghostly eyes watched everything until it went away.

Back at Danny's apartment, police were covering up the two dead bodies while waiting for them to be removed. Danny's apartment was now a crime scene. Paul Corillo arrived, along with Marie and Danny's mother.

"Oh, dear God," exclaimed his mother. "Danny!"

"It's okay," said the police officer to his mother. "Danny Marco was not here. In fact, we are looking for him. Do you have any idea where he is?"

Marie responded, "If we knew where the fuck he was, we would not be here!"

Paul stepped in. "Marie, take Mrs. Marco back to her car. I'll handle this."

She looked at Paul and then walked away with Ellen Marco. "Well, detective, where is Danny Marco?" asked the police officer.

"First of all, officer, yes, I am Detective Paul Corillo." He looked at the name on the officer's badge. "Sanders?"

"Yes, detective," replied Officer Sanders.

"How long have you been on the job?"

"Just about a year, sir. What is your point?"

"The point, Officer Sanders, is watch your mouth when speaking to a higher rank. You're talking to me like I'm a suspect!"

"Detective, I meant no disrespect, sir."

"Don't give me that bullshit. You're a young rookie trying to make his bones and look like a top dog. Not with me you're not. Understand, Sanders?"

"Detective, once again, I'm sorry. I was just—"

But Paul stopped him. "Shut the fuck up. Get a statement from anyone and get back to me. You think you can do that, Sanders?"

"Yes," said the young police officer.

"Good. Dismissed."

The officer walked away in humiliation. Paul looked up at the moon and started thinking, *My God, Danny, what happened tonight? Where the hell did you go?* He shook his head. *Did you take the meds I gave you?* Paul walked to where the first man had been thrown out the window.

"What can you tell me?" asked Paul.

The CSI leader replied, "Detective, it's just like at the warehouse. Look at him." He uncovered the body. "Look at the hole in his chest. It's unreal. I've never seen anything like this in my career. You think it's related to Marco?"

"What would it have to do with Danny Marco?" asked Paul.

"Come on, detective, it's no secret that these two were hit men for the Ginettis. And it's no secret ex-Detective Marco and Nicky Ginetti had a private war going on, and now this? It's just too much of a coincidence. And the driver of these two was found just blocks away, killed in the exact same way."

"You leave the theory to me and just do your job," said Paul.

"Detective Corillo?"

Paul turned around to the presence of Lt. Frank Mano. He grabbed Paul by the arm as they walked away to talk in private. "Paul, what the fuck happened tonight? And where is Marco?"

"Sir, I don't know where he is."

"Don't give me that bullshit. I am giving you a direct order. Where the hell is Marco?"

"Sir, I don't know."

"Come on, detective."

"Did you forget what happened to him that night? Ever since he was attacked, by whatever attacked him, he has not been the same. My God, his father is dead. The pizzeria is gone. He's been suspended until further notice, and now these thugs tried to kill him. We should try to find him and help him, not persecute him!"

"Stand down, detective," replied Lieutenant Mano. "We need to find him and find out what the hell happened tonight before there is another hit by the Ginetti crew. But we have another problem."

Paul looked at Lieutenant Mano with confusion. "What else could there possibly be, sir?" asked Paul.

"That thing that attacked these men and the driver, whatever it was, it was caught on camera and posted on social media and has gone viral."

Paul thought, *Oh, dear God, Danny.*

"Detective, just check your phone, and you will see what I mean."

Paul took out his phone and went to the Internet. He found what he was looking for and hit play. His facial expression said it all.

Meanwhile, back at the Ginetti residence, in his soundproof room, the Untouchable Don was with his associates going over what they had just heard over the phone—a growling sound from a beast that they could not explain and the last words of his hit man before the werewolf killed him.

Even in the soundproofed room, his voice was loud. "Can someone please tell me what the fuck happened tonight? It was supposed to be a clean hit, and then shit happened!" He was pacing back and forth while speaking with his associates, who did not have an answer

71

for him. "First Nicky, and now this. What the fuck are we missing?" He looked at the man closer to him. "Any word on our inside guy?"

"Nothing, Don Ginetti."

"How about the streets?"

"Sir, there is word that when our man was killed, people saw what killed him. They said it was a hairy-looking guy with sharp teeth and claws. And it howled to the moon."

Don Ginetti just looked at him. "What the fuck are you talking about? Howled to the moon? Are you saying that it was some sort of a wolfman?"

"Sir, there is no other way to describe it, but yes, from what people are saying, that's what it was."

"Has everyone lost their fucking mind!" screamed the don. "A wolfman? Oh, great, and who is next? Frankenstein and Dracula? Don't give me that shit! It was probably Marco dressed up like that, or he hired someone with a lifelike costume to kill our boys."

"Then, sir, how was he able to jump over cars and run on top of a building?"

The don turned to the other associate, his face red. "That's what I'm asking, you fucks!"

Another associate looked at his phone. "Don Ginetti!"

"What?"

"Sir, you may want to see this." He turned on the TV to the news. The don and his men watched.

> Breaking news from Brooklyn. Another brutal slaying happened again tonight in the Dyker Heights section of Brooklyn.
>
> Two armed men broke into the home of a NYC detective and were brutally slain. Near the incident, witnesses said they saw something chasing a car and described it as a hairy beast.
>
> Yes, you heard it, a hairy best. This beast was recorded by pedestrians as it went after a man whom police are assuming was one of the burglars.

Please note that what you are about to see is graphic, and viewer discretion is advised.

As you can see, this beast jumped onto the roof of the car and crashed its hand inside the windshield, pulling out the driver by the neck. With one hand, it dug into the man's chest.

This part we are blurring due to the nature of the killing.

When it released the man, you can see it looking up and howling at the moon before turning its attention to the onlookers and growling at them before turning away and escaping.

The police are unable to locate it and are advising everyone to stay indoors. Many are saying this could be a vigilante looking for justice and concealing his identity.

As for the NYC detective, he is missing at this time, and his identity will not be disclosed until he is found.

Thank you for joining us.

The associate turned off the TV, and they all looked at Don Ginetti.

"So, it's been Marco all along. If that's not him dressed up as this wolfman, then he has help. Possibly his partner Corillo or someone else. Whoever it is, we need to find him before he finds us. Reach out to your source at the police precinct and to everyone we have out there. I'm going to put an end to this bullshit and put Marco in a grave next to his father."

The don's phone rang. "Hello? Wait one minute." He put the phone down and addressed his associates. "You guys, out and start getting me some answers." As the last one left and closed the door, he spoke again to the caller.

"Salvatore, on behalf of the families, we are very sorry for your loss."

"Thank you," replied the don.

"Now on to more urgent matters. We saw the news regarding this beast killing your men. What can you tell us?"

"It's all bullshit. It's that Detective Marco. He killed Nicky, and now, he is coming after us looking like Bigfoot. I won't let that happen."

"And how do you know it was Marco?" asked the caller.

"How do I know? That prick Marco and Nicky have been at it since the day at the pizzeria. I told Nicky to stay away, but his ego got the best of him. Now that Marco is suspended, he figured the best way to get Nicky was with a costume. He killed my sister's son, my nephew. I had to strike back, but he beat us to the punch. There will be no next time for him. I promise you that."

"Salvatore, you are letting your personal feelings cloud your judgment. We know Nicky was family, but at the same time, you are moving too fast. From what we understand, Marco is missing, and they are looking for him and the other individual. Until they are found, we want you to stay low and let this pass. Your personal vendetta will hurt not only yourself but also all of us if you kill Marco. Please let this pass, mourn your nephew, and let's move on."

"With all due respect, no!" exclaimed the Don. "I can't let Marco get away with this. My sister is a mess and wants to know what I'm going to do about it. I'm going to find Marco and finish him regardless of what the other bosses think. It wasn't their nephew who was killed. It was my nephew. If it were you, you would be doing the same thing right now."

"I was afraid of this," said the caller. "Salvatore, we go back a long way, and I supported you in everything you did, but now, I must take a step back. If you go after Marco, you will not have the support of the other bosses, and anything that happens will be on you and only you. You will be on your own. Do you understand what I am saying? Please rethink this."

Don Ginetti took a deep breath. "Sounds like you all made your decision. I'm sorry, but it's my decision, and I'm moving forward."

"Very well," said the caller. "I was hoping it would not come down to this. This will be the last time you hear from me. All I can do is wish you luck. Goodbye, Salvatore." The caller ended the call.

A HOWLING IN BROOKLYN

Don Ginetti now stood alone. He thought to himself, *So they won't support me. Fuck them all! I don't need them. Once I get rid of Marco, I will own the police force and Dyker Heights. Everyone will know who is in charge. Me, the Untouchable Don. The other bosses will beg me to come back. Now to find Marco.*

CHAPTER 4

Ellen had just finished watching the news of what had happened last night and was on the phone with Marie. "Oh, dear God, Marie. What in the world is going on? I tried calling the precinct, and all they can tell me is that there is an investigation going on and they are trying to locate Danny. They are not telling me anything else. For all we know, he could be dead!"

"Ellen, please get a grip on yourself. You don't know that. You need to stay positive. How do you think I feel? We're getting married soon, and so much has happened ever since that night at that damn cabin. Why couldn't they just have gone to Atlantic City? I had to open my mouth and say no so he could save money. And then the problem with Nicky Ginetti, and look what happened to him. The media is saying he was brutally slain. I can't say I feel sorry for him," said Marie.

"He was trouble the day he was born," replied Ellen. "Who knows how many people wanted him dead. His uncle spoiled him and gave him anything he wanted. He thought for sure he was invincible as long as Don Ginetti protected him, and look what happened to him. Do you think this has anything to do with Danny?"

"I'm not sure," said Marie. "We need to get ahold of Paul Corillo. He signed Danny out of the hospital. If anyone knows, it's Paul."

"Good luck getting information out of him," said Ellen. "He and Danny have been friends since childhood, and they will not talk behind each other's back. They are so stubborn."

"That's for sure," agreed Marie. "I'm going to try and call Paul. I will let you know if I hear anything. Please stay positive. Danny is alive."

"I hope so, dear," replied Ellen. "Call me, please, as soon as you get any news."

"I will. Talk to you later."

Danny, where are you? thought his mother with tears in her eyes after speaking with Marie. Suddenly, her dog started making motions to go out the back door to the yard. "You need to go already? All right, calm down. I've never seen you so jumpy. No more treats for you after dinner." But her dog continued to jump by the door and looked back as if saying, *Please let me out.*

"Okay," said Ellen Marco.

She unlocked the door and opened it, and the dog went running out to something lying on the grass. She was shocked to see her son Danny lying on the grass, naked and dirty. "Oh, dear God, Danny." She ran to him and saw he was still alive. She hugged him as he started to come to.

"Where am I?" asked Danny.

"You are home, my baby, in the backyard."

"How did I get here?" He looked at himself. "Mom, please get me something to wear." Danny started to recognize where he was: the house where he had grown up as a child. He got up and ran into the house, and his mother brought him his father's robe. He put it on. She hugged him.

"We have been worried sick about you. What happened to you?"

"Mom, I promise to tell you all about it, but first I need to shower. I smell like I was in a sewer."

"You shower, and I'll call Marie."

"No!" Danny protested, startling his mother.

"What in the world is wrong with you? She is almost your wife. She has every right to know you are here. I can't keep that from her."

"Mom, please listen to me. Let me call Paul first, and then he can get Marie. I want to make sure she is not being watched."

"Watched? By whom?"

"The Ginettis," said Danny. "Mom, please let me handle this, okay?"

"Fine, Danny. I just don't understand any of this."

"I know, Mom, and I don't either. Please make me some breakfast. I'm starving."

"Okay, sweetie, but promise me you will call Marie."

"I promise. I swear I will."

She went back to the kitchen to make breakfast. When he saw that she was occupied with that, he took her cell phone and called the one man he could trust, Paul Corillo.

Paul Corillo arrived at noon at the home of Ellen Marco. He stepped out of his car and looked around to make sure he was not being watched. When he was satisfied, he headed to the Marco residence. He looked behind him again and knocked on the door. Within seconds, the door opened. Danny Marco was behind the door so anyone watching would not see him.

"Hurry and come in," he said.

Paul stepped in, and the door was slammed shut. Danny looked from the window of the door to see if Paul had been followed.

"Relax," said Paul. "I wasn't followed."

"Can you be sure of that?" asked Danny, looking at Paul. "Those pills you gave me had no effect. Instead, it just made it worse."

Paul shook his head. "Danny, I'm sorry. We are running out of options. Ginetti's men are looking for you. The department wants to question you regarding last night. Do you remember anything?"

Before Danny could answer, Ellen Marco came from her bedroom and was shocked to see Paul. "Paul, when did you get here?"

"I just arrived, Mrs. Marco. I came to check on Danny." He smiled at her.

"What is going on?" asked Ellen Marco. "Did he tell you I found him outside in my garden sleeping on the ground with no clothes on?"

"Mom?" said Danny.

"Danny, stop!" said Ellen. "I received a text this morning from a friend saying two dead men were found outside your home, and another man was killed trying to get away from a hairy-looking beast."

Danny and Paul looked at each other and back at her. "Mom," said Danny.

But he was cut off again by his mother. "I don't want to hear any more. It's been too much with the loss of your father, and now this? Danny, please tell me what is going on. I'm your mother, and I demand to know!"

"Mom!" Danny grabbed her by the arms. "You just don't understand the nightmare that is happening to me. Ever since that night at the cabin, my life has been turned into a damn nightmare."

"Danny, calm down!" Paul pulled Danny away from his mother. Ellen Marco was shocked at how Danny was acting.

"Mom, I'm sorry. Please forgive me, but it's best you stay in the dark. It's too hard to explain."

At that moment, there was another knock on the door and then a voice. "Ellen, it's Marie. Is Danny with you? I just saw Paul's car outside."

"Oh no, not now," Danny said.

Ellen went to open the door, but she was stopped by Paul. "Wait, Mrs. Marco. Stay with Danny in the corner. I will open the door."

"I don't understand any of this," said Ellen.

"Mom," Danny said. They looked at each other in silence, while Marie kept knocking and raising her voice to be let in. Paul took a breath and opened the door.

Marie looked at Paul. "What the hell is going on?" But before she could finish, he grabbed her and pulled her in fast and slammed the door shut. "Oh dear God. What is wrong with everyone?" Then she saw Danny. Marie ran to him and hugged him. "Damn it, Danny, you have been here all this time and never bothered to call me? Everyone is looking for you. There was a murder at your home. What is going on?" She turned to Ellen. "Why didn't you tell me he was here?"

Suddenly Danny exploded. "Marie, shut the fuck up, now!"

There was silence again in the Marco home. Danny closed his eyes and breathed slowly to regain his composure.

"Wait," said Paul. "Let's all just try to calm down and breathe. This is affecting all of us, and it will just get worse before it gets better."

"You guys must explain what is going on," demanded Marie. "Everything was going so well until you were attacked at the cabin." Danny looked at Paul, and they could read each other like a book. How would Danny explain to his mother and his fiancée that he was attacked by what might have possibly been a female werewolf and that now he was werewolf? And how would he explain Lisa Jacobson to Marie? She would think he wanted her.

"Guys, we are waiting," said Ellen Marco.

Danny shook his head and smiled and then looked at Paul.

"Danny," said Paul, "you just can't keep this to yourself anymore."

"Let's all take a seat," suggested Danny.

"Wait," said Marie. "Tell me, Danny. Is there another woman?"

Danny must now tell her about Lisa Jacobson, but how would Marie and his mother react to what happened that night?

"No, there is no other woman. But something did happen that night at the cabin, and it involved a woman and her father."

"Did you sleep with this woman?" asked Marie.

"No. Will you please just listen to me and stop interrupting me, Marie!"

"Easy, Danny," said Paul. "Let's all just sit down and stay focused."

They sat on the couch, Danny with Marie and Paul and Ellen on the opposite couch. Danny Marco took another very deep breath and looked at everyone and began.

He started with the night Marie was leaving for work and his dream of the werewolf speaking to him from the TV and then the dark figure he saw outside. His mind played back every detail as he continued to tell his mother and Marie the events that led to that night—the dreams he was having and the feeling of being watched yet not knowing who was watching him, and then the knock on the door, and Sebastian and Lisa Jacobson. Danny explained how Lisa tried to convince him that he belonged to her, but he assumed it was a bad joke by the guys and wondered why no one came out to check up on him and her. Then after the Jacobsons left, he went back out to get some beer and thought he heard her voice. He turned around and saw something with red eyes coming for him. He remembered drawing his revolver and started shooting, and then everything went dark.

Marie shook her head in disbelief, as did Ellen Marco. But before she could say anything, Paul then continued, "Ladies, please hear me out." He told them that they had run outside and found Danny on the ground in pain with blood coming out of his shoulder. They had to get Danny out of there and fast, and that was when it began. He mentioned the mysterious red eyes he saw in the darkness as he and his fellow officers started firing their guns at whatever was out there in the dark, and then they heard the howling of what sounded like wolves. Moving ahead, he told them that after he had signed Danny out of the hospital that evening, Danny decided to stake out Nicky Ginetti's warehouse to find the missing evidence that proved Nicky had killed his father, but they were caught by Nicky's crew.

Danny took over and explained how he was getting beaten in another room and thought for sure he was going to die, until a full moon appeared at the window, and he felt himself changing into something. He had felt such rage that needed to kill and be free. The thing that he turned into was a werewolf. Paul then explained how he saw this werewolf kill the men who were beating Danny. Then it turned to the men holding Paul.

Paul finished by saying that Nicky Ginetti and another man had him at gunpoint as they tried to get away, but it was too late. He then looked for Danny. But when he ran outside, he was shocked to see this hairy beast holding Nicky Ginetti by the throat. With its other hand, it ripped into Nicky Ginetti's chest and killed him. Nicky was the last one to die. Then he said that he aimed his gun at the thing, telling it not to move. And then he saw something shining on it, reflecting the moonlight. He mentioned the gold cross that belonged to Danny's father, Peter Marco. Ellen Marco had given it to Danny in the hospital. He told them the thing, the werewolf, was wearing the gold cross, and that was when he knew it was Danny. Incredible as it sounded, it was Danny. Then they started to hear sirens getting closer and closer. The werewolf turned, leaped over a car, and disappeared.

Ellen Marco and Marie were in total shock at what they had just heard. However, they were not ready to accept it.

"So, Danny, you are telling us that you are a werewolf, and you turn into a werewolf when the moon is full?" asked Marie.

Danny could only say yes.

Shaking her head, she looked at Ellen. "Are you buying this, Ellen?"

Ellen was at a loss for words. "As of now, I don't know what to believe anymore."

"Mom," said Danny. "You need to understand. I know this is hard to believe, but as absurd as it sounds, and Lord knows even I can't accept it, it's true. I am a werewolf."

"Wait just a second," replied Marie. "So the other night, with those two men that were killed, that was you?"

Paul answered, "Marie, it wasn't Danny who killed them, but the thing he turned into, the werewolf. Marie, that night, before Danny went to bed, he needed something strong to knock him out and prevent the werewolf from coming out. I reached out to my contacts, and I got Danny Temazepam."

"Temazepam?" asked Marie. "You need a prescription for that."

"I know, Marie," replied Paul. "But I was able to get it without a prescription with the help my contacts."

With her head down, Marie shook her head. "This is just insane! I guess it didn't work." She looked at Danny.

Danny said, "I was dreaming. I saw myself back in the woods, running and breathing hard. I felt like I was hunting, but I didn't know what my prey was. As I was dreaming, Salvatore Ginetti sent a hit squad to kill me."

"What?" said Ellen Marco. "Oh dear God, no!"

"Mom, please," said Danny.

"So you're telling me that the pills didn't work, the killers were inside your room that night, and as they were about to finish you,

you turned into a werewolf at the full moon, and it killed them, right?" asked Marie.

"Marie, you saw the news. There's your answer," Danny replied.

"Then how did you end up in the backyard?" asked Ellen. "This morning, the dog started barking by the back door. When I opened the door, I found Danny asleep on the ground with no clothes and all dirty."

Marie looked at Ellen and then at Paul and Danny. She got up, shaking her head, and walked away, and then she finally broke out and turned. "Danny, is this the best you can come up with? If you do not want to get married, then let's end this now."

Danny got up and walked toward her. "Marie, I know this sounds crazy, and I would not believe it myself if I were in your shoes. My life has been turned upside down, but it's all true. I'm a fucking werewolf!"

"Don't come near me," said Marie.

Paul and Ellen jumped up and walked toward them. "Marie, you need to calm down," urged Paul. "This is affecting all of us, and we need to stay calm."

"Fuck you, Paul!" screamed Marie.

"Marie!" said Ellen.

"No, I don't want to hear this anymore!" Marie looked at Danny. "You and your werewolf bullshit! You could never stop watching it on TV no matter how many times I told you! You just would not. Danny, just admit it. You met another ass at the cabin, you fucked her brains out, and you want her!"

"That's not true. I love you so much," said Danny. "How do you explain me getting attacked?"

"Oh, please, dickface. It was probably a bear that attacked you, and you guys assumed something else to cover it up!"

"Marie, that is not true," interrupted Paul. "There were no reports of bears anywhere that night. It was checked by local authorities. No one knows what attacked Danny, but now we do. As incredible as it sounds, it's true."

Marie was not yet done. "Yeah? Well, what about those two? Sebastian and Lisa Jacobson?"

"Paul tried to find them, but there was no one who fitted their description," explained Danny.

"Oh, please."

"Marie, please, you have to believe me," pleaded Danny. "I would never betray you. You are my life!"

"Yeah, your life? Did you say that to Lisa also?"

Danny raised his arms up and looked at Paul.

"I will tell you this, Danny. I don't believe any of your bullshit! Yes, you got hurt. The Ginettis tried to kill you, and somehow you were able to kill them, but no way am I going to believe that you are a *werewolf*."

"Marie, please," said Danny.

"No! Do not come near me!"

"Marie," said Ellen.

"No, Ellen. Your son found himself another bitch to party."

"Marie," yelled Danny. "You are out of line, and to my mother."

"No, Danny. You did this to us and your family. I'm so done with you."

"Wait! Just wait," said Paul. "We can't fall apart."

"Marie, I am putting my career on the line for you," explained Danny. "We have to stick together and pull through this now!"

"I don't want to hear any more of this," said Marie. "I have to get out of here and now."

"Marie, please," pleaded Ellen.

"Marie, stop," said Paul.

"Leave me alone, all of you!" screamed Marie.

While this was going on, Danny could not help but feel someone was outside the door. He looked toward it. "Guys, guys, stop! There is someone outside."

"What? I didn't hear anyone knock," replied Ellen.

But before Danny could check, the door was forced open and the police moved in. "Everyone on the ground now!"

"Hold on a second. I'm Detective Danny Marco, and this is Detective Paul Corillo."

"Stand down," said Paul.

"I know who you both are, and I'm ordering you all on the ground now!"

"Who gave you the order to come into this is house?" asked Paul. "It belongs to his mother, Ellen Marco."

Ellen and Marie were crying in fear, not knowing what to do.

"You assholes are scaring my mother! Put down your weapons now!" said Danny.

But before he could say anything else, Danny Marco was shot with a Taser gun. He felt a strong electrical bolt go through his body, and then he went down, convulsing.

"Oh dear God!" said his mother. Marie ran to her and held her back, while Paul stood in front of them.

"What the fuck is wrong with you guys? We are detectives. Did you not hear us?" asked Paul.

"Back away," said the police officer as he pointed his gun at Paul.

Paul stepped back, and the other two officers put cuffs on Danny. "Leave him alone," screamed his mother.

"Ellen, I'll take care of this." Paul looked at her and then at the police. "You guys are in so much deep shit!"

"Calm down, detective," said the one officer. "You think we wanted to do this? Arrest a fellow police officer? We are just following orders."

"Orders? Who gave the order, dirtbag?"

"Stand down, Detective Corillo." Paul looked at the figure walking in and went into shock as he saw who it was.

Lieutenant Frank Mano.

"Frank, you did this? To Danny and to his family? Are you fucking insane? You could have done this another way."

"Detective, you will respond to me as Lieutenant," said Frank Mano. "You knew where Detective Marco was all along. You could have brought him in for questioning, but you didn't. You want to kiss your pension goodbye, Paul? I had you followed, and sure enough, here you are with him."

"You son of a bitch," exclaimed Paul. "I guess the night at the cabin was nothing but a lie to you! I thought we were all brothers. Danny almost died!"

"Don't give me that brothers bullshit," replied Frank Mano. "What happened then and now are two different things, and you know it. I'm sorry what happened to Danny that night. I can't explain it, and I won't. But at the same time, I have to explain to the powers that be why you and Marco went into a stakeout without my knowledge, and as a result, Nicky Ginetti is dead. What happened yesterday all points to Marco."

"You ass! His uncle sent a hit team to kill Danny!"

"Yes, and those men are dead. Everything points to Marco."

"Then how do you explain that thing that the witnesses saw? It was caught on video by so many people."

"My guess is it was Marco for all I know!"

"Stop that!" yelled Ellen Marco. "He is my son, not an animal! And you came into my husband's pizzeria acting like a friend. Damn you!" Marie held Ellen back as she screamed at Lieutenant Mano.

"Mrs. Marco, I am sorry. I am truly sorry, but I have a job to do."

"Danny," said Marie, with tears in her eyes.

"Marie, I will make sure nothing happens to him. But this has to be done. Get him up," said Lieutenant Mano.

"Sir," said the officer, "he's unconscious."

"What? Impossible!"

"You fuck! How much voltage did you use? He's not an animal!" exclaimed Paul.

"Oh, Danny," said his mother, crying in Marie's arms.

"You bastard," Marie uttered to Lieutenant Mano.

"I hope you are happy with yourself," Paul said to Frank Mano.

"This is crazy," replied Lieutenant Mano. "He should not be unconscious!"

"Sir, we followed procedure," explained the officer.

Shaking his head in disbelief, the lieutenant said, "Take him to the hospital now!"

"I'm coming too," said Paul.

"No, you will not. Get your ass to the department. You have a lot of explaining to do to the top brass."

Paul looked at Ellen and Marie. "I have to go, but I promise once I get this squared away, I will contact you and keep you both updated on Danny. Please do not give up on him or me." He hugged them both and left with the officers carrying Danny.

Lieutenant Mano turned to Ellen and Marie. "Ladies, please understand. I had a job to do. Danny is still my friend."

"Still your friend?" asked Ellen Marco. "Get the fuck out of my house, you son of a bitch!"

Without saying a word, he turned and left. Ellen and Marie hugged and cried.

Hours later, after leaving the police precinct, Paul Corillo was exhausted. His day had gone from bad to worse, and it would just worsen before it ended. He knew soon he wouldn't be able to protect Danny once everyone knew the truth about him.

"Paul!" called a voice. He turned and saw Officer Ray Amato approaching him. They shook hands. "Paul, I've been hearing what's going on, and I just can't believe all this. And now Danny is in the hospital thanks to Lieutenant Mano."

"Yes, and to make this day even better, I've been suspended from active duty till further notice," Paul replied.

"Are you kidding me? Why?"

"After Danny was taken in, I was ordered here for answers, which I didn't have. They think I'm protecting Danny and felt it was necessary to suspend me until they have all the facts."

"I can't believe this. Both you and Danny are suspended all because of the night at the cabin. I am starting to regret ever going there."

"We can't change the past. But for now, Danny needs me more than ever. The Ginettis will stop at nothing to kill him."

"Paul, I'm with you if you need help," said Ray.

"You don't have to do this, Ray."

"Bullshit! You think you guys were the only ones grilled! I had to give a full statement about that night. And when they read about the howling, they thought we were drunk or high. I was ordered not to talk about this to anyone. I've been laying very low ever since."

"What about Messina?" asked Paul.

"He decided to go on a long vacation, that prick. He doesn't want to be bothered by us. Just when we need to stick together, he runs away."

"You can't blame him," replied Paul. "Look where we are now. He made his choice, so let us move forward. Right now, Danny needs us."

"Wait, all this talk about a hairy-looking beast? I saw it on YouTube. Are they kidding? Seriously? A werewolf? I thought it was a joke, but I'm hearing more about it, and I just cannot believe it to be true. It can't be true. Paul, please tell me it's not true!"

Paul Corillo just looked at Raymond Amato.

"My God! That's just impossible!"

Paul looked around him and then said, "We can't talk about this now. I'll fill you in later. I must get over to the hospital to check on Danny. It's after 5:00 p.m. Lord knows what is going on."

"Well, good luck on that. There are two police officers standing outside his room, and no one gets to see him without clearance from that dick Lieutenant Mano."

"Clearance or not, I'm going to see him. If Marie and Ellen are there, I need to be with them before something happens."

"What's that supposed to mean?" asked Ray Amato.

"I can't explain it now. I need to go."

"Wait, I'm going with you. My shift is just about over. Let me get changed and we will go."

"You don't have to do this."

"I know I don't. But Danny is my friend."

"Okay, I will wait, but hurry."

Ray nodded and ran in. Paul looked up to see the day would soon end and night would fall again. He started thinking, *Danny, please hang on. God help us.*

CHAPTER 5

ICU, Lutheran Hospital, 5:30 p.m.

In a private room, Danny Marco lay unconscious from the Taser shot he had received earlier. He was hooked up to a heart machine and IV. Next to him was the attending physician and Lieutenant Frank Mano.

"Doctor, why doesn't he wake up?" asked Lieutenant Mano.

"I wish I knew," the doctor replied. "Exactly how much voltage was used with the Taser gun?"

"Only fifty thousand volts, doctor, and no more. I've seen guys get up after it passed, but for some reason, it hasn't for him."

"How do you know your fellow officers didn't increase the voltage before firing at him?"

"Doctor, it's standard procedure not to increase the voltage, and after it's fired, it shuts down."

"Well, something went terribly wrong. You are very fortunate he is still alive."

"Doctor, I need to speak with him. Is there something you can give him to wake him up?"

"Certainly not. It could make his condition worse. Let him rest. All we can do is monitor his condition, but until then, there is nothing more we can do."

Lieutenant Mano shook his head. "Fine. Doctor, he is to have no visitors without my approval."

"And my approval," replied the doctor. "I'm in charge of his well-being, not you."

"Fine, but the two police officers outside the door are staying until further notice."

"That is fine with me as long as they do not interfere."

"You have my word on that." Then Lieutenant Mano saw Danny's closed eyes moving. "Doctor, look. Is he waking up?"

"No, he is not. He is experiencing REM."

"What?"

"Rapid eye movement, meaning he is dreaming and following his dream. That is a good sign. He is dreaming. But what he is dreaming, I don't know."

"Okay, doctor. Thank you again."

"I will come check up on him later."

When the doctor left, Frank Mano looked at Danny and his closed eyes moving in every direction. "What the fuck are you dreaming about? Danny, I'm so sorry. If there was another way…" Then his cell phone rang. He quickly answered. "This is Lieutenant Mano."

"Lieutenant, this is Commander Davis. I read what happened at the Marco residence. What the hell were you thinking?"

"Sir, please wait and let me explain. Just give me a moment." He looked at Danny, turned, and left.

He went out of the room and informed his officer to call him if anything happened. He walked away and started relaying the events at the Marco residence with his commander.

*****

Inside his room, Danny Marco was in a deep dream. In his dream, he was the hunter searching for his prey in the woods. He heard the voice of Lisa Jacobson. "Come to me, my love. I wait for you."

He then heard Marie. "Danny, how could you do this to me? I loved you so much."

He then heard his mother. "Danny, please come back to me."

Finally, he heard Paul's voice. "Danny, don't worry. I will protect you."

90

But Danny was still running and hunting, and his thirst for blood was getting stronger until he stopped and saw Nicky Ginetti standing outside the cabin with a hole in his chest, covered in blood. "Hey, Danny, Mr. Police Officer." He laughed. "You think this is over? My uncle is going to get you and get you good." He continued laughing.

Danny lunged for him, but Nicky vanished. He started hearing Nicky laughing more and more until he heard howling. Danny looked up at the night sky and then the moon. He felt energy coming to him from the shining moon until he howled.

Suddenly he heard another voice from within the cabin, a male voice. "Danny, please come inside. We need to talk, son."

Son? He recognized the voice and could not believe who it was. He opened the door and stepped inside the cabin, and to the right, sitting on the couch, was his dead father, Peter Marco. Peter was wearing the white T-shirt covered in blood the night he was killed at the pizzeria by Nicky Ginetti. Peter was smiling as he looked at his son.

"Danny, please sit down, son."

Danny sat down in shock as he said to his dead father, "Dad? How is it that you are here? You were shot by that bastard Nicky Ginetti. I'm sorry I wasn't there to protect you, Dad." He started crying into his hands.

"Danny, look at me now."

Danny looked up to his father, tears in his eyes.

With a smile, his father looked at Danny and said, "Danny, you couldn't always be there for me. You have your life to live, and you need to move on, my son. You can't blame yourself for what happened to me. Do you understand me?"

"Yes, I do."

"Good, but now you have more problems to worry about, Danny."

"What do you mean?"

"Really? Danny, you are not well. In fact, your life has taken a change ever since you were attacked by the wolf."

Surprised, Danny responded, "Dad, I don't know what's happened to me, but at night when the moon is full, my body changes, and I have a thirst for blood and a need to be free. I change into something I cannot control, and when I do, I kill and kill again and again. Dad, this is a nightmare I want to wake up from. I just want to go back to a normal life and marry Marie. But I can't. Not with this nightmare living inside me that comes out at night. I can't do this to Marie or to our family. Dad, I killed Nicky Ginetti! Well, the beast inside me did when he and his goons tried to kill me. They came for me at night, and I killed them. Last time this happened was at my place, and when I woke up, Mom found me in the backyard sleeping on the grass and covered in dirt. I didn't remember anything the night before."

"Danny, I know what has happened."

Danny was confused. "How, Dad?"

"Danny, I know, and that's all I can tell you. I know Paul and Marie were at the house trying to make sense of what is going on, and I know Lieutenant Mano and his team burst into my house and stunned you and knocked you unconscious. And now you are at the hospital still unconscious and under guard," said Peter. "But, Danny, it's still not over."

Danny could not believe what he was hearing from his father. "Still not over? Dad, they are going to kill me, right? Tell me the truth! Are they going to kill me? Is this all a dream and I can't wake up?"

Suddenly from outside the cabin, a thunderstorm began, shaking the cabin with loud thunder. The two looked around and then at each other.

"Danny, we haven't much time. You need to listen to everything I say."

"What do you mean not much time, Dad? I don't understand."

"Listen to me, son. Tonight, Don Ginetti will try again to finish you off unless you wake up and finish this once and for all!"

"What do you mean finish this, Dad?"

"Danny! You must take out the entire Ginetti crew. Everyone, from the snitches on the streets to the muscles to the top man, Don

Ginetti. You must eliminate them all! Once you do that, then you do the right thing and turn yourself in."

He was shocked at what his father had just said. He wanted his son to kill every member of the Ginetti family. "Dad, you're asking me to kill. I can't do that! It will make me just as bad as the Ginettis."

"But it won't be you who kills them. It will be the beast inside you, the werewolf."

Danny was shocked. "Let the werewolf kill and erase the entire Ginetti family? Just like that, Dad? You think it's that easy, turn myself in? I'll be locked away for life, and I'll never see our family again. Is that what you want?"

"Danny, if you don't, the Ginettis will kill you, your mother, your sisters, and Paul. They will walk away with their hands clean, just like they did when they killed me."

Suddenly they both heard laughter. Danny knew that laugh. Walking to them from the kitchen, drinking beer with a hole in his chest and covered in blood, was Nicky Ginetti.

*****

At the same time that evening at the hospital, a lone police officer stood guard outside Danny Marco's room. It was 9:00 p.m. on a cloudy night. It was quiet as usual, but things could change in a heartbeat. The lone police officer was under strict orders from Lieutenant Mano that no one should enter Danny's room without his authorization. Outside the hospital, his childhood friend Paul Corillo and Ray Amato had just arrived.

"It's already dark. Thank God it's a cloudy night, but we must get to Danny's room fast," said Paul.

Confused about what had happened to Danny Marco, Ray Amato tried to make sense of everything that had happened since the night at the cabin till now. "Paul, this is just insane! I just cannot accept the fact that Danny is that beast I saw on the news, a werewolf. How can anything like this be real?"

"Ray, there are a lot of things in this world that cannot be explained, and this is one of them. But right now, we need to get to Danny. For all we know, Ginetti may have a hit team already inside."

"I wish we had backup," said Ray Amato.

"And what do we tell them?" asked Paul. "That Detective Marco was bitten by a werewolf and killed Nicky Ginetti? And now Don Ginetti has vowed to kill Danny?"

"I understand. It's just so weird."

After they went inside to the front desk and showed their IDs, they were told by the guard that two women had just gone up to see Detective Danny Marco. Paul looked at Ray. Two women?

"Oh God, Marie and Ellen are here." Paul looked at the guard. "How long ago did they arrive?"

"Just a few minutes ago. I told them he is on the fourth floor."

"How did we miss them?" asked Paul. "Come on, Ray, let's move."

Both ran into the next elevator. The security guard quickly got on the phone. "I need to speak with Lieutenant Mano regarding Detective Danny Marco."

Standing guard outside Danny Marco's room, the police officer on duty was approached by another fellow police officer. "Hi, I'm here to relieve you."

The officer looked puzzled. "I didn't get notice of a relief."

"Yeah, well, with all the bullshit going on, you think they have time for something like this?"

"I don't know. I think I should call this in," said the first officer.

"You really want to piss off Lieutenant Mano after all the heat he is taking 'cause of the Taser on Marco? Come on."

"I suppose you are right."

"Okay, then. Go to the cafeteria. There is a hot-looking ass serving food," the police officer responded, smiling.

"I think I will. You want some coffee?"

"Nope, I'm fine. Go check her out, you dog."

Smiling, the first police officer walked to the third elevator and got in. The second police officer on guard quickly got on his cell phone and called a number. "All is clear."

A door opened to his left. A male nurse came out with a covered tray. He approached the second officer, the fake cop. "Go in and get this done," he said.

At the same time the male nurse went inside, the first elevator doors opened. Marie and Ellen Marco exited and headed to Danny's room.

"This is not good," said the second officer.

Inside Danny's room, the male nurse uncovered the try. On the tray was a .45 automatic pistol with a silencer. Meanwhile, the fake police officer was approached by Marie and Ellen Marco.

"Hello, officer. We are here to see Danny Marco. I'm his mother, Ellen Marco, and this is his fiancée, Marie Marconi."

The male nurse inside Danny's room covered him with the blanket and called Don Ginetti. "Don Ginetti, I'm in."

"Good," replied Don Ginetti. "Get it done now. I'm tired of all the bullshit! I want him dead. You will get your payment after you send me a photo with a bullet in his head!"

"I understand," said the hit man. He put down the phone, checked his pistol, and was ready to fire, aiming for Danny's head, when he heard commotion outside Danny's room. He lowered his gun and went near the door to hear what the commotion was about. He went back to his phone. "Don Ginetti, we have a problem."

"What the fuck do you mean a problem?"

"This is so ridiculous," Ellen Marco said outside Danny's room. "I have every right to see my son. You get Lieutenant Mano on the phone right now."

"Mrs. Marco," said the fake police officer, "try to understand. I cannot let anyone inside without orders from Lieutenant Mano. You must stay calm!"

"You watch how you to talk to her," demanded Marie. "How dare you! She lost her husband, and now her son is not well. You better let us inside."

He held up his hands. "No one is going inside. Do you both understand? Please go to the cafeteria for some coffee while I call Lieutenant Mano."

"Bullshit! We're not going anywhere," declared Marie. "Call him now!"

"What the hell is going on here?" They turned to see Paul Corillo and Ray Amato arrive.

"Paul, he will not let me in to see my son," said Ellen. "I will not go anywhere until I see him."

*****

Danny Marco and his father, Peter, were shocked to see Nicky Ginetti standing there in the cabin. Danny could not make any sense out of what he was seeing. "Well, well, look at what we have here. Mr. Police Officer Danny Marco, his dead dad, and me. Hey, let's order a pizza." He started laughing.

Danny got up. "You son of a bitch!"

But Peter Marco stopped him. "It's okay, son. He cannot hurt us. He is just playing with your mind."

"Yeah, listen to your pops, Danny. You haven't much time until you hear a loud ring in your head, Danny boy," teased Nicky.

"What the hell are you talking about?" Danny asked as the storm grew louder outside.

"Danny," said Peter. "We haven't much time. Don Ginetti has sent a hit man to kill you!"

Danny was confused and shaking his head. "Dad, what are you trying to tell me?"

Peter Marco stood up and grabbed his son by his arms. "Listen to me, son. You were knocked out by a Taser at the house. Do you remember? Try to remember. We are running out of time."

*****

Back at the hospital, Paul confronted the fake police officer. "Why won't you let her see her son?"

"I have orders from Lieutenant Mano that no one is to go in without his approval regardless of who wants to see Marco. No one gets in. Now you should all leave before I have you all locked up!"

Shocked at what the fake cop said, Paul responded, "How long have you been on the job? I've never seen you before."

The fake cop started getting nervous while the hit man inside Danny's room with the gun in his hand listened to what was going on outside.

"What the fuck is going on in there?" asked Don Ginetti from the cell phone.

The hit man grabbed the phone and spoke slowly. "Sir, it appears that Marco's mother and fiancée are here, and to make matters worse, I heard two other men speaking to our guy."

"Who are they?"

"I don't know, sir, but I am stuck here in Marco's room on the fourth floor. Our guy needs to get these people out of here!" Suddenly he heard Danny Marco from under the covers breathing hard. The hit man looked at him and spoke to Don Ginetti. "Sir, we have another problem!"

*****

Back at the cabin in his mind, Danny started to remember when he was tased and knocked out. "Dad, I remember. Oh my God, I remember. Then this, all of this, is not real," he said as he looked around, scared and confused. "You're not real. You're dead just like that shit Nicky Ginetti!"

"I'm truly insulted," remarked Nicky.

"Don't pay attention to him, son. Look at me. You need to wake up and fight your way out of this, now!"

"How, Dad?"

"Danny, listen to me. The hit man is about to kill you. Wake up! Release the beast inside you!"

Danny was still shocked and could not believe what his father just said.

"Danny," said Peter Marco. "The Ginettis have caused nothing but problems for so many good people. They have killed and laughed while good people have suffered and died because of them. Nothing that would have sent them all to prison could stick to them, until now. Danny, my son, you must destroy the Ginetti family once and for all. Wipe them all out until there is no one left. You have been given a special gift by Lisa Jacobson. Use it now!"

"It's not a gift!" reasoned Danny. "It's a fucking nightmare I can't escape. Lisa Jacobson is not human! And how the hell do you know about her?"

"Oh, Danny boy," said Nicky, "you are so dead." He started laughing.

Danny looked at Nicky. "Shut the fuck up!"

"Or what? You will kill me? That's a joke, since I'm already dead, and soon you will be too." He laughed again.

"Danny, look at me," said his father. "The storm is getting louder. Please, you are running out of time!"

*****

Back at the hospital, Paul and Ray showed their badges to the fake cop. "I will ask you again. What district are you with, and why haven't I heard of you until now?" asked Paul.

"I don't think he is a cop," said Ray Amato.

Ellen and Marie stood behind Paul, stunned. "What is going on here?" asked Ellen Marco.

"That's what I want to know. Everyone, stand down now." They turned and saw Lieutenant Mano and the officer who went to the cafeteria approaching them. "Everyone, shut up now," ordered Lieutenant Mano. He then looked at the fake cop and the name on his fake badge, which said "Parrish."

"Officer Parrish, where did you come from? I never gave authorization for a relief."

"Sir," said the other police officer. "I should have checked."

"I'll deal with you later," replied Lieutenant Mano. Looking back at the fake cop, he asked again, "Who is your commander?"

"Sir, I think he is a fake cop," suggested Paul. "He may have been sent here to kill Marco."

"Now why would I do that?" asked the fake cop, smiling with his hand on his gun.

"Freeze!" ordered Officer Ray Amato as he and the other police officer aimed their guns at him.

"Who the hell are you?" asked Lieutenant Mano.

In his hospital room, Danny Marco started to move from under the covers and gave out a light growl. Confused, the hit man reached for his phone. "Don Ginetti?"

"What the hell is going on?" asked the don. "Kill him now!"

"Sir, I can't. There is commotion going on outside the door, and something is going on with Marco."

"What? Is he awake?"

"I don't know, sir."

"What do you mean you don't know?"

"Sir, I put a blanket over his head and was ready, but he kept moving, and I am hearing growls coming from him."

"Growls? What? Does he have a fucking dog with him?"

"Sir, something is not right here."

"Don't you bail out until he is dead!"

"Sir, until I find out what is going on outside his door, I am stuck. Sounds like our man has been made."

"Oh, shit!" exclaimed the don. "Now what?"

*****

"I will ask you again. Who are you?" asked Lieutenant Mano.

"Sir, he is a fake cop sent here by Don Ginetti," said Paul Corillo.

"What is going on?" asked Ellen Marco, scared and in tears. Marie held her back behind Paul and Ray Amato.

"What the hell is going on?" They turned to see hospital security running toward them.

In an instant, the fake cop drew his gun and aimed it at everyone. "Don't move," said the fake cop. "I'm getting out of here."

"You have no place to go," replied Lieutenant Mano. "Lower your weapon now!" He did not comply.

"You have no place to go," said Paul Corillo. "You are outnumbered. Don't let this get ugly. Stand down now!"

*****

Back at the cabin, Peter Marco looked out the window to see a full moon. He turned to his son. "Danny, it's time. The moon is out. Save yourself and wake up. Save your mother and Marie. They are at the hospital. All hell is about to break loose!"

Danny was confused, scared, and sweating. He could not make out anything more until he felt the moon's energy. "Oh, dear God. It's happening again. Dad, get out of here now!"

"Danny, I'm already dead," replied his father. "And soon you will be. Please, son, wake up!"

"Forget it, Peter," said Nicky Ginetti. "He is a scared chicken, just like you. Say your prayers, Danny boy, 'cause in a few seconds you will be dead like me." Nicky started laughing.

Peter Marco looked at Danny. "Danny, it's time. Let the beast out now."

Danny covered his face with his hands. Shaking, he now knew. Suddenly he growled, stronger and stronger, until he looked up, and his eyes were red for blood.

*****

Back in his hospital room, the hit man saw more movement from under the covers and didn't know what to make of it. He saw from the window the clouds had passed, and it was a full moon. He turned to the door, where he heard loud voices telling the fake cop to drop his gun.

Don Ginetti was screaming on the phone, "What the fuck is going on?"

Outside the door, Paul ordered, "Drop your weapon now!" Ellen and Marie stood there in fear.

"You have no place to go," said Lieutenant Mano. "Don't let it end like this."

The fake cop knew he would go to jail and did not have any options left. He was ready to die to avoid going to jail. He had made up his mind to shoot his way out.

As he prepared to open fire, from inside the room, the hit man was standing by the door, his gun up, when suddenly he heard the growls from Danny Marco getting louder. He approached Danny very slowly with his gun aimed at him. Danny was still moving under the blanket and growling. The hit man walked closer to the bed. With one hand holding the gun, the other hand quickly removed the blanket. The man under the blanket was no longer Danny Marco. The hit man looked into the red eyes of the beast, a werewolf! And that would be the last thing he would ever see again. The werewolf attacked, and the hit man screamed.

Out in the hallway, they all reacted in fear to the scream inside Danny's room. "Oh my God, Danny," said Ellen Marco. "He needs help!" Then they heard the growling getting louder and louder as it approached the door. They started to step back, including the fake cop, who did not know what was going on. He moved to the left. Lieutenant Mano and the others stepped to the right, all guns drawn and aimed at the door, as the growls continued to get louder. Paul Corillo could only imagine what was about to happen. He knew what he heard was not Danny.

"Whoever is in there, step out with your hands up! Now!" ordered Lieutenant Mano.

And just like that, the werewolf came crashing through the door. It stood on its hind legs, body covered in hair and armed with razor-sharp teeth and bloodthirsty eyes. The blood of the hit man dripped from its paws. Still in hospital gown, it was no longer Danny Marco but the werewolf.

Both women screamed in fear as the werewolf released a strong, loud, and fearful growl.

"What the fuck is that?" asked Ray Amato. His gun was still aimed at the werewolf.

"Stand down," ordered Paul Corillo. "Don't shoot, please. Don't shoot it. It's Danny!"

"What?" exclaimed Lieutenant Mano.

Both Marie and Ellen could not believe what they had just heard. "What the hell is going on?" asked Marie.

"Shoot it," ordered Lieutenant Mano.

"No!" protested Paul.

Suddenly, on instinct, the werewolf decided to escape. It turned to the fake cop, who fired, but the werewolf pushed him out of the way and started his escape from the hospital. Lieutenant Mano and the other police officers opened fire at the werewolf as it ran. They started to pursue it, while Lieutenant Mano called for emergency backup on his police radio.

"This is Lieutenant Mano. We have an emergency. Shots have been fired. Need Emergency Services at my location at Lutheran Hospital. We are chasing what looks to be a hairy beast."

"What are you chasing, sir?" asked the responder.

"Just do as I say now!"

Paul turned to Ray Amato. "Get them out of here now. It's not safe."

"What about Danny? We can't leave him here," said Ellen Marco.

"I will stay with him. Now, please, Mrs. Marco, you all have to get out of here. It's dangerous."

"What the hell was that thing?" asked Marie.

"Marie, I'll explain later, but for now, please, you have to get out of here."

Ray Amato looked at Paul. "I'll get them out of here."

As they started to leave, Paul turned to see that the fake cop was gone. In all the commotion, he managed to get away. Paul quickly looked into Danny's room and turned away at the sight of what Danny, or the werewolf, had done to the hit man. He looked down the hallway and joined the chase. He could not let them kill the werewolf. If the werewolf died, then Danny died.

He heard gunfire and followed the sounds. The werewolf was running in random directions, looking for a way out. Hospital staff members were screaming at the sight of what was coming toward them. They stepped out of its way in fear, not knowing what it was.

Lieutenant Mano, the other police officers, and hospital security followed close by.

"Everyone, on the ground!" screamed Lieutenant Mano as he and the other police officers opened fire on the werewolf with little effect.

The werewolf saw a window and started running for it, only to be met by other security hospital guards. They tried to stop it, but the werewolf threw them back like rag dolls, injuring some of them.

The werewolf turned, saw a window, and knew it could escape from there. Then it heard Lieutenant Mano and turned to face him.

"Freeze," ordered Lieutenant Mano. "You have no place to go. Stand down."

Their guns were aimed at the werewolf. Paul Corillo arrived, breathing heavily from his run, with his gun drawn. "Please don't kill it."

"What the fuck are you saying, Corillo? Is that Danny in that costume?"

Suddenly the werewolf growled again. They looked at it. The werewolf turned toward the window and started running for its escape. Lieutenant Mano and the other police officers started firing a hail of bullets at the werewolf.

"No!" screamed Paul.

The werewolf made it to the window and crashed through it, landing on the ground, and then it stood up to see dozens of police officers on the scene. It growled again and started running and leaping over cars. The other police officers fired at the werewolf, again with little effect. It continued running, followed by police cars.

Lieutenant Mano, Paul, and the other officers made it downstairs and outside. "Report," ordered Lieutenant Mano to the officers outside.

"Sir, whatever it was, we couldn't stop it."

"What? How is that possible?"

"Sir, it just came crashing through the window and landed on its feet. I've never seen anything like it. We fired at it, but it didn't go down. It's incredible. It took off in that direction. We have units chasing it."

"Unit," said a voice on the police radio.

"Copy," replied the officer.

"Sir, whatever it was, we lost it. I've never seen anything that can leap over cars and run as it did, but we lost it."

"Copy," said the officer.

"I want the whole area searched," said Lieutenant Mano. "Get as many officers here as you can. We need to find this, and find it we will, tonight."

"Yes, sir," replied the officer.

He turned toward his fellow officers and gave them new orders. Then he turned to Paul Corillo. "You have some explaining to do, Corillo. Why did you disobey my orders to fire at that thing? And I'm trying so hard to make sense at what you said before. That was Danny Marco? What are you trying to tell me, Corillo?"

"Sir, I don't think now is the right time," answered Paul.

"You're damn right about that, and you will tell me everything because nothing makes sense ever since that night at the cabin."

"Sir, I understand," replied Paul.

"No, you don't. I have to call One Police Plaza and give them a full report on tonight. They will not believe a word of this. Not one word!"

Another police officer approached the lieutenant. "What is it?" he asked.

"We found a dead man in Danny Marco's room. He had a hole in his chest."

"A gunshot?"

"No, sir. It's almost as if someone just ripped his chest off. There was blood everywhere. We found a gun next to him and a cell phone, but no Marco."

"What?"

"Sir, Danny Marco is nowhere to be found."

"Search this entire hospital and bring the gun and phone to CSI. I need to know what the hell is going on."

"Yes, sir." The officer turned and left.

Lieutenant Mano looked back at Paul Corillo. "Sir," said Paul. "I truly believe Don Ginetti is behind this. He sent a hit man to kill

Danny and planted the fake cop by Danny's room. His plan almost worked."

"Speaking of which, where the hell did that fake cop go?" asked the lieutenant. "Wonderful! We have a fake cop in the district, a dead hit man, a missing man, and an animal running loose in Brooklyn. What the fuck is next? Dracula? Corillo, go home. Now!"

"But, sir, I want to help you find Marco."

"I said go home, Corillo. You have done enough for the night. I'll call you if I need you, so keep your damn phone on and your mouth shut, understand?"

"Yes, sir."

"And, Paul, so help me, if Marco gets in touch with you and you don't tell me, I promise you it will be your ending. Understand?"

"Yes."

"Now get out of here!" Lieutenant Mano turned and went back toward the hospital.

Paul was outside, rubbing his head and thinking, *Where could Danny have gone? And how many more hit men did Don Ginetti send?*

Suddenly he felt a tap on his shoulder. He turned to another police officer. "Detective Corillo?"

"Yes."

"I was ordered by Lieutenant Mano to drive you home, sir."

"Unbelievable. I can get home on my own."

"Sir, please, if I don't drive you home, I will not hear the end of it from Lieutenant Mano," said the young officer.

Paul took a deep breath. "Yeah, you are right. He doesn't let things go. But first, I must find some people I came with."

"Oh," said the officer. "You mean Officer Ray Amato and two women?"

"Yes."

"Well, you don't have to worry," said the young officer. "The ladies are waiting for us as we speak."

"Okay."

"Right this way." The officer led him away.

Above another building, a pair of glowing eyes were observing the scene, and then it went away.

CHAPTER 6

Thursday morning, October 24

Danny Marco was being chased. He did not know who was chasing him, but he was determined not to be captured. It was dark, and the moon was full. Clearing the bushes, he came to the cabin where his nightmare began. He looked inside from the window and saw no one. He heard a female voice from the darkness.

"Danny, my love. Let me help you. I am the only one who can. Come to me now."

He knew who that voice was. Lisa Jacobson, the woman who turned Danny into the beast that prowled at night for blood. Danny tried to open the door, but it was locked. He turned and saw lights in the bushes getting closer and closer.

"Danny," said Lisa Jacobson. He looked and saw her standing just a few feet away from him, looking exactly the way she did when he first met her. Those mysterious eyes looked at him with lust. "I chose you, my love. You belong to me. We are destined to be together. Come with me now before they find us."

Danny's back was against the cabin door. He shouted at her. "Leave me alone! You ruined me and my life. You caused me so much pain. Get the fuck away from me or I will kill you right now!"

"Danny, you don't know what you are saying," said Lisa Jacobson. "I can help you, and we can be together. Take my hand." She started to walk closer to him.

Danny was enraged, and he felt his blood burning. He looked up to see a full moon.

"They are coming for you. You must not let them take you." She pointed to the bushes.

He looked and saw lights and heard voices. "There he is," said the voice. "Get him now!" Danny looked out at the lights and growled.

Suddenly, he woke up. A dream. He had been dreaming. He found himself lying in the backyard of the house where he grew up, behind some plants his late father, Peter Marco, had planted. He was still wearing his hospital gown and was dirty. He got up slowly and looked around him, hoping no one saw him, except his mother's dog barking from the window. Danny quickly ran to the back door, only to find it open. He went in and closed the door. The dog quickly ran up to him and started licking him, happy to see him.

Danny called out, "Mom? Are you here?" No answer. He went to her room and saw she was not there. He wondered, *Where could she be?* He went to look out the front window and saw a police car parked outside. He quickly went back. The dog was still barking, so he got dog food and put it in a bowl for the dog to stay quiet. He went back to the front window and saw the police car still parked outside. He saw the police officer talking on the phone but could not hear what was being said. Then he saw the car start up and the police officer drive away. Maybe the officer was called for an emergency or was told to leave. He didn't know, but he was happy the patrol car had gone for now.

He went into the kitchen, got a drink of water, and sat down on the chair with the dog next to him. Danny was all dirty from sleeping outside. He had no recollection of what had happened last night other than the dream he had of seeing his father inside the cabin with Nicky Ginetti. He was confused and didn't understand what was going on. He picked up the phone and tried calling Paul Corillo. No answer. He dared not leave a message, so he hung up. He tried called Marie, and again, no answer. He hung up. He started to get worried and thought, *Where could they be? And where is Mom?*

Nothing was making any sense, and with no memory of what had happened the night before, he slammed his hands on the table, startling the dog. He rubbed his eyes and got up. He drank more water and got some food. He sat down in the living room. With nothing to do, and not daring to go outside, he turned on the TV and watched the news to see if anything was on the media regarding last night.

Then the news commentator said,

> Since the events last night at Lutheran Hospital, police are again looking for what they said was a hairy beast that attacked hospital guards and police. From what we understand, police were guarding someone of interest when all hell broke loose. One man was killed by this so-called hairy beast. The man killed was thought to be a male nurse, but it turned out he wasn't. Witnesses stated that this thing went on a rampage inside the hospital before jumping out of a window four stories up without getting hurt.

> Police fired at this thing, but it managed to get away with all the heavy police presence in the area. The police are not saying who the victim was, nor do they have any comments on the hairy beast, but there is a manhunt for this thing.

> Police are asking everyone to be cautious when out at night and to call if they see this so-called hairy beast. Whatever this thing was, whether it was just someone in costume or something else, the police will not stop until it's found. And with the Internet exploding with videos of this thing, it's just a matter of time before it's exposed as a hoax or a Halloween joke. In the meantime, sources are saying the person of interest who was being guarded was an NYC detective. Their identity has not yet been confirmed at this time, and police will not disclose any more information until further notice.

> In other news…

Before the news commentator could continue, Danny turned off the TV and sat on the couch in silence. Now he knew what had happened last night, but it still did not explain where his mother was, and also Paul and Marie. He thought about calling his sisters, but he couldn't; the phone lines could be bugged by the police.

What the hell is going on? He rubbed his forehead and looked down. *Why did this happen to me? Why did we have to go to that fucking cabin? Why did that bitch Lisa Jacobson pick me? Why? Why?*

There were so many questions in his mind, yet very little answers. His whole world had been turned into a nightmare. He leaned back on the couch, and the dog jumped on the couch next to him to give him some comfort. Then he started to remember the dream he had of his father inside the cabin and what his father had said to him: "Kill the entire Ginetti family. It's the only way to put an end to this."

Kill them? I'm not a killer!

Was it all just a dream, or was his father really speaking to him, telling Danny to get vengeance on the Ginetti family? Confused and frustrated and worried about his mother, he leaned back and fell asleep again.

Danny Marco was in a deep, exhausted sleep when suddenly he woke up to the sound of the phone ringing. He got up and went to answer it, but stopped and decided to let the answering machine record whoever was on the phone. After a few rings, the recorder came on. "Hi, you reached Ellen. Please leave a message, and I'll get back to you."

Then a familiar voice came on the phone, a voice he never expected to hear, much less call. "Marco, I know you are there. Guess who this is. I'll give you one clue, asshole. Don Salvatore Ginetti. Pick up the phone! I know your mother is not there. How can she be when she is here with me?"

Danny was shocked at what he had just heard. Did Don Ginetti have his mother? He didn't believe it!

"Hello? Okay, let's try this." Suddenly his fear came true.

"Danny? It's Mom."

Danny was in disbelief. They had his mother. He quickly grabbed the phone. "Mom, are you all right? I've been so worried—"

But that was cut quickly by Don Ginetti. "So you are home. What did you think this was, a prank call?"

Danny was enraged. "You son of a bitch! Let my mom go. She has nothing to do with this."

"Hey, watch your language, kid. That is very disrespectful." Don Ginetti started to laugh.

"What do you want?" asked Danny.

"First, lower your fucking voice. Second, go to your mailbox. You will find a disposable phone and a note with a number taped to it for you to call. Get it and call me back, and don't waste time calling me back, Marco. You have exactly two minutes." He hung up.

Danny rushed to the front door, but before he opened it, he looked to make sure there were no police cars or unmarked cars nearby. It was all clear. He opened the door slowly and went to the mailbox. He found the phone with a note, a number to call back. He closed the door and locked it. He looked again from the window and went back to the couch. He took a deep breath and tried to calm himself down. They had his mother, for God's sake. He called back the number written on the paper.

"Well, that was fast," said the Don. "I wish you cops would answer your 911 calls much faster."

"Cut the bullshit," said Danny. "What do you want with my mother? What kind of man are you? You bastard!"

"Hey, I said watch the language, or I will show you what kind of man I am with them."

"Them?" asked Danny, confused.

"Oh, I guess my memory is not as good as it once was. Sorry, Danny. Them, your buddy Paul and Marie. I invited everyone here to dinner and thought I should give you a call for an extended invitation."

Danny could not believe what he had just heard. Don Ginetti was able to kidnap his mother, Paul, and his fiancée, Marie. How? How did he do this with all the police at the hospital?

"Hello? You still there, Danny boy?"

"Fuck you!"

"Hey, I'm not going to tell you again about your language. Your father didn't teach you any manners?"

"Leave my father out of his. He is dead because of you."

"No, not me. My nephew Nicky killed your dad. The kid never listened, but that is not the point. You, or your friend in the costume, killed Nicky. Now it's personal."

Danny was getting scared. "Personal? You have my family and friend. Killing them won't bring back that punk nephew of yours. Let them go. You want me? Then release them, and I will come to you."

There was silence on the phone, and then the don said, "Nothing will make me happier than to have your head over my fireplace, but that is too easy. I don't want to hurt your mom, but you brought this on yourself."

"Me? None of this would have happened if Nicky had stayed away, but he didn't. He ruined my family's business and hurt my family. He walked away with a fucking smile on his face. No! If anyone is to blame for this, it's him, your dead shit-faced nephew. He brought this down on all of us!"

"I said watch your fucking mouth, kid. Yes, I know, Nicky was out of control, and he didn't listen. He never listened. I told him to stay away from your pizzeria knowing you're a cop, but he decided to do things his way. Listen, kid, I'm truly sorry about your father. I truly am. Whether you believe me or not, I don't care, but I truly am. But you took him from me. He was my sister's son, and she is waiting for me to do something about this. Do you understand me, Danny? I cannot let this go. You killed my nephew."

Danny screamed back, "I didn't kill him!"

"No, maybe not you, but your friend in the fucking costume did. And don't think I'm not looking for him too. Fucking news is calling him a werewolf! Are you fucking kidding me? A werewolf?" said Don Ginetti. "I saw pictures of the hole in Nicky's chest. Your friend must have had sharpened knives on his hand to put a hole in my Nicky. We had to have a closed coffin for his wake."

"Wait a minute," said Danny. "You saw pictures of Nicky's dead body? How? That was never given to the press."

"That's for me to know and you to find out, but you don't have time to find out."

Danny started to think back to when Paul told him that Nicky was not found guilty for killing his father. The murder weapon was never found. There was a leak in the department. That was the only answer.

"Hello. You still there?" asked Don Ginetti.

"Yes, yes, I'm still here. What do you want from me?" asked Danny.

"Simple. You! I will give you instructions where to meet, and I will have you picked up and brought to a location. Then and only then will I let your family go."

"Fine! I'm waiting."

"Not so fast," said the don. "We can't do this now."

"What? You want me. Let's do this. I'm ready. Let my mom and the others go."

"There is too much heat on the streets now," said the don. "Everyone is looking for you. I can't have any more mistakes. It all comes to an end. I will give you instructions on October 31."

"What? That's five days from now. Why?"

"Danny, come on and think. October 31. Halloween, kid."

"Why on Halloween? That doesn't make any sense at all."

"It does. Think about it. Everyone will be dressed up in their Halloween crap, running around dressed as monsters and superheroes. It's perfect. While the streets are packed with people running around and having a good time, the cops will never notice you, and it will be easy to get you to me."

"This is insane," exclaimed Danny. "I have to wait five days for you to get back to me? And what about my mom and the others?"

"You have my word, Danny. They will not be harmed. They will be taken care of as long as you listen and follow my instructions. You have no choice, Danny. And you better not report this! My people will be watching. Well, what's your answer? It better be yes."

Danny was upset and frustrated. Don Ginetti had him by the balls, and he had no other option but to agree. "Fine. You win."

"Good. That is the answer I wanted to hear. Remember, they will be fine as long as you listen to me. I'll get back to you in five days."

"Wait."

"I'm not changing my mind, Danny."

"No, it's not that."

"What is it?" said the Don.

"How the hell were you able to get my mom, Marie, and Paul with all those cops there?"

"Really? You think I'm going to tell you? You're the cop. You figure it out. Bye, Danny. We will speak again on October 31." The phone clicked off.

Son of a bitch, thought Danny. *He must have inside men in the department. When all broke loose, his men must have picked them up. Mom, Paul, and Marie thought they were cops and went along with them. Damn it!*

Danny had nothing left to do. They had his family and friend. He couldn't go to Lieutenant Mano for help. There was nothing more to do but wait till October 31. In the meantime, he had to check on the weather and pray there would be no full moons out for the next five days. Heaven help him.

To be sure, he got up and went to his mother's computer. He logged on and typed in "weather forecast." He saw that that night would be very cloudy and windy, with no full moon till Saturday night.

Okay, he thought. *So no full moon tonight, but how will I pass the time?* If he stayed in for the next five days, he would lose his mind. But if he went out, there was a chance he would be spotted by the police, and if he got caught, he would not be able to save anyone. Finally, he decided he would take a chance and go out, but when night fell, not during daylight. He could blend more easily in the dark than during the day, and with his police training and experience, it should be no problem. He hoped. He looked at the clock: 10:00 a.m.

Hours passed, and by 9:00 p.m., he looked out the front window. No unmarked cars that he could make out. He looked as far back as he could from both sides of the window. Satisfied, he went to the closet to see if his mother still kept his dad's clothes after he'd died. Sure enough, he found pants that just fit him, old sneakers, and a sweatshirt with a hood. He looked in the mirror and was sure he would not be noticed. He petted the dog, gave him some dog food, and promised he would be back.

He went to the back door to the yard. He checked again from the window. Satisfied, he opened the door slowly, stepped out, and quietly closed the door. He bent down and walked toward the garage. He walked very slowly until he got to the bushes and tree. He looked around and hoped the neighbors didn't see him. When he was sure it was all clear, he started to walk quickly past the garbage cans to the sidewalk and then started walking. With the hoodie up and his head down, he blended into the darkness and walked with people near him. He had made it outside but was still cautious of everything around him. While he was walking, a pair of glowing eyes watched his every move from a rooftop building.

On Eleventh Avenue and Seventy-First Street, he stayed alert as he walked with the people in front or behind him, just in case. So far, there was nothing out of the ordinary, until he saw three men leave a store. All three men were laughing, and they got into a black Cadillac. He recognized one of them. He was a member of the Ginetti crew. His name was Joey. On the streets, they called him Joey Knuckles.

As the car pulled away from the curb past Danny, he could see Joey laughing with his crew, and then he looked at Danny, but Danny looked away as the car drove off. Concerned, Danny went to the store they had left. He looked into the store window and saw a woman in her sixties scared to death and being consoled by another woman. He could see the fear in their eyes. That was when he knew, this visit had been a collection by the Ginetti crew on the stores, protection money. Danny started to get angry. He could not believe the pain and fear that Salvatore Ginetti was causing. He wanted to call it in, but he knew he couldn't. He wanted to do something so they wouldn't bother the store owners again. But what could he do?

Upset, confused, and angry, then he thought of something. The last time he had seen Joey Knuckles was at a social club bar and pool hall. The back of the club was where they ran their illegal operation. But what could he do once he found it? He couldn't go in and demand the money back or call it in. He was getting frustrated, then he thought of something.

He started walking as fast as he could without drawing attention to himself. He got to Sixtieth Street and Eleventh Avenue. His hunch paid off. He saw the car that Joey had driven off in along with the other guys. He knew they were all inside. Now what could he do? Should he make an anonymous phone call to the police department? There had to be something else he could do. He closed his eyes. He started to remember what his father said in his dream. "Danny, you must take out the entire Ginetti family once and for all. Wipe them out until there is no one left." He opened his eyes. For the first time, everything was now starting to make sense. *Take out the Ginetti crew until there is no one left but the man himself, Salvatore Ginetti.* Danny needed to come up with a plan, and this time, he would get help, and not from the local police department. He had a plan.

He quickly went back to his mother's house. Before going in, he checked again if anyone was watching. With the coast clear, he went back into the house, while again a pair of glowing eyes were watching him from behind. He took off the hoodie but didn't turn on the lights just in case and logged back onto the computer to check the weather. Now it said there was no full moon till Friday night. *Perfect.* He now had a plan and knew what he needed to do if there was going to be any peace in the neighborhood. He scrolled down on YouTube and saw the video link of the werewolf that someone was able to catch and post online. He started thinking, *If I ever needed you, now is the time!*

*****

Friday night, October 25

Danny arrived at the social club where Joey Knuckles brought the money. It was 6:00 p.m. No one was there yet. He looked carefully both ways. *How would I get in and hide?* From the open basement in front of the club, he saw a man come up from the stairs and go into a van, get a box of what looked like booze, and go back down. *A delivery. Perfect.*

He walked across the street and looked again to make sure he was not being watched. He waited for the delivery guy to come back. He got another box and went down. Danny waited, then moved to the van, got a box, and went down the basement. There was little light, and no one else was around. He quickly moved and hid behind a cart and put the box down. He heard the delivery guy coming. He heard him walk up the steps, then heard him say, "I thought there was another box." He heard the van door close and then the cellar door close. Finally, he was inside. Now he needed to act fast.

He got up from behind the carts and walked past some boxes to another door. He first listened for anyone inside. He didn't hear anything. He opened the door and looked inside: a meeting room with tables, chairs, a bar, and large-screen TV. *So this is where they meet.* Now, he just had to lay low until they all showed up. He went back out and closed the door. He walked past the boxes and carts to a window by the steps where he had come in. *A window. Not large, but a window.* He cleaned the window so he could get a good look at the dark sky. He was ready.

He took off his jacket and went back to where he was hiding. He looked at his watch: 7:30 p.m. Now he just had to wait till they all showed up, and soon they would meet an unexpected guest hiding. *God help them all*, he thought to himself.

CHAPTER 7

It was now 11:00 p.m. The sky was dark, and the moon was starting to shine. Inside the social club in the back room downstairs, Joey Knuckles, along with the other crew members, started to come in and throw the collection for the night on the table.

"Now this is what I call a good night," said Joey. "See, guys, Mr. Ginetti will like this a lot. Hey, maybe he will give us a raise."

They all started to laugh. There were seven of them. The TV was on, and they were smoking and drinking. Joey looked over to the bartender. "Didn't we get the new order of booze yet?"

"Yes," answered the bartender. "I'll open a bottle right now."

"Good, 'cause tonight, we party. I got some ladies coming over soon, guys."

They all started laughing.

"Hey, Joey," said one guy. "What about the lady at the store from last night?"

"Are you fucking kidding me?"

They all started to laugh. Joey took a drink, when suddenly he and the other men heard a growl from the front room behind the closed door where Danny Marco was hiding. Joey slowly put the glass down on the bar, and they all looked at each other.

"What the fuck was that?" asked Joey.

"Sounded like a dog," said one of them.

"Lower the TV volume," said Joey.

They stood there, and again, a growling sound came from the other room.

Joey looked at the others. "Okay, who brought the dog?" They started laughing. "Seriously, guys, if you are going to get a dog, don't leave it in the dark. That's inhumane."

"Do you even know what inhumane means?" asked one of the men in the room.

"Very funny."

They all laughed again. Another growl was heard, and they looked at the door.

"Poor thing must be hungry," remarked Joey. "You guys are terrible. Is this the way you treat your families?" They all looked at each other, confused. "Tell me, none of you know about the dog?" They all agreed; not one of them knew. "Well, someone brought the dog here, and I'm going to bring it home with me since you jerks don't care."

"But, Joey, none of us brought a dog here," said another guy.

Joey waved his hand. "Enough with the bullshit. I'll handle this." Joey walked over to the door, opened it, and went in, closing the door behind him.

The men just looked at each other and then resumed what they were doing. They could hear Joey Knuckles talking from behind the closed door. "Okay, doggie, where are you? Don't be afraid. Joey will save you from these jerks."

"Jerks?" one man said, and they laughed. Then they heard Joey, and it was the last thing they would ever hear again. "Where are you? I can hear you. Ahh, you are behind the box. What the fuck?"

He screamed. The men in the back room all jumped. "What the hell?" said one man. Then they heard a roaring sound. Startled, they all stood up and reached for their guns.

"What the fuck is going on?" asked one of the six men.

Shaking and not knowing what to do, one of the men said, "Let's get out of here."

"No!" said the other. "We leave, and Ginetti will be up our ass 'cause of a dog!"

"Joey?" said one man, but there was no answer.

They were all baffled and didn't know what to do. Suddenly the growling came louder by the door. The men looked at each other; their guns were drawn and pointed at the door.

"It's just a fucking dog," said one of them.

"Yeah? Then why don't Joey answer us?"

"Guys, cover me," said one of the men. "It's just a dog!"

He approached the door while holding his gun up. The other man walked closer to the door while the others watched, not knowing what was about to happen. As he got closer to the door, sweat ran down his forehead. "This is fucking nuts." He shouted again, "Joey, are you all right? What kind of dog is in there?"

Then without warning, a hairy paw went through the door, into his chest, and through his back. "Jesus Christ!" yelled the other men. The hairy paw pulled back, and the man fell down dead in his own blood. They heard a loud roar. And smashing through the door and standing tall was a hairy beast with razor-sharp teeth and blood in his eyes. No, it was not a dog, nor was it Danny Marco—his alter ego had again been released.

The six men in the room stood face-to-face with a werewolf!

"What the fuck is that?" screamed one of the men.

Without warning, the werewolf attacked, clawing the remaining six men in the room. Meanwhile, upstairs was filled with people and loud music. They heard nothing. Downstairs, the werewolf showed no mercy as it attacked. Gunshots were fired, but the werewolf was quick, and it clawed the last man as he tried to get away. The room was filled with death, and blood was splattered everywhere. The werewolf saw that it was victorious once again. After looking at its bloody paws, it looked up and howled in victory.

Upstairs in the social club, a man was walking with his girlfriend. Holding hands, they went past the door that led downstairs to the men's room. They looked at each other and started kissing, and he said to her, "Well, babe, it will be a minute unless you want to come and watch the show."

"You jerk," she replied. "There is nothing there for me to see."

"Really?"

119

They both laughed. Suddenly they heard sounds coming from the door that led to the basement, and then they heard heavy breathing.

"Well," said the man, "I think someone is getting a happy ending tonight."

They both laughed, and this time, they heard a loud growl. Their smiles turned to shock. The young woman stood behind him in fear.

He exclaimed, "Shit, was that a dog?"

From there, the door was ripped open. They covered their eyes to avoid the splinters, and when they looked, standing before them was the werewolf. It roared at them, and the young woman screamed as they both backed away in fear.

The werewolf had blood in its eyes and looked around. It needed to escape and be free. It looked toward the left, to the sound of music and people talking. It looked at the couple again, roared, and then ran toward the sound. Inside the social club, men and women were drinking and dancing to the music from the DJ. They were having a good time, when suddenly the werewolf burst out. It roared at the people inside. People started to scream and scatter. The werewolf picked up chairs and threw them across the room toward the DJ, and the music stopped. Bouncers tried to stop the werewolf, thinking it was a prank, but the werewolf clawed one man and threw the other over the bar, shattering glasses and bottles. People started running out of the club, screaming in fear.

Outside, the pedestrians saw the commotion and called 911. Inside, one bartender took out a gun and fired at the werewolf, hitting its arm. It was not happy. It lunged for the bartender and threw him through the front window, shattering the glass into pieces. The werewolf saw a way out. A few people were still inside screaming and trying to stay away from what they were seeing. The werewolf quickly jumped out the window, onto the street, and into the night. It looked around, then raised its head up to the moon, and released an incredibly strong howl. People across the street were stunned and quickly grabbed their phones to take a video of what they were seeing. They could not believe if it was real or someone dressed in a costume.

Several police cars arrived on the scene. The werewolf saw flashing lights and roared at them. Policemen jumped into position with guns drawn and aimed at what they saw.

The first police officer said to the other, "You have got to be kidding me. Halloween is not till a couple of days."

Another police officer got on the police speaker and said, "Stand down with your hands up. You are surrounded by the New York City Police."

The werewolf did not care, nor did it understand. It just needed to escape and be free.

The police officer then said, "You make any move, and we will shoot you if necessary. I repeat, stand down now!"

The werewolf growled, and without warning, it lunged toward one of the police cars. The police started shooting at it, but the werewolf with its quick reflexes dodged all the firepower from the police, leaped over a police car, and escaped, with police officers still firing at it.

"Jesus," said another officer. "How can anyone move that fast?"

The werewolf had struck again, and it was only the beginning for what Danny Marco and the werewolf had planned for the Ginetti family.

The police started to make sense of what had just happened, and they talked with witnesses inside the club. From above, a pair of glowing eyes had watched everything that transpired below.

One man in the club looked around at all the confusion. He saw that no one was around him, so he took out his phone and made a phone call.

It was past midnight at the Ginetti residence, and Salvatore Ginetti was sound asleep with his wife when he woke up to the sound of knocking and a voice behind his bedroom door. "Mr. Ginetti? Sir, I need to speak with you right away!"

His wife woke up also, confused and scared. "What is going on?"

"Relax," said the don. "It's probably nothing."

"Nothing?"

He turned to her. "Please, just try to relax. I'll deal with this."

"Mr. Ginetti," said the voice behind the door.

"I'm coming!" he shouted. "Give me a minute." He put on his robe, opened the door, and stepped outside his bedroom, closing the door behind him. He grabbed his guard by the arm and walked away from the door, saying, "What the fuck is wrong with you? You trying to give my wife a heart attack?"

"Sir, please excuse me, but you need to hear this." He handed his cell phone to Don Ginetti.

"Yes," said Don Ginetti into the phone. "What the fuck is going on?"

Suddenly he was in shock, and his eyes widened as the caller told him what had just happened at his social club.

"Are you fucking kidding me?" he screamed. Shaking his head and rubbing his eyes, he told the caller, "All right, all right. Listen to me. Stay low and don't say a word to anyone. You hear me? I'll send someone over to get you and bring you here. Understand?"

"Yes, Don Ginetti," replied the caller.

The don closed the phone and handed it back. "Go to the social club and bring him here, now!"

"Yes, sir." The man ran, calling out for more men to get in the car, and they raced to the social club.

Don Ginetti was getting angry and red-faced. He shouted, "Goddamn you, Marco!"

At that same time at his home in Bensonhurst, Lieutenant Mano woke up to the sound of his phone ringing. He picked up the phone, noticing that his wife didn't wake up to the noise. He answered, "This is Lieutenant Mano." When the caller told him what had happened, his face turned to shock. "What the hell? Was anyone hurt…? Fine, I'll be there in thirty minutes. I want the whole area secured until I get there. Understand? Good." He ended the call, got up, shook his head, and screamed, "Marco!"

His wife woke up in fear.

CHAPTER 8

Saturday night, October 26
Another Ginetti location: cement contracting
firm on Coney Island, New York

From inside, men were screaming in fear, and a hail of gunfire erupted, when suddenly blood was spattered from the inside. A dark figure came crashing through the windows, landing on its feet. The werewolf had struck again, killing more of the Ginetti crew. Howling at the moon, it started running in the middle of the street, stopping moving cars dead in their tracks, leaping over cars with incredible agility, and scaring people who didn't know if what they were seeing was fake or real.

Meanwhile, 911 was flooded with calls. "This is 911. Please state the location of your emergency."

The caller responded, "I'm not on drugs, and I'm not drinking, but I just saw a hairy thing running wild across the avenue. It leaped over my car. It was big and scary looking. It turned to look at me, and I saw its red eyes and sharp teeth. It just looked at me and growled. I took off and sped away."

"I'm sorry," said the operator. "You said you saw something that jumped over your car and you sped away? What was it, and how fast were you driving?"

"Did you hear me? Listen to me! Something hairy with sharp teeth and red eyes jumped over my car and just looked at me and took off. I wasn't about to be its main course, so yeah, I took off speeding. What would you have done?"

The 911 operator responded, "Thank you for that clarification. A police car has been dispatched. Would you care to give me your name?"

"Why?" asked the caller. "So you can lock me up, thinking I'm nuts? Find this thing!" He hung up.

"Hello, sir?"

*****

Sunday night, October 27

A warehouse district on Staten Island was attacked. From inside, men were running and shooting at what was following them. One by one, they were picked up and torn to pieces by the werewolf. One man was on his phone calling for help. "Louie, something is in here and is killing us." He looked back and fired more shots.

Louie said, "What the fuck is going on? What is it?"

The man looked back, and it was the last thing he saw. "Holy mother of God!" He fired more shots.

The other person on the phone, Louie, only heard one thing—the howling of the werewolf. "Jesus Christ," said Louie to his other associates in the room. "They are all dead!"

"What?" asked one man. "What killed them?"

"Listen." Louie turned on the speaker of his cell phone. They heard growling, sniffing, and then a horrifying howling. Louie dropped the phone. The men stepped back and looked at one another with shock and, this time, fear.

Meanwhile, 911 was again flooded with calls reporting a hairy-looking monster with razor-sharp teeth running along the streets of Brooklyn at night. Police were being dispatched in dozens trying to find this thing that was attacking members of the Ginetti crew.

Back at the police precinct, Lieutenant Mano was beside himself yelling on the phone while looking at the map on the wall, which indicated that the werewolf had struck all locations owned and operated by the Ginetti crew. He slammed the phone down, not knowing what to do next. He called in more men to set up a manhunt for whatever was killing the Ginetti crew.

One officer responded, "Sir, if we see it, what would you recommend?"

The other officers looked down. They could not believe what this officer had just said.

Lieutenant Mano went up to him; fear was written on the young officer's face. "What should you do? How about leave a trail of dog biscuits and see what happens? Get out of here, all of you!"

After all the officers had left, he sat down at his desk, breathing deeply and trying to understand what was going on. He wondered where the hell Danny Marco and Paul Corillo were. His phone rang. "Yes, what is it?"

"You have a call, sir. It's—"

But he interrupted the caller. "I don't care who it is. Not now!"

The caller responded, "Sir, it's the police commissioner."

"Damn it!" he said, slapping his forehead. "Oh boy, what else could go wrong tonight? Okay, put the pencil pusher on the phone."

Another voice responded: "This is the pencil-pusher commissioner."

Lieutenant Mano's face turned white, and he thought, *Oh shit!*

*****

At the Ginetti residence, Salvatore Ginetti was screaming inside his study. There was one man outside the door, and the other men were inside. "What the fuck is going on?" he shouted. "That fucking Marco is taking out our crew. I want more men with more firepower at all the locations. Get him before he gets us, but don't kill him. Not yet. We still have leverage—his mother, fiancée, and friend. Doesn't he understand I could kill them all right now? I want him alive!"

"Don Ginetti," said one man. The don looked at him as well as the others. "Sir, how could you possibly think it's Marco killing our men? Our inside man is saying people are reporting a hairy-looking thing with sharp paws just jumping over cars like it was nothing and howling. Sir, I don't think it's Marco. He might have someone helping him. It's that, or this thing is real."

The other men looked at him, bewildered at what he had just said.

Don Ginetti just looked at him. "Really? You think he is real? Okay, then do me a favor. Go downstairs and wake up Dracula and tell him to find this animal and bite his balls off! What the fuck is wrong with you? Shut your mouth!"

There was a knock on the door. "What is it?" asked Don Ginetti.

The door opened, and another man told him, "Sir, I think you better put the TV on to the local news. You will want to see this."

"Well, that's fucking great." The don told one man to turn on the TV. He sat down with the others as they watched the news.

This is News One with a special report. Police are still looking for what people are saying is a hairy-looking beast. So far, it has struck twice, at a social club and a warehouse district, killing whoever was present and then running away with incredible speed and agility, leaping over cars and howling at the moon. Yes, you heard it, howling at the moon.

A source from NYPD has stated that the men killed were all members of the Salvatore Ginetti crew. As to what reason it has for attacking them, we don't know. But police are asking for everyone to be on guard and lock your doors and windows and turn off the front lights until this thing or person is captured.

Anyone with any information on the situation is to call 911 immediately.

With Halloween just days away, it makes you wonder if the Ginetti crew will dress up for Halloween to avoid a confrontation with this thing. Maybe Snow White and the Seven Dwarves.

The newsman chuckled, and then there was a blast at the TV. The men were startled. Don Ginetti had just shot the TV.

"Fuck you, newsman! How's that for a punch line?" He turned to the men in the room. "This is fucking insane! Our boys are getting ripped to pieces, and everyone wants to know what my next move is going to be. Does Marco think I am just going to sit here and let him or his friend make a fool out of me? No! The other bosses must think I've lost my fucking mind!" He looked at one man. "Phil, get the disposable phone and call Marco. Tell him to stop now 'cause if he doesn't stop, he can kiss his family goodbye!"

"But, sir, if we do that, he will never come to us," Phil reasoned.

"He will come to us. He has so much to lose if he doesn't."

"But killing his family just might push him over the edge. And if that happens, we will have no bargaining chip to deal with, and Marco will come after us at full force," said Phil.

"So what are you saying we should do? Nothing?" asked the don. "Just let him wipe us all out!"

There was knock on the door. "Yes," said the don.

Another associate opened the doors and peeked inside. "Sir, about the blast we just heard?"

"Not now." Don Ginetti looked back at Phil. "Do you know how this looks? I can't just sit here and do nothing."

"Sir," said the man by the door.

"Not now! And shut the fucking door! Our guy at the police precinct? Any information on Marco?"

"Nothing yet," answered Phil. "Marco hasn't been seen at his mother's home since this started."

"Bastard must have a hideout somewhere. Reach out to everyone. I want Marco found. Try to call him. Make sure our other places have more men and firepower to blow this thing away. If he thinks he has one over on me, then he's wrong. Nobody fucks with Don Ginetti!" He slammed his hands on the table.

There was another knock on the door. "What the fuck is it?"

The door opened, and it was the same man. "Sir, I do apologize, but again it's about the TV."

"Are you fucking kidding me? It's just a TV. I can buy a dozen TVs, blast them all, and buy another dozen. Why are you asking? Did the neighbors complain about the noise?"

"No, sir. Mrs. Ginetti would like a word with you."

Inside the room, all the men looked at the Untouchable Don. "Fuck," said Don Ginetti. "Tell Mrs. Ginetti I will be with her in thirty minutes."

Suddenly, they heard a woman's shout. "Salvatore! Get your fucking ass out here right now!" It was his wife, Josephine Ginetti. "What do you think our house is, a shooting gallery?"

The don looked down at his desk and up to his men who were looking at him. "Can my fucking day get any better?"

*****

Sitting at his desk was a very tired and sleep-deprived Lieutenant Mano. He had not been home in two days. He had not shaved and was wearing the same clothes. Boxes of half-eaten food sat on his desk. He didn't know where to start or how to end what was going on in Brooklyn. Members of the Ginetti crew were being eliminated by something he could not explain—from the police photos of the dead men and how they were killed, and from photos and videos taken by the eyewitnesses of a hairy-looking beast with a thirst to kill and agility to get away. He had listened to the 911 calls and people's descriptions about what they saw. He started to question his judgment. All his police training and experience gained over the years of serving the NYPD could not compare to what was going on now.

A hairy-looking beast? A werewolf? You only hear about these things on television. It's not real. It can't be real, can it? he thought to himself. He rubbed his eyes and drank the cold cup of coffee. *Snap out of it! None of this is real. A hairy-looking beast could not exist, for Christ's sake.*

He started remembering the night at the cabin when Danny Marco was attacked by an unknown animal. The howling he and the others heard in the middle of the night and the pair of glowing red eyes he had seen. *Could any of those things have something to do with*

Danny Marco? It's insane to think that any of the events of that night at the cabin could have something to do with Marco and what is going on now. It's insane to even assume the possibility, but the facts cannot be ignored.

That night at the hospital, he could not forget how that thing had just gone through the window with such speed. Then the hit man was found dead at Marco's apartment. Then afterward, Marco was tased at his mother's house and was knocked unconscious. Now his mother, Marie, and Paul were nowhere to be found.

And where the hell is Danny Marco? he asked himself. *I need to find Marco and fast. I need to put an end to this before anyone else is killed. I swear, once this is finally over, and it will be, I am done. I will turn in my papers for early retirement and just move away to somewhere no one will recognize me. Neither I nor my family will be humiliated by someone teasing us about a werewolf in Brooklyn. It will come to an end. It's just so insane to even admit to the idea of a werewolf in Brooklyn taking out the Ginetti crew. I just wish we never went to that damn cabin. That's how all this started.*

And Danny's father, Peter Marco. He didn't deserve this. That fucking Nicky Ginetti. He walked away with a smile on his face when the murder weapon disappeared. I would have loved to see if he was still smiling when he met his end. He had it coming.

I should not even think that. I'm a cop, and these people need to pay for their crimes and be sent to prison for life. But Nicky Ginetti, he had it coming, piece of shit that he was. If I were in Danny's shoes, I would probably have done the same thing. Then the neighborhood would go back to the people, and they would not have to live in fear of the Ginettis anymore. I hope it happens. But for now, I have to clean up this mess and stop the killings. Most importantly, I need to find Danny Marco.

He looked out of his office window. *Danny, where the hell are you?*

CHAPTER 9

October 28, Monday, 6:00 p.m.

D anny was laying low and out of sight from people who might be looking for him. From a rooftop, dressed in a windbreaker and wool hat, Danny Marco was staking out another known illegal operations site of the Ginettis', an auto repair shop with a wide entrance to the back for automobiles and trucks. Danny had seen this before, a chop shop. Stolen cars and trucks were brought to this location during the night hours. The vehicles were then stripped of their parts and sold. Danny was thinking of a way to get in and stay hidden till the moon was full. While watching the shop, he saw a van pulling up. Several men came out carrying large duffel bags.

This can only mean one thing, he thought to himself. *Don Ginetti has called for reinforcements. Those duffel bags could be carrying more guns and stronger firepower for my alter ego, the werewolf. So Ginetti is getting scared, and he's sending out more lambs to be sacrificed. It will be hard to get in there with all those extra guys watching and waiting. How will I get in undetected?*

So many ideas were running through his mind until he thought of something. *But will it work?* He was running out of daylight, and there would be a full moon tonight. He put his plan into motion.

At 12:30 p.m., the chop shop was busy as usual. While the Ginetti boys stood guard inside the shop, the mechanics were working on the stolen cars, taking them apart. There were sounds of drilling and banging from the hammers and other tools the men were using to strip the cars and box the parts. The lights were bright. Some of the men were nervous, having read about what had happened at the other Ginetti places. The headman came out of the office with a bullhorn to get everyone's attention.

"Guys, I know you are all on edge. But Mr. Ginetti has assured us we will all be fine with their presence." He was referring to the extra muscle standing behind him and around the shop with weapons. "So if you guys want to go home tonight, get to working. Get it done, and then we get paid. Back to work."

The sounds of drilling and hammering continued. A loud bell rang by the garage door. Three men approached the door. One signaled the other to open it. A button was pressed, and the garage door slowly opened to a tow truck. It was carrying on its flatbed a red Cadillac. The driver was confirmed and allowed to enter. The door was closed quickly while the three guards watched. Once it was closed, they turned around and watched as the flatbed truck drove to deliver its next victim to the choppers.

Overhead, the moon was starting to release a full brightness through the skylight. While this was going on, one guard looked at the other and asked, "You think he will show up tonight?"

The other responded, "Let him." He clicked his gun. "He will be in for a big surprise if he does. There is no way he is going to get past us. Let that thing or whatever it is show his face to me. It will be his end."

"You looking to score points and move up in rank with Don Ginetti?" asked the other guard.

"Whatever it takes," replied the other.

They laughed and then continued to watch, on the ready.

The red Cadillac was released from its flatbed to the next station of mechanics, ready to be ripped apart. "Well, let's get this over with," said one mechanic. "I'm beat, and I just want out of here."

"I'm with you," replied the other.

The first mechanic opened the door to release the hood. The other opened the hood.

"Very nice, and looking good. Let's get started," said the first one.

"I'll check the trunk," replied the other. He walked to the trunk and gave it a bang with the crowbar, and the trunk banged back. Startled, he stepped back a bit. But then he realized it might have been the sound of the next crew working on another car. He smirked, set the crowbar at the edge of the trunk, and, with a strong effort, opened it. He was caught off guard. A hairy paw just went through his chest.

"Well, how does the trunk look?" asked the other mechanic, closing the hood. He looked up to the top of the car and went into shock; he could not speak. He was looking into the hungry red eyes of the werewolf!

Suddenly the sounds of drilling all stopped and were replaced by the sounds of screaming. The werewolf was attacking at will, grabbing anyone it could, ripping them and tossing them over the cars. Sounds of gunfire erupted. The two guards who let the truck in were taken by surprise. "How the fuck did it get in here?"

They all ran for cover from the bullets. The werewolf was jumping from one end to another. Every man it came across, it killed without mercy. It took out other guards with a single blow of its razor-sharp paw. Blood spattered everywhere. There was total chaos inside the shop, dead bodies everywhere from the werewolf attack and thick smoke from the gunfire trying to kill it. Men were coughing, other men tried to hide, and others were screaming, while the remaining few tried to escape from the fury of the werewolf. One by one, they were slaughtered along with the guards. The werewolf was on its game; it destroyed some of the bright lights while on the hunt, roaring at everyone and killing them. The two guards who let in the truck were now afraid, hiding behind vehicles with their guns drawn and sweating and coughing from the smoke of gunfire.

"What the fuck?" said one guard. "How can one man take us all out? This can't be happening!"

"Stay alert," replied the other guard. "Kill whatever it is before it kills us!"

They looked around and fired their weapons where they heard sounds of roaring and more screaming. Their bullets hit some of their own, and they went down while the werewolf continued to attack.

"I'm getting the fuck out of here," said one guard. "No money is worth getting my ass killed."

"Stay low," replied the other. But the man did not listen. He got up with his gun drawn and looked around for the werewolf. Then he tried to activate the automatic door opener, but his hand could not find the control knob. He was shaking in fear.

"Get down," said the other.

Finally, he found the right button to press, and the door began to open, while the werewolf was still roaring and hungry for blood. Then he shouted, "Anyone still alive, get the fuck out of here now!" He turned to the other guard and said, "Let's go!"

As the other guard started to get up, the werewolf struck the guard who opened the door, and its bloody paw went into his chest.

"Holy God!" exclaimed the other.

The dead guard fell, and now the last guard looked into the eyes of the werewolf. The guard could not fire his gun, only screamed in fear. The werewolf grabbed the guard by his throat and jumped up. Blood poured down from the ceiling. The few men inside started running out of the opening in fear; some were covered in blood, not looking back.

Inside his office, the man in charge of the chop shop was hiding under his desk, shaking and not knowing what to do. He heard another scream and loud sounds from the werewolf. Then he heard more sounds of gunfire and then nothing. Suddenly he heard a crash through his office window. Lying a few feet from him was one of the two guards the werewolf had grabbed. His neck and chest were slashed and ripped open. His dead eyes looked at the man under his desk. The man in charge covered his mouth, trying not to make a sound. He was in complete fear. He was shaking and scratching his forehead. Should he take a chance and try to make a run for it or wait? But if he waited and the police arrived, he would be arrested for his illegal operation. So many thoughts ran through his mind.

Suddenly he heard the front garage door opening. Had help come from Don Ginetti? Or were his men trying to escape? He took a deep breath and slowly crawled out from under his desk, not making any kind of sound for fear of whatever might still be inside.

He went near the broken window and moved up very slowly. All he could see was smoke and flickering lights, and yes, the smell of death everywhere. He was terrified and sweating, and his heart felt like it was going to explode. Looking at the dead body in front of him, he crawled back to his desk. There was broken glass and blood everywhere. He started praying, "Oh Mary, mother of God, forgive me for my sins." Shaking, he reached for his cell phone, thinking that he was in the clear, and made a video call to Don Ginetti.

At the Ginetti residence, Salvatore Ginetti was sitting in his meeting room with his other associates when one of them got a video call.

"Sir, I'm getting a video call from our guy at the car shop."

Don Ginetti looked at him with a confused look. "Why the fuck is he doing that? Do not answer it. Text him, tell him to call." The associate complied and texted the man to call and not video call, but the caller did it again. "Don Ginetti, he is video calling again, and his text said, 'Trouble at the shop. Something is killing us.'"

The don's face turned red. "Now what?" He slammed his fists on his desk, and he told his guy to accept the video call and bring it over. "The rest of you, come stand behind me and watch also. What the fuck is going on tonight?"

The associate opened the video call and put his cell phone on Don Ginetti's desk. As the chat opened, Don Ginetti and his associates saw their man. They saw a man shaking in fear, sweating, and looking around. His eyes were wide open, and his hair was a mess.

"What the fuck is going on?" asked Don Ginetti. "You look like you just saw the devil!"

Speaking slowly, his eyes wide open, the caller replied, "Sir, it was here."

"What was there? What the fuck are you talking about? Was the place raided?"

"No, sir. It wasn't."

"Then what the fuck are you talking about?" Don Ginetti yelled. His men were still watching, not knowing what was going on.

"Sir, that hairy thing was here in the shop."

Don Ginetti was stunned. "What the fuck do you mean it was there? That place is secure. How the fuck did it get in there? Did you guys at least try to kill it?"

"Sir, try to kill it? It killed all of us. See for yourself." He turned the phone over to the body of the dead guard covered in blood and broken pieces of glass.

Don Ginetti and his men were taken aback. They could not believe what they were looking at. "What could have done this?" Don Ginetti looked at his men. They all had the same confused look. None of this was making any sense. Don Ginetti could only think of one man who could be behind all this.

"Marco. That son of a bitch!" Scratching his head and breathing heavily, he looked back at the video and the scared man. "Listen to me, you need to get the fuck out of there and fast before the cops show up."

"Sir, I can't." His eyes were wide open and scared to death. "Sir, I just can't move. I don't want to be next to die. This thing is hunting us!"

"Shut up! Get up and get the fuck out of there now!"

"Sir, you don't understand. This thing—"

But before he could continue, he saw a shadow in front of him, a very large shadow. And he knew he wouldn't be going anywhere but to his death. He looked at the phone one last time in fear.

"Mr. Ginetti? It's here." Suddenly he was grabbed from behind and pulled back screaming as he dropped his phone.

All Don Ginetti and his men could see was the ceiling, and they heard screams that abruptly ended. They were shocked and could not make any sense of what they had just heard. They looked back at the phone, still on video call.

"What the fuck is going on?" Nothing.

They looked at one another, and the don shouted, "What the fuck is going on? Answer me!"

There was brief silence, and then they heard light growling sounds getting closer to the phone. Suddenly the werewolf showed its horrifying face on the screen. It roared before smashing the phone.

Don Ginetti and his associates all gasped and stepped back on seeing the face of the werewolf. They were all shocked. "This can't be fucking real," said one of the associates as he wiped the sweat from his forehead. Everyone looked at him.

Don Ginetti shook his head in disbelief. He closed his eyes, then opened them. "None of this can be real. It just can't." Salvatore Ginetti had always maintained order by fear. Anyone who opposed him had never been seen again. No one ever questioned him, and no one ever got the best of him.

Now, for the first time, someone had gotten in his mind. This someone was quickly taking out his crew, and Don Ginetti was starting to believe that once this someone was done, he would be next. And that someone was Danny Marco. He looked up. "You guys go and get a drink, except for you, Pat." They looked at one another, wondering why only Pat could stay with the don. "Do you fucking guys have a hearing problem? Out!" shouted the don.

"Come on, guys, go," said Pat. He opened the door for them and then closed it after. He walked over to Don Ginetti and waited.

"Sit down."

Pat sat, ready to hear the next plan.

Sitting back in his leather chair, Don Ginetti lit a cigar and started to smoke. Looking at Pat, he said, "Remind me, what day is it?"

"Sir?" said Pat.

"Just remind me what the fucking date is. Is that too much to ask for?"

"No, sir. It's October 28."

"Just three more fucking days till Halloween. That is the date we gave Marco to come to us. And what does he do with the time till then? He starts going after me, hitting our spots and taking out our men. That fuck truly believes that by getting rid of our guys, he will have easy access to me. Does he really think that he could just waltz in here, kill me, save his family, and then go home like nothing happened?" He was still puffing on his cigar and leaning back in his leather chair. Pat just sat there and listened.

"Sir, may I suggest something?"

The don looked at Pat, still puffing on his cigar. "What is it?"

Nervously, Pat said, "Sir, why not reach out to the other bosses and see if they can spare some men to deal with this problem and help us get rid of Marco?"

Don Ginetti opened his eyes wide, and his face turned a burning red. He slammed what was left of the cigar on his desk, sending burning pieces of tobacco flying into the air and raining down onto his desk and the floor. "Are you fucking insane?" He stood up and leaned on his desk toward a very scared Pat, who was wishing he had never made the suggestion. "If I reach out to the other bosses for help, that would be a sign of weakness! They will think I don't have it anymore, and then they will vote to take me out and take control of Bensonhurst. That shit will not happen as long as I'm alive and breathing. Do you understand?"

"Yes, sir," answered a very scared Pat, sweating and breathing hard.

The don stood up and fixed his suit jacket. He wiped his forehead with his hand, and then stepped back, turned, and looked out the window. It was late in the evening, and the moon was full. He turned to look at Pat and sat back down on his leather chair.

Looking at Pat, he started, "Even if I were crazy enough to call for backup, I can't."

"I understand why you can't."

"No, no, you don't. What I'm about to say stays in this room. Do you understand? If you open your mouth to anyone, I will slice out your tongue."

Pat was getting nervous again but maintained his composure. "I will not say a word to anyone."

"Good." With his hands folded on his desk, Don Ginetti said, "The other bosses have turned their backs on me."

"Sir?"

"Just listen. They have turned their backs on me. They said I made this too personal with Marco. Plus he is NYPD. There is too much heat involved, and it was not good for business, so they left us out in the cold until the matter is resolved. If they think I will fold, they are wrong. I will put an end to this and to Marco. After all is

LUCIANO DI GIALLONARDO

done, they will come back to me and see why people call me the
Untouchable Don. When Marco comes to us on Halloween, he will
be taken care of, and all this shit about a fucking werewolf will be
over. Has everyone lost their fucking minds? A hairy beast running
around and killing our men? What the hell is wrong with everyone?"

"But, sir, how do you explain how brutally the men were killed?"

The don leaned forward from his leather chair. "Please don't tell
me you believe this bullshit about a werewolf?"

"No, sir, I don't, but how do you explain the massacre? As far
as how our guys were ripped apart, I still say Marco had help in this
to make it look like a brutal slaying just to scare us and hype up
the media. And what of his family? What do we do with them after
Marco is dealt with?"

"They are expendable as far as I care."

"You mean you won't release them?" He looked at the don with
confusion. "His mother, fiancée, and Detective Paul Corillo? You
would consider murdering two women and an NYC detective? Sir,
that would go against the rules."

Lighting up another cigar, Don Ginetti took a few puffs and
put down the lighter. He took another puff, leaned back, and blew
out the smoke; he was looking at the cigar, and then looked at Pat.
"Like I said, they are expendable. Are you questioning me?"

"No, sir. I fully understand."

"Good. Now go home and get some sleep. We have a lot to do
tomorrow."

"Yes, sir." Pat got up. "Good night, Don Ginetti."

The don just nodded while taking another puff from his cigar.
Pat turned around and walked to the door and stepped out, closing
the door behind him. Standing outside the door, Pat started to wonder if Don Ginetti was taking this so personally that he would risk
everything by killing two women and a detective just to show the
other bosses that they made a mistake turning their backs on him.
And how many more men would he sacrifice? Lord knew what the
outcome would be. Pat walked away.

From inside his office, Don Ginetti was standing by the window, looking up at the full moon. He took another puff from his

138

cigar, thinking to himself, *Nicky, I promise you, this will all come to an end. And Marco will be dead.*

Back at the chop shop, the garage door was still open, and all the lights were flickering. The werewolf came out from inside the shop, breathing hard and looking around, its paws covered in blood. It looked up, howled at the moon, and quickly made its escape.

Meanwhile, on a rooftop, a pair of ghostly eyes were watching.

CHAPTER 10

October 29, Tuesday, 9:00 a.m.

From his office at police headquarters, a very tired and unshaven Lt. Frank Mano sat in his desk drinking a hot cup of coffee. He rubbed his red eyes and scratched the top of his head while reading the latest report on the attack of another Ginetti front, the chop shop of stolen vehicles. Lieutenant Mano reviewed the report and examined the photos of the dead men and how they were literally ripped apart by something or someone. This made him stop drinking the coffee and sit back. He rubbed his eyes again and wondered, *Could Danny Marco have done this?* He just could not imagine Danny Marco going off the deep end. It just didn't make sense that he could do this. *Could the death of his father have made him snap after Nicky Ginetti was acquitted of murder? I need to find Danny before Don Ginetti finds him. Damn it, Danny. Where the hell are you? And where the hell is Paul, your mother, and Marie?*

He wondered if Paul and Danny were working together to get rid of the Ginettis. But it still didn't make any sense. Paul's wife had been calling every day, wanting to know what had become of him. Shaking his head and scratching his forehead, Lt. Mano started thinking back to before all hell had broken loose; they had gone to the cabin for Danny's getaway bachelor weekend. How he wished they never went, but he could only dwell on the past. What's done is done, and he needed to find Danny Marco before anyone else was killed by whatever was doing the killing. *"Reports of a hairy beast that looks like a werewolf." Has everyone gone insane?* he wondered.

He refused to believe that a werewolf was doing the killings. It just couldn't be true.

There was a knock on the door. "May I come in?"

"Yes, please come in, Lieutenant Gabriel."

"You look like shit, Mano," remarked Lieutenant Gabriel. "How long have you been up?"

"I don't even remember. This case is just getting insane, and I think the worst is yet to come. I was wondering how long it would be before Internal Affairs stepped in. I guess you guys want in on this whole werewolf thing, right?"

"Maybe. Have you seen the latest news development?"

"Not really."

"You haven't seen the breaking news yet?"

Lieutenant Mano rubbed his forehead and looked up from his desk. "What can the media say that I don't already know?"

"Well said," replied Lieutenant Gabriel. "There is only one way to find out." He turned toward the TV opposite Lieutenant Mano, took the remote, and turned it on. He quickly went to the morning news. "Listen to this," he said.

Lieutenant Mano watched from his desk as the news reporter began.

This is News One, coming again live from Brooklyn. Authorities have confirmed this supposed mechanic garage to be a chop shop. During the night hours, police responded to sounds of gunfire and screams. When the police finally arrived, they were met by the smell of death. A dozen if not more men were brutally ripped apart by something or someone. The stench of death was everywhere, and there was so much blood. Sources said something razor-sharp just ripped these men to pieces.

The bodies were carefully removed and sent to the medical examiner's office. Other sources said this may have been an illegal crime front controlled by Don Ginetti, but it has yet to be proven at this time. One thing we can say, during the night, many people living nearby were awakened by the howling of what they thought was a wolf.

Another resident, who wished to remain anonymous, spoke with me earlier this morning. She said when she woke up from the howling, she looked from her apartment window and saw a hairy-looking beast come running out of the shop. Its paws or hands were covered in blood, and its eyes were blood red. She watched in fear as it ran up a building, and then it was gone.

Could this have been the same person who has been attacking other Ginetti fronts, a vigilante dressed up as a hairy beast or what other witnesses are calling a werewolf? Yes, you heard it again, a werewolf in Brooklyn. With Halloween just days away, you just can't help but wonder if there will be a full moon out on Halloween.

But all jokes aside, people are asked to take precautions when going out at night, and if anyone sees this thing, this werewolf, please call the police immediately. That's all we have for now.

Lieutenant Gabriel turned off the TV and put down the remote on Lieutenant Mano's desk. "So tell me. Where are we on this case?"

"We?" asked Lieutenant Mano, raising an eyebrow. "No one told me we were working on the same case, Lieutenant Gabriel. Doesn't Internal Affairs believe I will solve this? You know I will."

Raising his hands, Lieutenant Gabriel said, "Now relax. Just relax, Frank."

"Frank?" Lieutenant Mano smiled, relaxing back in his chair. "Okay then, since we are being formal, tell me, Robert, why of all days are you here today? Is it because you are so close to retirement that you want to solve one last case that I can't and retire with news headlines and a big fat thank-you from the police commissioner and the mayor, possibly earn a promotion if not retirement?"

"Hey, relax. Just relax." Lieutenant Gabriel pulled a chair to sit down. Scratching his thinning gray hair, he took a deep breath and looked at Lieutenant Mano. "Listen to me very carefully, Frank. The office just sent me here to see if you needed any help with this. That's all. I'm here as a second pair of eyes if you need something looked over or need any calls to be made. I can help you if you want."

Smiling from his desk, Lieutenant Mano responded, "Trust me, Gabriel, I really don't need your help, but I do appreciate the offer. You just wasted your time coming here. You could have called me."

"Damn it, Frank. Why are you such an ass? I'm offering you some assistance, that's all!"

"And as I said, I do appreciate your help, Robert, but right now I am fine."

Lieutenant Gabriel shook his head, smiling and looking at Lieutenant Mano. "I swear you are one hard ass. You really are. Just answer me this one question."

"Okay," Lieutenant Mano said, curious.

"Where the hell is Danny Marco? And why can't you find him?"

"That's two questions."

"Will you stop with the bullshit? You know what I mean."

Getting up from his desk, Lieutenant Mano stared Lieutenant Gabriel straight in the eyes. "Listen to me very carefully, Robert. If I knew where the fuck Marco was, we would not be having this conversation. I've had patrol units at his mother's house and his apartment. But we can't find him, and in case you didn't hear, his mother and fiancée are both missing, as well as Detective Paul Corillo. I have four missing people and a pile of slaughtered bodies, and to top it all off, everyone thinks there is a werewolf loose in Brooklyn. Anything else you want to know, Lieutenant Gabriel?"

Lieutenant Gabriel stood up from his chair. "So you want to play hardball? Fine. It's no secret that you and Marco are close friends outside of work."

"What is that supposed to mean?"

"It means that I think—no, wait, it means that we *all* think that you are protecting Marco, his family, and Corillo, and somehow these slayings are connected to Marco and possibly you. That's what I think. And if I find out that I'm right, trust me, your career is over with the NYPD. And you, Marco, and Corillo will be locked up."

Shocked at what he had just been accused of, Lieutenant Mano, with anger setting in, calmly walked around his desk and got face-to-face with Lieutenant Gabriel. Holding his temper in check, he said, "Listen to me very carefully, Robert. You are treading on very thin ice. You come to my office pretending to be my friend and offering help when your real agenda was to accuse me of abusing my authority as a police lieutenant and possible misconduct? You got some pair of balls on you, Robert. This is my case. I will find Marco and everyone else who is involved, and I will bring them all in. And whoever this wacko pretending to be a werewolf is, he will be apprehended as well, and then this case will be closed."

Then he walked over to the door of his office, opened it, and looked at Lieutenant Gabriel. "Do me a favor and get the fuck out of my office now or so help me."

Without saying a word, Lt. Robert Gabriel walked toward the door and left the office of Lt. Frank Mano, who slammed the door after him. Lieutenant Gabriel stopped and looked back. Shaking his head, he walked over to his driver, who was waiting. "Go get the car ready and meet me outside. I'll be down in a few minutes."

"Yes, sir," said his driver as he walked into an elevator.

Lieutenant Gabriel walked down the hallway to the far end of the building. He looked round, and once he saw that he was alone, he took out his cell phone and made a call. "It's me. We have a problem."

*****

Tuesday, 12:30 p.m.
Dyker Heights, Eleventh Avenue and Seventy-Fourth Street

Inside a residential home, a lone woman was trying to make sense of all that had happened since her husband, Paul Corillo, and three others had taken Danny Marco out for a getaway bachelor's weekend that turned into a nightmare for Danny and resulted in the disappearance of her husband. This woman had waited frantically to hear news of what had happened to Paul and why. While her children were at school, trying to keep their young minds focused, their mother could only stay home and wonder, waiting for information regarding her husband. She had every right to be frightened and fear the worst. She was Kathleen Corillo, wife of missing NYC Detective Paul Corillo.

Nothing has made any sense since that night at Lutheran Medical, she thought. *And since those reports of a hairy-looking beast inside the hospital room where Danny was. After that, Danny and Paul, as well as Danny's mother and his fiancée, all just disappeared without a trace, not even a clue, as to where they could be. Somehow, I truly believe the Ginettis are involved in this. I don't know why I believe they are involved.* Looking at their picture, she could only pray and speak out loud, "Oh, Paul, where are you? Please come home to me safe."

Lost in her own thoughts, she was suddenly brought back to reality by the sound of the doorbell. She looked around and stood up. She adjusted herself and looked in the mirror before she opened the door slightly with the chain lock still on. No one was there, but when she looked down, she saw a familiar dog tied to her fence with a note. The dog was wagging its tail, happy to see her. She closed the door for a second and unchained it. When she opened it again, the dog was jumping up for attention.

"Well," said Kathleen, kneeling. "Are you lost?" She petted the dog and reached for the attached note. *Why do you look so familiar?* She started to read the note.

Kathleen,

I have no time to explain, but I need a favor from you. Please look after my mom's dog while I search for her, Marie, and Paul.

I'm so sorry for what you are going through, but I promise you, I will find them and bring

Paul home to you unharmed. You have my word. Until then, please don't call the police. I'm asking you to trust me. I will be in contact again soon.

Danny

"Dear God," she muttered. "Danny?" She stood up and looked up and down the neighborhood block but didn't see him. She put her hand to her mouth, and tears began to flow. She shouted, "Danny, where are you? I need to know what is going on!" There was no response. She wiped the tears from her eyes. She looked down at this precious dog and gave it a hug, and the dog responded by licking her face. She smiled for a moment. She looked back out again and then at the dog. "You must be hungry. Let's get you something to eat. Wait till the kids see you." Smiling, she brought the dog in and closed the door.

Hiding from her view was Danny Marco. Knowing his mother's dog would be in good care, he now set out to find his mother, Marie, and Paul. *I swear*, he thought, *if Ginetti has hurt them in any way, he will unleash the beast on him without mercy. Enough is enough. I will hammer in the final nail in the Ginetti coffin once and for all, and Don Ginetti can join his fuckin' nephew in hell. All this bullshit will come to an end.* Wearing his dark gray hoodie, unshaven, his face full of anger, he looked both ways and left. Meanwhile, on a rooftop, a pair of glowing red eyes were watching his every move.

*****

Tuesday, 2:00 p.m.
The Ginetti residence

Two men stood guard at the private study of Salvatore Ginetti. They both looked at each other with fear and confusion after hearing the Untouchable Don arguing with his wife, Josephine. The don was wearing his comfortable dark gold robe and smoking his cigar. He was upset, his face taut with nerves and his eyes wide open. Josephine was pleading with her husband for permission for her to step out to Dino's Restaurant and arrange for a private party. She wanted to plan a surprise birthday party for her friend on Friday night, but the don would not permit it, fearing for her life due to the reports of a hairy-looking man on a killing spree.

Facing her husband, coat on and ready to go out, Josephine made her plea. "I just don't understand you, Salvatore. I've been in this house for a week not doing much at all, and now my friend Carol's birthday is coming up, and I want to do something special for her. Why can't I go and talk to the owner of the restaurant? We are such good friends with him."

She did not know that the restaurant in question was also another Ginetti front for illegal loan sharking. Shaking his head in frustration and taking another puff from his cigar, Don Ginetti rubbed his eyes and put the cigar in the ashtray. He looked at his wife. "Josephine, have you been watching the news at all?"

"I understand what is going on. And I understand your concerns, but this is ridiculous. I'm so tired of staying in and not being able to do much. I need to get out."

"We can have the party here. I can arrange to have a full caterer complete with live music. Doesn't that sound better than going out to Dino's?"

"That's just it. I need to get out. I don't want to have the party here. We need a change of scenery to relax and not look at the same walls. Do you understand me, Salvatore?" she asked. "I promise you I won't be out long. I will come straight home."

This is not a good idea, he thought, but he didn't want her to get more upset than she was now. He made up his mind. He put out the cigar and smiled at her. "Okay, Josephine, you win. You can go."

Smiling at her husband, she embraced him with a kiss. "Thank you so much, Salvatore. You won't regret it."

I hope not. "But wait," he said to her as she was walking away. "What is it?"

"You don't think I'm just going to let you go alone, do you?" He shouted to his men, "Guys."

The door opened, and one of the men outside looked in. "Yes, Mr. Ginetti?"

"Get the car ready and drive my wife to Dino's Restaurant. Wait for her and then drive her back home."

"Yes, Mr. Ginetti."

Shocked and confused, she asked, "Really, Salvatore? Is this necessary?"

"Either they go with you, or you don't go."

Upset and just wanting to leave, she agreed. "Fine!" Mrs. Ginetti turned to both men. "Let's go."

After they left, Don Ginetti reached for the phone and called Dino's Restaurant.

*****

Tuesday, 2:00 p.m.

A very tired and determined Danny Marco walked down Eleventh Avenue and Eighty-Sixth Street, staying cautious and keeping his guard up against any unmarked police car or members of the Ginetti crew. Danny Marco would not stop until he eliminated the Ginetti crew, and then he would make his stand against Don Ginetti to get his family and friend back. He didn't know what the outcome would be, but no matter. His life had changed forever since the night at the cabin when he met Lisa Jacobson. She did this to him. She ruined his life. Danny and Marie were going to start a life of love and happiness together. But now all that has changed. Would Marie even consider marrying him, knowing what he has become? A predator of the night. A werewolf. He loved Marie so much, but Lisa Jacobson had to step in claiming to be his soul mate, that they were meant to be together.

What bullshit, he thought. *Why did she pick me out of so many others? I would never wish this hell on anyone, and I can't change the fact that I'm a werewolf. I joked about it so many times, and it's real. I'm a werewolf. As insane as it sounds, you would expect to see this on TV, but it's true. Werewolves do exist, and I am one of them. But when this is all over, where do I go from here?* He stopped for a moment and rubbed his tired eyes and face. People walked past him, not knowing if they knew who he really was. No matter, he had a job to complete.

When he looked at the storefronts, he saw what he was looking for—another Ginetti front that he would permanently put out of business, killing those inside working for Don Ginetti. He walked across the street to get a better view and staked out where he could get in and hide until midnight. He looked at all the angles, the windows, and the entrance to the basement cellar and the side entrance, anywhere he could blend in and be unnoticed. He came up with an idea to get in through the side entrance. If he could get in that way without anyone watching or any delivery being made, it should work. But just as he was about to come up with a plan, he noticed a burgundy-colored Cadillac pull up to the curb. Thinking that it could be Don Ginetti, he quickly moved away, far enough to not be noticed but still have a good view. Two men emerged from the driver's seat and passenger's seat. They looked both ways. Then the driver signaled the other to go in while he waited outside with whoever was in the car.

Walking around the car to the back door, the man waited until the other man came out. They exchanged words, which Danny could not hear. Then the driver opened the door to let out the passenger. Danny was caught off guard when he saw who it was—Josephine Ginetti, wife of the Untouchable Don, Salvatore Ginetti. She had arrived at Dino's Italian restaurant. He saw no one else coming out of the car, and the driver closed the door.

Of all places to get a bite to eat, she comes here. Bitch! He watched as she waved off the two men, as if saying, "Don't come in with me." But one man did go in while the other stayed outside. *Now what could I do? Will she stay there? Is she meeting someone? Damn it. Not now, but she is here.* Danny shook his head in disbelief, put his hand to his mouth, and decided not tonight. He must think of another plan to hit the Ginetti front.

Josephine Ginetti has nothing to do with this. It's her damn husband Don Ginetti. She is innocent. But then again, so are my family and my best friend, Paul Corillo. Don Ginetti has them until Halloween night. He is calling the shots. Damn it. No, I cannot walk away. I've come this far.

He looked again at Dino's Restaurant. The Cadillac was still parked outside with a Ginetti guard standing guard. He saw a van pulling in by the side entrance. *A delivery? I must do this.* He prayed Mrs. Ginetti would be gone afterward, and he would be ready.

He decided to do it. He started walking back up from across the street opposite the restaurant. He blended in with other pedestrians so as not to be noticed by the other guard standing outside. He crossed the street, still with his head down, and moved at his own pace until he reached the corner with the restaurant just a few feet away from him. Now, he had to get to the side entrance without raising any eyebrows. He was thinking of what to do, when suddenly from the corner of his eye, he noticed two very attractive women in tight jeans and nice size racks walking past him. This could be the diversion he needed to get into the side entrance. Praying and hoping the guard would do what he thought he would do, he started walking casually just a few feet from the two women, and just as they were about to go past the restaurant and the guard, Danny stopped and watched.

As the two women walked by the restaurant, the guard outside smiled at them. "Ladies," he said. The two women smiled and giggled, and the guard turned to look at them as they walked. That was what Danny needed. He started to walk and then made a quick right turn to the side entrance of the restaurant just as the guard turned back.

Once a dog, always a dog. Some things never change.

As Danny walked toward the van outside the side entrance, he saw that there was no driver. He went to the back of the van where the doors were open and saw a stack of tablecloth, drinking glasses, and other items; but the one thing that caught his eye as a sure way for him to get inside was a waiter's black jacket. He quickly took off his hoodie and put on the jacket while looking around to see if anyone had seen him. Just as he got rid of the hoodie, someone came out the side entrance wearing a white shirt. Maybe the cook.

"Well, why are you just standing there?" said the man in the white shirt, thinking that Danny was one of the waiters. "You could have at least shaved before you came. Lucky for you I don't send you home. Going to be a busy night. Grab some of the tablecloth and bring it in. Then go shave please. I can't have you looking like that while serving food. And comb your fucking hair for God's sake. Where the hell did the owner find you?"

Danny Marco needed to go along with the act, and fast, or all was lost. Looking at the man, he responded. "Hey, sorry. I just rushed out of my house. My old woman's been breaking my balls every day on stupid shit. I just had to get out of the house. You know what I mean," said Danny.

Laughing, the man responded, "You don't have to tell me about a bitchy wife. I know far too well, but leave your personal shit at home next time, okay?"

"Got it."

"Okay. Now let's get busy. We are going to have a long night. I need to get back to the kitchen and start cooking before I get chewed up by the owner." He walked away.

Yep, he is the cook.

CHAPTER 11

Carrying a tablecloth, Danny walked toward the dining room and put the cloth on a table. The lights were not fully bright yet, so he took advantage of it. Acting like a waiter, he started to put the cloth on one table while others walked past him. He took a chance and walked away. He was trying to find the cellar until he heard voices coming from a few feet away, a male and female voice. *Maybe the restaurant owner?* He listened and made sure no one was around. He took out his phone, turned it off, and put it to his ear, pretending he was on a phone call so no one would question what he was doing standing there.

"Mrs. Ginetti, again I am truly sorry," said Dino, the owner. "But our banquet room is booked till Saturday. If you would have called earlier in the week, maybe we could have accommodated you and your guests, but right now there is nothing I can do. I do apologize."

"Really," said Mrs. Ginetti. "Let me ask you, Dino. Has my husband by any chance got to you and told you not to book me the room? And don't lie to me."

"By no means did he. You have my word he didn't."

But Danny knew Dino was lying to Mrs. Ginetti. *Typical Ginetti bullshit*, Danny thought. *His wife can't go anywhere without his permission for fear she would be taken against her will. Against her will?* Danny started thinking, still listening to the conversation in the office.

"Oh, please, my husband thinks he can do anything he wants and no one can say otherwise. I feel like a prisoner in my own home, and now I can't even plan a birthday party because he won't allow it."

"I assure you, Mrs. Ginetti, that is not the case."

Hearing this conversation in the hallway gave Danny an idea of a new attack on Don Ginetti. It could either backfire or improve his chances of saving his family. But he must act fast.

"Mrs. Ginetti, I think we should leave," said another voice. *The driver*, thought Danny. *He's been quiet all this time.*

"We will leave when I say so, thank you," said Mrs. Ginetti. "I'm not done yet."

Danny had a daring plan, but he couldn't do it alone. If his plan worked, he would have the edge over Don Ginetti, but he would need help and fast. *God, forgive me for what I plan on doing.* He walked over to the bathroom and checked that no one was around. He heard nothing but the sounds coming from the kitchen. He made a quick call.

Sweat ran down his forehead, and his heart pounded. He was nervous and should be. If his plan failed, it was all over. "Yeah, it's me, Danny. No time to explain, but I need your help and fast."

Outside Dino's Restaurant, the second guard was still waiting for the driver and Mrs. Ginetti to leave. From there, a police car parked behind the Cadillac, and a police officer stepped out, along with his partner. The guard looked up, shook his head, and looked back at the police officer approaching him.

"Is this your car?" asked the police officer.

"Well, yes," answered the guard.

"Well, yes? Is this your car?" asked the police officer.

Taking a deep breath, the guard tried to keep his composure. "Yes, officer. I drove my client here so she can book a room for a birthday party. We won't be here long, officer."

"Don't be funny, pal. You can see my name right here," said Officer Amato. The police officer on the scene was Danny's friend, Officer Raymond Amato. He was the one Danny had called for help. "This is a no-parking zone. See the sign?" He pointed to the sign that said "No Parking between 6:00 a.m. and 7:00 p.m."

"It's only 2:30 p.m. Why didn't you park in the parking lot? You think you're better than others that you get to park in a no-parking zone?"

"Look, officer," said the guard, raising his hands.

"Lower your hands," ordered Officer Amato.

"Damn it. Look, officer, we are not breaking any laws. Just give me a few minutes to get the people inside, and we will leave."

"Who's inside?"

The guard was hesitant to answer and was getting very nervous. People walking by stopped to watch.

"Well?"

The guard shook his head, his face turning red. He answered, "I'm waiting for Mrs. Josephine Ginetti."

"Ginetti? You can't do better than that? Bullshit. Let me see your license and registration right now."

"Come on."

"You want to go to jail?"

Suddenly from inside, the man in white, the cook, came out, and things got worse. "Jesus Christ," he said. "Don't you cops have anything better to do?"

"Sir, stay out of this," said Officer Amato.

"And you can go stuff your mouth with a doughnut," replied the cook.

Suddenly an argument broke out between the cook and Officer Amato; the Ginetti guard was in the middle, trying to calm them down while other people looked on. This was just what Danny Marco needed, a distraction.

Meanwhile, back inside the restaurant, the owner said, "Mrs. Ginetti, again, I do apologize to you, but we are booked. If you like, I can make a reservation for you and your husband for this evening? My way of saying I'm sorry."

"Unbelievable." She looked at her driver and said, "Come on. Let's get out of here. I'm sure there is another restaurant that won't say no to me."

But before Dino could say anything, Danny Marco came running in with a look of concern. "I'm sorry to interrupt, sir, but there is a situation escalating in front of the restaurant."

Dino stood up with his eyes wide open. Mrs. Ginetti and the driver listened. "What is going on?" asked Dino.

"There is a car parked outside at the no-parking zone," answered Danny. "The police came and asked the driver to go park in the parking lot, but then the cook came out and told the cop to go eat a doughnut. Now there are people gathering outside to watch the commotion."

Dino brought both hands to his head, and his face turned red. "Goddamn cook. He just can't mind his own business. He always seems to get involved in things that don't concern him. We need to put a stop to this before this goes live on social media."

The driver stood up, along with Mrs. Ginetti, who was getting nervous. "Mrs. Ginetti, we need to get out of here now."

"Hold on. You can't just leave now," said Dino. "There is just too much going on outside. She needs to stay here until all is clear. In the meantime, your guy needs our help outside."

"But I can't leave her alone," replied the driver.

"I'll stay with her," said Danny Marco.

"No," Mrs. Ginetti protested. "I'm not afraid to show my face outside." She stood up.

"Wait," said the driver. "With all due respect, Mrs. Ginetti, it's best you stay here until we can get things settled outside."

"Fine." She took a deep breath. "I dare not embarrass the Ginetti name." She sat down.

"Good. Come on, Dino."

When the driver left, Dino started to follow but then turned with a confused look on his face, looking at Danny. "What a minute. Who the hell are you?"

Danny felt his heart racing. He needed to think of something fast. "I was just called for tonight, sir. Was told it's going to be a busy night, so I came right over."

Shaking his head, Dino said, "I would appreciate it if someone had told me. What's your name?"

Danny thought of a name fast. "I'm Nicky." Mrs. Ginetti's face turned white as she looked at him.

"Fine, please stay with Mrs. Ginetti. This should not take long. And, Nicky, when we come back, please go shave. We can't have a waiter with a five o'clock shadow on his face."

"Will do, sir."

Dino left and headed for the front of the restaurant. Danny turned and smiled at Mrs. Ginetti, the woman who was married to one of the most dangerous men in Brooklyn, Don Ginetti.

"Well, this is a bit awkward," said Josephine Ginetti with her head down.

Danny thought that he might have been made. "I'm sorry?"

She smiled and looked back up. "I'm sorry. It's just that when you said your name, I nearly cried."

"Why is that?" asked Danny.

"Well…" Mrs. Ginetti took a deep breath and looked at him. "My late nephew, his name was Nicky. He was brutally killed, and the police never found out who did it. It's just a shame how the police will not help when they find out your name is Ginetti. It's just so awful how the police treat people. And now they are harassing us again outside."

Keeping his cool, Danny Marco turned away from Josephine Ginetti. He closed his eyes and started to remember when he woke up in the hospital and was told that his father was dead, and how he died, and how Nicky Ginetti got off because the murder weapon had disappeared from the evidence room. *A mole in the department? Maybe.* He shook his head and opened his eyes. Mrs. Ginetti was looking at him with a bit of confusion.

"Are you all right?" asked Mrs. Ginetti.

Danny was breathing slowly, trying to calm himself. He responded with his back to her. "I understand full well what you mean, Mrs. Ginetti. Your nephew was killed, and there was no justice."

"Exactly," she said. "What a shame on the NYPD."

"You know what else is a shame, Mrs. Ginetti?" He turned and looked her directly in the eyes with anger. She was caught off guard by his look. "It's a crying shame how Nicky Ginetti got away with murder after he killed my father at Marco's Pizzeria. And he walked out of the courthouse with a big fucking smile on his face. That's the biggest shame of all, Mrs. Ginetti. Thanks to your husband. Because of your husband, my mother lost her husband, the family business, and nearly lost me, her son, while your shitty-ass nephew and your husband got away with the murder of my father, Peter Marco! You tell me, Mrs. Ginetti, where was the justice for my father? Bitch, I'll tell you where it was. It was in the dirty money your fucking husband paid off to lose the murder weapon, and your son-of-a-bitch nephew just walked with that arrogant smile on his face."

Josephine Ginetti was stunned and unable to speak. Her heart was racing, and fear came over her, knowing that the man she was facing was not a waiter, and his name was not Nicky. No, she was now starting to realize that the man she was talking to was the son of Peter Marco, NYC Police Detective Danny Marco. Shaking and not knowing what would happen next, she tried to scream for her driver, but Danny quickly covered her mouth with his hand. He could strangle her and leave her for dead, but he saw the fear in her eyes as tears started to flow down onto his hand.

He took a deep breath, looked behind him and back to her, and said, "Not a word. Not a damn word, Mrs. Ginetti."

Outside the restaurant, the owner of Dino's, his chef, Mrs. Ginetti's driver, and the bodyguard were engaged with Officer Amato, verbally trying to calm things down before it got worse.

"This is all bullshit!" said the chef. "You can't even park your car for a minute without you cops harassing us."

"Enough." Dino pointed to the chef. "You, get back inside and cook now!"

The chef, angry as hell, turned and went back into the restaurant. With a crowd of people still watching, he begged Officer Amato to just write the driver a ticket and leave. This was not good business for his restaurant.

"This is just unreal," said the driver to Officer Amato.

"You need to get the fuck out of here," said the guard to Officer Amato.

"Shut up," replied the driver.

"You guys really want to go to jail, don't you?" said Officer Amato. "I'm calling this in."

"No!" the driver protested. "Just give us a ticket, and we will leave."

"Fine." Officer Amato wrote up the ticket and handed it over to the driver. "Next time, read before you park, or do you guys need for me to get you both prescription glasses?" Both men turned red but did not say a word. "You boys have a nice day."

"Okay, people, the show is over. Go on with your business." The officer went back to his patrol car, got in, and left. He hoped that Danny had done what he had planned to do.

"Finally," said Dino, rubbing his head and starting to relax.

"I can't believe what the fuck just happened," remarked the driver to the other.

"Don't blame me," the guard said. "I had everything under control until that wacko came out and made things worse."

"It's a good thing Mrs. Ginetti didn't come outside to see this."

Suddenly to their left, a screeching white van came out from the side entrance, turned, and sped away. All three men looked.

"Now where is this fucking cop now?" asked the guard.

"Forget it," said the driver. "Let's get Mrs. Ginetti and get out of here. I've had enough drama for one day."

All three men went inside and headed toward Dino's office. "You left her alone in the office?" asked the driver.

"Relax. She is not alone," answered the guard. "A waiter came in and told us what was going on outside, and he said he would stay with her until this was over. I need a drink."

When they went inside Dino's office, they were stunned to see no one was there. "What the fuck?" said the guard. "He said he would watch her."

"Maybe she went to the bathroom?" said the driver.

"What? And the waiter went inside with her?" asked the guard.

"Let me check," said Dino. He left for a moment and came back. "No one is in the women's room."

"What the fuck?" remarked the driver.

All three men were confused, trying to understand what was going on.

Looking at Dino, the driver asked, "Who was this waiter you left her with?"

"He was new, called in tonight to work."

"And you believed him?" asked the guard.

"What did he look like?" asked the driver.

Dino rubbed his eyes and said, "Well, I do know he needed to shave. He looked horrible, and we have a high standard on clean-shaven waiters."

"What? Who the fuck works as a waiter with a beard?" asked the driver.

"No, no," said Dino. "He needed to shave, but he didn't have a beard."

Both men looked at each other and started to get angry at Dino. "A guy with a 5:00 p.m. shadow working as a waiter?" said the guard.

"Shut the fuck up!" exclaimed the driver. Then he looked back at Dino with anger. "Tell me, Dino, besides his beard or whatever, did he tell you his fucking name?"

"Well, of course," answered Dino. "He said his name was Nicky."

"Nicky?" The driver looked at the guard.

Both men were confused and did not understand what was going on. "So you're telling me a guy with a fucking beard got called tonight 'cause you were down a waiter, and he told you his name was Nicky, and you just left him here with Mrs. Ginetti? And all you can remember about this fuck is that he needed to shave? Do you know how this sounds, you prick?"

Dino was scared and nervous, and he should be.

"Do you have the job applications?" asked the driver.

"Well, of course we do," answered Dino. "Why wouldn't I?"

"Don't get fucking smart with me, Dino. Let's see those applications now!"

Dino was sweating and nervous, praying he had the signed job application. He knew if he did not have it, it would be his end. He pulled out all the job applications from his desk drawer. The driver and guard started checking each one, looking for the name Nicky.

"Nicky is not on any application," said the guard.

Dino was shocked. "I do not understand. How was I caught off guard?" He sat back in his leather chair.

The guard looked at the driver. "How the fuck are we going to explain this to Don Ginetti? His wife has been taken."

"We?" asked the drive. "You left her with this Nicky, and you didn't even stop to think."

"Hey! Do not even try that bullshit with me!"

"Gentlemen, please stop this yelling. This day has been just horrible. Please tell me what is going on," said Dino. "I've had enough surprises for one day."

Angry and frustrated, the guard threw the job applications at Dino and walked around the desk. Dino was getting scared as the guard grabbed him by his shirt.

"Listen very carefully, asshole. Next time, pay attention to who your employees are and not who needs to shave. Understand, Dino Dog?"

Dino nodded without saying a word. He let go of Dino and looked at the driver. "I can already hear Don Ginetti. This is not going to be good."

As they proceeded to walk out of Dino's office, the guard stopped, turned around, and said, "Listen, Dino Dog, if I were you, I'd close down tonight, maybe for the next couple of nights, maybe a couple of months, and lay low until things cool down or until we find Mrs. Ginetti. For your sake, pray we find her alive."

"But I booked reservations tonight," said Dino. "What do I tell the guests?"

With a smirk on his face, the guard answered, "Either you cancel all reservations tonight or, trust me, we will book you for an unmarked grave. Understand, Dino Dog?" He turned and left.

Dino was shaking. He had no choice but to cancel all reservations. His phone rang, and it startled him. He picked up the phone.

"Hello, this is Dino's. I do apologize, but we are not taking any reservations at this moment. We are currently renovating and will be closed. For how long? That remains to be seen," said Dino and hung up.

CHAPTER 12

Tuesday, 3:00 p.m.

Inside a motel room, a man was pacing back and forth while two women sat at a table. There were half-eaten plates of food, bottles of water, and coffee cups in disarray on the table. The room had three beds, a dark carpet that was not cleaned, and one bathroom. The TV was on, but they were not watching. These people were tired and fed up. They wanted to go home, but they could not. The two windows were sealed shut, and all they could see from the window was a dirty parking lot. A lone car was parked outside; the individuals who drove the car brought them food and a change of clothes when they needed it. They were not allowed to have any cell phone or computer. These people had been taken and were being held against their will until one man was ready to release them. That man was Salvatore "the Untouchable Don" Ginetti. The three people he had kidnapped were Danny Marco's mother, Ellen Marco; his fiancée, Marie; and his best friend, NYPD Detective Paul Corillo. He had them taken the night at the hospital when a hit man was ordered to kill Danny Marco with the help of the fake cop, and then all hell broke loose. Now Don Ginetti was using them as leverage until Halloween night.

Ellen Marco looked up at Paul. "Paul, please, for the love of God, sit down. I cannot take it anymore." She started to cry. Marie put her arm around her to comfort her.

Paul sat down next to her. "Mrs. Marco, I am so sorry. Damn it, I am so sorry." He rubbed his eyes and scratched his head. "I am sorry to the both of you for getting caught in the middle of all this.

I wish there was a way out of this mess, but there isn't. For now, we must be strong and ride this till the end."

"I just do not understand," said Marie. "Ellen doesn't deserve any of this. She lost Peter, the business is gone, and now Danny, wherever he is, is on the run from the Ginettis because of that prick Nicky Ginetti. How long will they keep us here? Or will they kill Danny and then kill us all?"

"No!" Ellen was crying out loud and shaking. "Please not my Danny. Oh, dear God."

"Ellen, I'm sorry. I'm just so frustrated at what is going on. We don't belong here. Please calm down."

Paul stood up. "Yes, we don't belong here at all, but as of now, we have no choice. I miss my wife and kids. Lord knows what is going through their minds, but there is nothing I can do about it."

Ellen looked at Paul. "I just do not understand what is going on. Everything that happened had something to do with the night at the cabin. Everything seemed to have changed the night you were all there. I know we talked about this before. You and Danny seemed to have an answer for every single question we asked you, but, Paul, Danny a werewolf? I just cannot believe this to be true. I know in my heart you are keeping something from us. I don't know what it is you are hiding, but I know you are. Please, Paul, for the love of God, you are like a son to me. I have watched you and Danny grow up together and graduate from the police academy. I know you cops carry a code of protection for each other, but this has gone way too far. What really happened to Danny the night at the cabin? And does it have anything to do with Nicky Ginetti's death? Paul, please as a mother and friend, you need to tell us what the hell is going on before it's too late."

"And stop this nonsense about a werewolf," added Marie.

Paul looked at them both and thought, *How will I ever get them to believe that Danny is a werewolf?* "As strange as it sounds, it's all true. Danny Marco is a werewolf. If someone had told me this, I would not have believed it myself. My best friend is a werewolf because of Lisa Jacobson. Damn it, I wish we never went to that damn cabin."

"Damn it, Paul," said Marie, startling him. He came back to reality, looking at them both.

"What?" asked Paul.

"What is it?" asked Marie. "You had that faraway look as if you were in another world. I said your name twice, and then I had to get loud. I'm sorry, but you were in another world."

If only that were true, he thought.

Ellen touched Paul's hand. "Son, are you going to tell us what is really going on? We have a right to know."

Paul looked up, took a deep breath, and looked down again at them. *We told them the truth, and they didn't believe us.* "Ellen, Marie, what we told you about what happened to Danny is true. He is a werewolf. What else can I say or do to prove to you that what we told you is all true?" He started laughing.

"What is so funny, Paul?" asked Marie.

"I am sorry for laughing. But honestly, as incredible and weird as it sounds, I should be in Bellevue Hospital for believing this. But, ladies, I don't know what else to say or how to convince you both that what we told you is the truth. Danny is a werewolf."

"Fine," said Marie. "This is just unbelievable! You are sticking to your story that Danny was bitten by a wolf, this Lisa Jacobson who told him she was his mate, and now he is going around killing the fucking Ginettis. Is that what you really want us to believe?"

"What else can I say?" said Paul. "What else?"

Marie got up and walked away, angry. Paul and Ellen just looked at each other.

*****

In another undisclosed location, Josephine Ginetti was sitting and fearing for her life. She had been taken away against her will by Danny Marco. When he saw her at Dino's, he had come up with a plan that would buy him time to save his family. She was his bargaining chip. This went against everything he was trained for as a police officer and an NYPD detective. He knew he had broken the law, but he had no choice. It was time to play dirty with the Ginettis.

He sat down facing her. "Please do not be afraid. I will not hurt you, but you need to understand. Your husband has kidnapped my mother, my fiancée, and my friend, who is also an NYC detective. He has made this personal ever since that son of a bitch Nicky Ginetti was killed. Mrs. Ginetti, none of this would have happened if your nephew had left my family alone. He would not let it go. He wanted the family pizzeria. He kept pushing and pushing. And my poor father, Peter Marco, was killed fighting to save his business. And I was not there to save my father from that prick nephew of yours. You want to know why I wasn't there, Mrs. Ginetti?"

She was so scared that she didn't respond, but Danny continued to talk to her. "It's because my friends took me out for my bachelor's getaway weekend in Pennsylvania. And while I was there, I was attacked by a wild animal and left in a coma. When I came out of it, I was shocked to find that Nicky had just walked away from a murder conviction because the murder weapon he used to kill my father just disappeared from evidence. No doubt in my mind your husband had paid someone off to get rid of the murder weapon and Nicky's shirt, which had my father's blood on it. Do you understand me, Mrs. Ginetti? Your family killed my father and destroyed everything. And Nicky walks away with a fucking smile on his face. Where is the justice in that?"

Terrified, Josephine Ginetti finally spoke. "I am so sorry for the loss of your father and all the trouble you are having. And yes, my nephew Nicky, he was just out of control. We tried so hard with him. We really did. But every time we thought he was finally coming to his senses, he would turn around and get himself into more trouble. The things he did was unforgivable, and now he will have to face the judgment of God for his sins. But taking me will not bring your father back. Things will just get worse for you the longer I am with you. Please, let me go, and I promise you I will talk to my husband. I will make sure he releases your family, and my family can put this behind us. We both need closure."

"Closure? How can I have any closure? He will not let them go until Halloween night. My life for my family. He wants me dead! An eye for an eye because of Nicky! My God, even in death, that son of a bitch still haunts me." He scratched his messy hair.

"May I ask you a question?"

"Yes." Danny rubbed his eyes.

"Please tell me, did you kill Nicky? Word is that a hairy beast killed him without mercy. I for one do not believe in monsters. But from the news and social media, I think everyone has lost their minds on this so-called beast, unless it was someone dressed as a beast. So I ask you again, did you kill Nicky?"

Danny smiled and thought, *Yes and no. Yes, part of me killed that bastard. The werewolf killed him, not me.* "No, I didn't kill Nicky, but I wish to heaven I did. However, it wasn't me."

"Then who killed him?"

"Nicky had many enemies. It could have been anyone. But it does not change a thing. I will not let you go. My family comes first. And as long as I have you, your dirtbag husband won't dare try anything."

Frustrated, Josephine Ginetti spoke louder to Danny. "Listen to me, I'm so sorry for what has happened to you and your family, but what you are doing will only make things worse for you. Please, let me just speak to him. I am sure he will listen to me and let them go."

"No. I am sorry to drag you into this, but again, your husband made this very personal." He reached into his pocket. "This is a disposable phone your husband left for me. Let's just wait for him to call before it gets dark."

Confused, she looked at him and asked, "Why? What will happen in the evening?"

Danny just looked at her, wiping the sweat from his forehead. "Trust me when I say all hell will break loose."

From there, the disposable phone rang. They both looked at the phone and at each other. "Right on time," said Danny. He picked up the phone and hit answer. "I was wondering if you were going to call."

From the other line, Danny and even Mrs. Ginetti could hear the screaming angry voice of Don Ginetti. "You worthless piece of shit! How dare you take my wife? You think that you have an advantage over me, you prick bastard. I will bury your family ten feet under. And as for you, I have special plans for you. Now let me speak to my wife, asshole!"

"Salvatore!"

Don Ginetti was stunned to hear his wife on the phone. "Josephine! Are you all right? Did he hurt you?"

"Salvatore, never mind that! What the hell is wrong with you? You have his family, and you will kill them all for Nicky? And what do you think Danny will do to me?"

Don Ginetti was breathing heavily and trying to stay calm. His heart was beating fast. "Josephine, you just don't understand. My sister wants revenge for Nicky's death. I can't let this go."

"And what about the Marco family? Nicky created a huge mess that got him killed, and you had to clean up his mess again, as always. There is no logic in this, Salvatore. Nicky was trouble, and you know it. It's sad that he is gone. However, there is nothing more we can do but move on. For the love of God, Salvatore, please stop this before anyone else is killed."

Rubbing his forehead and trying to stay calm for his wife, he replied, "Josephine, yes, Nicky was nothing but trouble and so much more. He did cause these problems, and I told him many times to stay away from Marco's Pizzeria. But once Nicky made up his mind, that was it. There are rules that have to be followed, and Nicky made up his own rules."

"Fuck your rules! Let the Marco family go!"

"Okay, that's enough." Danny Marco pulled the phone away from Mrs. Ginetti and spoke to her husband. "Hey, old man. I think your wife has more balls than you."

With his face turning red and squeezing the phone, Don Ginetti responded, "You bastard! I swear to God I will put a hole in your fucking head."

"Do that and you will never see your wife again."

"Fine," said Don Ginetti. "You win for now, but trust me, this is not over. We will set up where to meet and exchange."

"No!" said Danny.

This put a confused look on the face of the don and his wife. "No? What the fuck do you mean no? I'm willing to let go of your family for my wife, and you say no? You really want to turn this into a bloodbath with your blood, you prick bastard!"

"Shut the fuck up for once in your life and listen, 'cause as of now, I'm the boss in charge, and I will give the orders," said Danny.

"What?" The don was screaming in his office. His guards standing outside his door heard everything and were getting nervous. "You are going to give me orders? This should be interesting. Let's hear it, boss man." Don Ginetti leaned forward in his leather chair.

"Fine. We will resume the meetup on Halloween night. But before Halloween is here, you are going to text me all your illegal operations and locations and how many men are in each one. I want them all. Once my hairy friend disposes of all your garbage, then we will meet on Halloween night. I want to get rid of your entire gang and leave no one alive, and I will, 'cause if you don't comply with my demands, then let's just say my hairy friend will be in the mood for Italian food. Right, Mrs. Ginetti?"

The don quickly stood up in his chair, red-faced, and slammed his fist on his desk. "Don't you dare!" said Don Ginetti. "As for my operations, you seem to know where they all are. Why ask me? You have taken out most of my guys and cost me money, you shit!"

"Don't worry about that. You just do what I say, and she will not be harmed. One more thing, old man. Do not alert anyone, 'cause if you do and something happens to me, your precious wife will be having dinner with that little shit Nicky. I'll be waiting for the text. You have exactly five minutes starting now. Bye."

"Wait! Let me talk to my wife again." But the line was dead.

Don Ginetti stared down at his phone, then hurled it across the room and screamed. Both his guards came into the room.

"Don Ginetti, are you all right?" asked one guard.

Sitting in his chair with a confused look on his face, the don said, "Is everything all right? Are you fucking kidding me, you prick?" He reached into his desk, pulled out his gun, and pointed it at his guard. "I should blow your fucking head off for leaving my wife alone at Dino's."

Hands up and terrified, one guard replied, "Sir, we are sorry, but it just happened so fast. Please, sir."

Don Ginetti put the gun down on his desk and sat back in his chair. Both guards were somewhat relieved. "Get the burner phone," said the don. "Start texting our hideouts to Marco and write down how many men are in each one."

"Should I have our people ready to take him out once he shows up?" asked the guard.

"No!" said the don. "I made a deal with him. He will eliminate our boys to save his family and then meet up on Halloween night to make the trade. His family for my wife."

Confused, both guards looked at each other, and then one of them said, "Sir, are you saying you are going to let Marco kill our boys and we are not going to do a thing about it? You are going to sacrifice them without a warning?"

The don pulled out a cigar and lit it. Puffing smoke, he looked at his guards. "Correct. Again, he has my wife. If Marco is taken down, his wild friend will kill her. Now do as I say, asshole. He gave me five minutes. We have barely two minutes left. Start texting the locations to him now. And don't warn anybody."

"Yes, sir." The guard began texting the Ginetti locations to Danny Marco.

Have your fun, Marco, the don thought. *This is just a setback for me, and payback will be a huge bitch!* "And one more thing," said Don Ginetti, looking up at his guard. "Call that dick Dino and tell him he is permanently out of business."

*****

Back at his hiding location, Danny Marco received the text he was waiting for, with addresses of the Ginetti operations and how many men were in each one. Danny wrote each one down.

Josephine spoke to him. "Are you really going to have that hairy thing kill me? Then you do know who killed Nicky?"

Looking up at her, Danny replied, "No, I will not harm you in any way. I have a heart. Your husband doesn't. And no, I don't know who killed Nicky. He had enemies from here to the Bronx. As for me, I have to do what I must to save my family, and that means taking out the entire Ginetti crew. I am sorry, but I must tie you up and make sure you will be here when I get back."

He quickly tied up her hands but not too tightly. As he put a rag over her mouth, she said to him, "May God forgive you."

He leaned down to her ear and responded, "No, may God forgive your husband for all the pain he has caused my family." Then he quickly gagged her mouth. He moved to leave and looked back at her. "I'm sorry. But family always comes first, and I will do whatever it takes to save mine." He turned and left. Then he walked out the door and locked it. He looked at the disposable phone, and sure enough, he started to receive more text messages of the Ginetti operations in Brooklyn as well as Staten Island. *Shit, eight locations in Brooklyn and one in Staten Island. This can't be all of it. Can I pull this off? There better not be anyone waiting for my other half.*

His detective half was telling him he was wrong and to let her go, but his other half was telling him, *Do not stop now. Remember what your father said to you in your dream. Eliminate everyone in the Ginetti family.* His mind was made up, and now he knew what to do next. He looked at his watch: 6:00 p.m. Soon night would fall, and the moon would rise.

He looked at the burner phone. The first address was a pool club on Cropsey Avenue in Brooklyn. The back room was used for illegal gambling and collections. There were seven men. *Time to get to work. Don't let me down, my other half.*

As he started walking away, a pair of mysterious glowing eyes were watching him from above and quickly came down behind him. He heard a familiar voice.

"Danny?"

He quickly turned around.

*****

Back at the undisclosed hotel room, Paul Corillo was again telling Ellen Marco and Marie the events that occurred that night at the cabin—Lisa Jacobson and the mysterious animal that attacked Danny and turned him into a werewolf, the same werewolf that killed Nicky Ginetti and other members of the Ginetti crew. But trying to get them to believe him was a lost cause. Marie and Ellen Marco just could not accept the fact that Danny Marco was a werewolf. Marie had her face in her hands and was shaking her head, while Ellen was trying to make some sense of everything.

"Look," said Paul. "I have told you this over and over. At first, I didn't believe it myself. These things cannot exist, but in this strange world, they do. How is it they do? I don't know. But I know for a fact Danny is a werewolf. We must accept it regardless of how insane it sounds."

"Stop it! Just stop it." Marie lifted her face from her hands. Her face was red and tearful. She looked at Ellen and then at Paul. "How stupid do you think we are?"

"Marie, please understand—"

But she cut him off. "No! Enough. Do you honestly expect us to believe this bullshit you've been telling us all day? I told Danny so many times he had to grow up, watching those old werewolf movies and wearing that ridiculous mask to scare me. But he would not. He thought it was a big joke."

"Marie—"

"No. Wait. I am not done yet. And then there is this Lisa Jacobson. Tell me, Paul, that night they were out alone, did you guys plan this for him to get his last fling?"

"Now stop right there," said Ellen Marco. "Danny would never betray you like that. He loves you."

"Loves me?" said Marie. "From what Paul said, she was practically all over him. I should have known better. Danny was never ready for marriage, so you guys made up this bullshit about him being attacked by a wild animal when in fact he screwed this Lisa Jacobson on the porch, and you guys cheered him on."

Ellen slapped her in the face, which caught both Marie and Paul off guard. "Enough."

"Then how do you explain the animal attack that put him in a coma, Marie?" asked Paul. "We were shooting blindly in the forest.

Whatever it was, it got away from us, and we almost lost Danny. When he finally came to at the hospital and found out what happened to Peter, he was blinded by revenge. I tried to stop him, and I followed him to the warehouse where Nicky was, but we got caught. They were tuning him up in another room, and that was when we heard the scream. Not Danny, but the guy who was beating him up. And that was when I saw it. I could not believe what I was looking at. It was hairy and had sharp paws and teeth. And it was out for blood. It was fast and agile. It killed Nicky and his crew. At first, I thought this thing had broken into the warehouse. If I didn't see the gold cross on the werewolf, I probably would have shot it."

"Oh, dear Lord," exclaimed Ellen. "I put it around Danny's neck for protection."

"A lot of good it did him," remarked Marie.

"I told him, or it, that I was sorry for not believing him," Paul continued. "When it heard the sirens, it ran away."

"Do you think he understood you?" asked Ellen.

"Honestly, I don't know," answered Paul.

"Ellen, please, you cannot believe any of this bullshit. It just can't be true, and I will not accept it. I will not accept the fact that Danny is a werewolf going around killing people," said Marie.

"No, he is not killing people. He is only going after the Ginettis." Paul took a deep breath, looked at them both, and said, "After he takes care of every member of the Ginetti crew, he said he would turn himself in."

"Turn himself in?" asked Ellen with a look of shock.

"Yes, he said he will turn himself in."

"Are you fucking kidding me?" asked Marie. "He will go to prison, and we will never see him again. They will probably dissect him just to see how he turns into a werewolf. Oh God, what am I saying?"

"There must be another way," said Ellen.

"I'm afraid not. What Danny is doing is saving all of us and putting an end to the Ginetti family," Paul explained.

"Oh, dear God, this is a fucking nightmare. I just want to wake up," said Marie.

Suddenly they heard the door unlocking. They all stood up. Paul stood in front of them. The door opened, and two big men came in.

Smiling at them, one said, "Sorry, folks, but it's checkout time."

"Oh no." Ellen held on to Marie.

"Relax, lady," said the other man. "We are just going to move you to another location. Just listen, and no one will get hurt."

Ellen Marco's fear had now turned to anger. She walked around Paul as he tried to hold her back and went up to one of the men. "You bastard!" she said. "You should be ashamed of yourself. You and your friend are nothing but two bullies. Your mother must be so proud of how you turned out, you waste of life."

Paul quickly grabbed her and pulled her to him. "Ellen, stop it! They don't give a damn about us." He looked back at the two men. "Guys, she is just upset. A woman her age doesn't deserve to be treated like this."

"Hey," said one of the men, "don't worry about it. I have been called worse, and I'm sorry she was dragged into this. Just get ready to go, please. It will be dark soon."

Dark soon? Paul thought. *Danny, wherever you are, put an end to this once and for all.*

CHAPTER 13

Tuesday, 10:00 p.m.
Cropsey Avenue, Brooklyn

Outside the Bar and Pool Club, the scene was quiet like any other night. Neon signs outside the bar shone brightly, people walked by, and cars drove along like any other night, except this night, pedestrians stopped in fear at the sound of gunfire inside. Bright flashes of gunfire could be seen as people ran to avoid getting hit by a bullet and cars sped away. Within seconds, a man was thrown out the front window, followed by more gunfire, and this time people were running out of the pool hall in fear for their lives. Screams were heard, and there was more gunfire. Then the sound of a growling monster grew louder and louder as it got closer to the window and leaped out. It stood up high with its razor-sharp claws dripping blood. It was breathing heavily from its razor-sharp teeth. With the eyes of death, the werewolf had struck again as it looked up and howled at the moon before escaping into the night just as scared witnesses started calling the police.

"Nine-one-one, where is the location of the emergency?"

"Please send the police here. I just saw that hairy monster."

"I'm sorry," said the operator. "Did you say you saw a hairy monster?"

"That's exactly what I am saying. This is no fucking joke. It threw a guy out of a window. And then it jumped out the window, looked up, and just screamed."

"Screamed?" asked the operator.

"Screamed, barked, whatever. It's real and it's here. Send a fucking SWAT team here."

Danny Marco, as the werewolf, had struck again, attacking another Ginetti location. And keeping his word, Don Ginetti could not do anything about it but sit in his leather chair in the dark smoking his cigar while his men and his illegal operations were being destroyed by the werewolf. All he could do was think about his wife, Josephine.

Nicky caused this huge mess, he thought to himself. *Nicky, you were my nephew, my sister's kid. I loved you, Nicky, but damn you! You just never listened to anyone but yourself. You just couldn't leave Marco's Pizzeria alone, and for what?*

Then he heard a familiar voice coming from his left. "I had to show you I was more than just your nephew and your errand boy, Uncle Sal."

He looked, and there sitting in the leather chair to his left, his shirt soaked in blood, was his nephew, Nicky Ginetti. Shocked, the Untouchable Don sat up, staring. "What the fuck is this? You are not here. You are fucking dead, Nicky. Your fucking ego killed you, you worthless bag of shit. You caused so many problems, and now that you are dead, you are still causing me more problems."

Nicky laughed. "Yeah, Uncle, and now I'm dead. Are you happy about that?"

"No, you are not here. I'm dreaming. You're just in the back of my head trying to drive me nuts, you shit." The don rubbed his eyes. He looked to his left, and Nicky had disappeared. He started to relax, but it was too soon.

"Oh, I am here, Uncle."

Don Ginetti looked to his right, and Nicky was standing there by the edge of his desk. Don Ginetti was taken aback and jumped back in his leather chair. For the first time, he was scared and shaking. Don Ginetti was talking to a ghost, or was he? "Fuck! Are you trying to give me a heart attack? What the fuck do you want? You are all out of chances, Nicky, and I don't think your mother would want to see you like this."

With blood still on his shirt and coming closer to the don, Nicky sat on top of his desk and looked at him with a cold look. "Relax, Uncle Sal. I'm not looking for any more chances from you. And please leave Mom out of this. She cries every night because of you."

"Because of me?"

"Of course. She blames you for my death. She yells every night at Dad, telling him it's your fault that I'm dead and that you should have had more control of the situation and kept me out of the family business."

"What?" The don slammed his hand on his desk. "What bullshit! I did everything I could for you to keep you out of trouble. But every time I did, I would hear of so many different problems you caused, and I had to bail you out of them, but did you stop? No, you didn't. You just kept doing what you wanted to do, and it drove me out of my fucking mind. You had a huge target on your back, and the only reason why you were still alive back then was because of me, you prick!"

Leaning back in his leather chair and trying to regain his composure, the don took a deep breath and looked at Nicky. "And let me tell you something else, you little ballbuster. I never wanted to bring you into the business. It was your father who begged me to just keep an eye on you, you little fuck. I bet that is one detail your dad forgot to tell her, right? And where is your dad now? With his wonderful job, keeping his nose clean."

Raising his hand, Nicky Ginetti looked at his uncle with a smile. "Okay, okay, Uncle Sal. You made your point. Fine."

"Okay, then. Now do me a favor and get the fuck out of here. You are freaking me out with that bloody shirt."

Nicky looked down at his bloody shirt. "What? This old thing?" And he laughed.

"What the fuck are you laughing at?" asked the don. "I told you not to go back to Marco's Pizzeria, but again you didn't listen, and you killed Peter Marco. That blood is his blood, and it's all on you, not me."

"Yeah, I killed the old man, but this is not his blood. It's my blood," said Nicky. "I was killed, or did you forget? Plus, Peter Marco turned down a business proposition that could have made us rich. But that's not why I'm here, Uncle Sal."

Confused, the don looked at his dead nephew. "Oh, no? Then please enlighten me. Why the fuck are you here?"

Nicky got up from the desk and walked around to the front while speaking to Don Ginetti. "Uncle Sal, it has come to my attention that you made a deal with Danny Marco. Correct?"

"How the fuck did you find out?"

Nicky stood in front of the desk and slammed his hands down, startling the don. "Come on, Uncle Sal. I may be, in fact, dead. But I am not stupid like you thought I was. I know things."

Smiling, the don sat back in his leather chair again. "Okay, smart-ass. Since you know things, tell me what you know."

"Oh, you want to go that route? Fine. So you have Danny's family, and you told him you were going to hold them till Halloween night and that he was to come to you at a place of your choice. Then Marco takes Aunt Josephine and turns the table on you. He tells you he wants all the locations of your operations so his friend the beast man can get rid of your boys one by one until there is no one left, and then he will meet up with you on Halloween night. Am I right so far?"

"Continue."

Smiling, Nicky continued. "And he warned you if you tell anyone he is coming, then that big, mean, hairy beast that put his fucking hand through my chest will have a late-night dinner, and Aunt Josephine will be the main course, right?"

The don stood up. "Watch it, Nicky."

But Nicky continued. "So here you are, sitting in the dark. Marco is hitting all your locations, and you are not doing a thing about it."

"What the fuck do you want me to do?" asked the don. "If I send word out that Marco is coming, I will never see Josephine again, you shit. Once I get her back, then this shit is over."

"What the fuck do you mean this shit will be over? You are letting Marco call the shots?" Nicky shook his head in disbelief. "Oh, you have got to be kidding me. The great and powerful Don Ginetti is shitting in his underwear because he is afraid. That is just too funny." And he started to laugh.

Don Ginetti stood up with anger in his face. He moved toward Nicky and attempted to slap him, but his hand passed through him, leaving the don in a state of confusion.

"Come on, Uncle Sal. Really? You can't hurt me if you wanted to. I am dead! You are so pathetic and weak. What would the other bosses say if they saw you talking to yourself?" He started to laugh, and the don turned around with his face in his hands.

Looking out the window, he said with his back to Nicky, "What the fuck do you want me to do?"

"Hmm, this is a first. You are asking me for help."

The don turned around, but Nicky was not there. He turned toward the window and saw Nicky outside the window. He jumped back.

"Relax, Uncle Sal."

"Get the fuck out of here. I don't want to talk to you anymore." He turned around, and Nicky was standing in front of him. "Jesus Christ, Nicky. Please go away!"

"Not until you listen to me, Uncle Sal, and you will. Sit down, now!"

The don sat down by the chair next to the window. Nicky looked at him. "Look at you. Just look at you, Uncle Sal. Now you are going to listen to me. Don't let that fuck Marco give you orders. You need to get rid of him and fast, on Halloween, before the moon is full."

"The moon? What the fuck does the moon have to do with this?"

"Because if you wait too long and the moon is full, it will be your downfall, and you will be hanging out with me downstairs. When Marco shows up with Aunt Josephine, make the exchange, but have someone ready to blow his brains out and fast, and then get rid of his family."

"Are you insane?" asked Don Ginetti. "Kill his mother, his fiancée, and Detective Corillo? That's not in our rules, you shit. I will not kill two women and an NYC detective. I will deal with Marco my way, but I will not kill his family."

"Fine. Do what you want to do, but don't say I didn't warn you when the time comes and that hairy man kills you."

"Hairy man? Are you kidding me? I don't buy that bullshit, all that talk of a werewolf on the loose. Give me a break. It's all bullshit."

"Uncle Sal, when will you learn? I am trying to help you get rid of your problem, but you seem to have all the answers. Fine, then. I will leave you in your dark world."

He turned around, but then turned back to the don. "Tell you what, Uncle Sal. Just to prove to you that this werewolf is real. When you get Marco, put him in a room with his family and then just wait till the moon is full on Halloween night."

Confused, the don said, "And then what? Serve them all espresso?"

"Uncle Sal, I swear you are such an asshole. The family needs a new leader. Just do what I say. Put them in the same room and just watch what happens."

"And then what?"

Laughing, Nicky responded, "And then what? You are Don Ginetti, the Untouchable Don. You figure it out. I am done. I have said enough. I am out of here, Uncle Sal. Say hi to my mom. It's now up to you."

"That's it? You're leaving?"

"Well, if you want me to stay longer…"

"No, no, no!" replied the don. "Leave now. Go back to where you came from. I have heard enough from you."

Laughing, Nicky said, "Uncle Sal, you just don't know what it's like where I am, but I have a feeling you will be there soon. I met a bunch of people who are dying to meet you. Get it? Dying to meet you." Nicky was laughing while looking at his uncle.

The don stood up. "Goodbye, Nicky." He turned to look out the window and then glanced back. Nicky was gone. Then he heard Nicky's ghostly laugh echoing in his study.

"Uncle Sal, I told you everything you need to know. Don't let Marco win. If he does, I... No, not I. We will all be waiting for you. And trust me, Uncle Sal, there is no air-conditioning here." There were ghostly laughs, and then nothing. Nicky was gone.

Don Ginetti got up, looked around, and covered his ears from Nicky's laugh. Shaking his head, he asked himself, *What the fuck? None of this just happened. I probably fell asleep and didn't realize it. Nicky is dead. He is fucking dead. Fucking little bastard, you did all this, and now I have to fix what you did for the last time. As for Marco. Marco is not a werewolf. He can't be. I will deal with that prick bastard myself. Once it's all finished, there will be no one to fuck with me ever again. No Marco, and no more bullshit about a werewolf or Nicky ever again. Has everyone gone fuckin' insane? I need a drink.*

He walked over to his minibar and poured himself a drink. As he started to drink the glass of scotch, he turned back and walked toward the window, only to see a full moon. He took another sip and said, "Bullshit! It's all bullshit." He turned around to leave, and Nicky was there, outside the window.

"No, Uncle Sal, It's not."

*****

Wednesday, October 30, 11:00 p.m.

Four men were playing poker in the storage room of a building. There were several beer bottles and half-eaten food on the table. The men were smoking. The white lines of smoke from their cigarettes blended with the light from above, so they could see who was cheating who. There were bills of money on the table. Someone was about to have a huge cash-out or would go home in a huge body bag. One man kept looking out the window, holding a gun, before looking back at his hand of cards. The other men were getting annoyed.

"Tim," said Sam. "Are you going to deal in your gun or are you going to play?"

"Let me tell you something." Tim put his gun down. "In case you have not been following the news, Sam—and in your case, I don't think you can read—someone or something has been killing our boys like roadkill. I don't know what the fuck is going on, but since we haven't heard anything yet from Don Ginetti, I am not going to sit around and wait to be killed next. So, as long as I have my baby with me, it's every man for himself. We shouldn't even be here. Let's close and get the fuck out of here."

"Let's all just relax, guys, and calm down," said Sam. "We are getting all worked up for nothing."

"Nothing?" said Doug. "I agree with Tim. It's been too quiet. Why haven't we heard anything from Don Ginetti?"

"'Cause the big man has no balls," put in Mike. "He has left his sheep to fight the wolf."

"Bullshit!" exclaimed Sam. "We are going to stay right here till morning, but if you guys want to leave now, go right ahead. I am sure Don Ginetti won't mind at all, and I am sure he will not mind what you called him, Mike."

"You would throw me under the bus, you fuck!" Mike said.

"Then don't say that bullshit ever again," replied Sam. "Let's just keep playing cards."

"Fuck you, guys." Doug got up. "I am not playing anymore. I am so done. You guys want to stay here all night and jerk off, then be my guests, but I have my lady waiting for me. I am out of here."

"What about the pot on the table?" asked Sam, smirking.

"Are you kidding me?" asked Doug. "That is just pennies to me, and if you guys want to play all night for it, then keep playing. Good luck to the winner, but tonight I will be the winner."

Doug stood up and put on his jacket. He coughed a bit. "Damn. You guys smoke too much." They all laughed. He reached for the beer bottle, took a last gulp of beer, and put down the bottle. "Good night, ladies." He walked toward the door.

"Do you need any blue pills?" asked Tim. They all laughed.

Doug turned. "Ask your mother if I need the blue pill." They all laughed. Doug turned toward the door and opened it, thinking, *Man, what a night this will be.* And that was the last thing he would ever think. A furry hand with sharp claws went into his chest and out his back.

Doug stood there, his face white and shocked, and his eyes looked in horror. Blood started to come out from his mouth as his eyes closed, and the razor-sharp paw came out of his chest. He fell to the ground as the other men watched in horror.

"Holy Christ!" exclaimed Sam as they all got up in fear. The werewolf had struck.

Tim screamed out loud, "Kill it!"

They reached for their guns and started shooting, but the werewolf was quick and too fast for them. It leaped and ripped Tim's head off, then landed on the floor as Tim's body fell.

"Oh, Jesus Christ," said Sam. He and Mike fired more rounds, but they did not get their target; instead, they blew out the light. "Fuck." Sam's gun was aimed in the darkness.

"Stay calm!" yelled Mike as they heard the werewolf growling. "Let's get the fuck out of here!" said Sam. "Go for the door!"

Mike was confused and tried to make sense of what was going on. Suddenly something grabbed him from above, and he screamed in horror.

"Mike?" Sam started shooting blindly all round him. "Show yourself, you fuck!" Then he heard a click from his gun. There were no more bullets left. "Damn it!" Sam noticed the door and made a run for it. He tripped over Doug's body and landed on his face, breaking his nose. Blood gushed out. He turned around in agony, only to look up at the beast, the animal, the werewolf! It grabbed Sam by his legs and pulled him in as it growled. Sam was in shock and fear; he screamed until there were no more sounds but that of the werewolf howling.

*****

October 31, Halloween, 8:00 a.m.

Police and the media were on the scene of the latest attack on another Ginetti front. Police had put up barriers, and only law enforcement was allowed inside to what some witnesses were saying was a very gruesome scene of slaughtered bodies. A makeshift tent had been added so no one, including the media, could see the carnage from last night. With more people gathering outside and the media demanding to see what was beyond them, more police had been called in to keep everyone at a distance while they investigated inside.

A dark-blue SUV arrived on the scene with flashing lights and sirens. Four men stepped out of the SUV. One of the men was Lt. Frank Mano. They started making their way to the crime scene but were stopped by the media.

"Lieutenant, can you confirm that this was another attack by this so-called werewolf who has been going after the Ginettis? And what is its purpose?"

He looked at the reporters' cameras and responded to the question. "As of now, we have no comment. Please let us do our job, and we will inform you all in due time. Thank you." He started to walk inside while more reporters were asking questions, but he ignored them.

"And there you have it," said the news reporter. "Until we can get more information, we advise everyone to please take extra caution when going out this Halloween night."

As Lieutenant Mano walked in, he was not surprised by the dead bodies lying covered up on the ground. Blood was everywhere. Several bullets were scattered on the floor with the smell of gunfire residue all over. There were shattered lights and broken beer bottles, covered dead bodies, and CSI teams photographing everything while shaking their heads and trying to understand what or who was doing this.

Lieutenant Mano could only suspect who did this and, if he were right, why all this? *Is Danny sending a message to Don Ginetti, or has Danny completely lost his mind?* he thought to himself.

"Lieutenant Mano?"

"Yes." He looked at the man walking toward him.

"Sir, I am Donald Jeffries of CSI. I know this is not the way you wanted to start your morning, but you needed to see this first."

"I understand. So far, what do you have?"

"Well, as you can see, whatever attacked these men wanted to be sure no one would live to tell about it." He looked down at the covered bodies.

One body was covered, and something round was covered next to it. Confused, Lieutenant Mano asked, "What is this? Was this guy's pet killed?"

"No," answered the CSI officer. "From the ID this person was carrying, his name was Sam. Whatever attacked him just ripped his head off."

"Ripped his head off?" Lieutenant Mano reached down.

"Would you like to see?"

"No. I will take your word for it. So the bottom line is another string of attacks on the Ginetti crew with very few answers. Anyone see or hear anything?"

"Just the usual people saying they heard screams, gunfire, and howling."

"Howling?" said Lieutenant Mano.

"Yes, sir. From what people are saying, it sounded like a wolf!"

"A wolf?"

"Yes, sir, that is what people are saying. What do you make of it?"

"Hey, it's Halloween, right?" Lieutenant Mano shook his head and thought to himself, *Danny, where are you? That thing I saw at the hospital... It cannot be real.* He looked back to the CSI officer. "How much longer will this be?"

"Well, I take it another two hours."

"Get it done in half that time and close this place up," ordered Lieutenant Mano. "There are too many people outside who want to get in. Once your team is done, close the place up and seal it. No one else gets in without my approval. Understand?"

"Yes, sir."

"Send me your final report when you are finished." He stepped outside to a swarm of more reporters asking more questions, but he ignored them all and got back into the SUV. "Take me back to my office."

The driver turned to him. "Sir, before we go, I found this envelope on the windshield with your name on it."

Confused, Lieutenant Mano took the envelope. "You didn't see anyone put this there?"

"No, sir."

"Fine. Let's get out of here."

The driver started the SUV. Lieutenant Mano looked at the handwriting on the envelope.

Why does this look familiar? he wondered. He opened the envelope, took out the letter inside, and began to read it. "Damn it!" he said. He took out his cell phone and speed-dialed a number. "This is Lieutenant Mano. I need you to call the district attorney's office in New York and get ready to have warrants issued to search and arrest. Don't give me that 'on what grounds' bullshit! I will text you all the information I have. Today, we bring down the Ginettis. They will be history."

*****

October 31, Halloween, 12:00 p.m.

Watching the news from his office in his secure home, the Untouchable Don sat in silence as he and his men watched the news of police and federal officers raiding and arresting members of the Ginetti crew at their illegal operations.

> This is John Logan with News One reporting. As you can see, members of the Ginetti crew are being arrested for illegal gambling, racketeering, and other charges. And not just at this location. Sources are saying many other locations have been raided, and more people are being arrested. Without question, this is the biggest takedown on organized crime in our city in years.
> Questions were asked to top NYPD officials as to how they received their source of informa-

tion, and their answer simply was that they have been working and planning hard to bring down these criminals and serve them justice. Whether it was a credible tip or not, today sparks a huge victory against the war on organized crime and their man, the Untouchable Don Ginetti.

This is John Logan reporting live from Brooklyn, New York, for News One.

The don reached for the TV remote. He turned off the TV, threw the remote on his desk, and sat back in his leather chair. He stared at his associates, and nothing was said until one said, "Sir, may I speak?"

Without saying a word, Don Ginetti nodded his head.

"I understand Detective Marco has your wife, and he had a good backup plan to get the cops and feds to take down our locations. By the end of the day, all our locations will be hit. How do we know Marco will not have another backup plan once we meet up with him for the exchange? And that hairy thing that has been killing our crew. It's probably just waiting for us, ready to tear us apart. Sir, I do not like this. We need to be ready for tonight in case it shows itself again."

Don Ginetti leaned forward and answered, "You think I don't know what Marco is up to?" He looked at his associates. "He planned this good. He got the cops and feds running around, hitting our spots to get them offtrack for what will happen tonight. Yes, he has my wife, and I had to make this deal with him. Our boys are unfortunately dead or in jail. But after tonight, we will rebuild again. The Ginetti family will rise again, stronger than ever. Marco thinks his plan is set. Well, I have a backup plan myself. He will regret it, and Halloween will be the perfect night for this. Call Marco and tell him the time and location for the exchange tonight. Tell him midnight. I swear to Christ. I will put an end to this bullshit! And if that werewolf shows up, I will chop his fucking head off and hang it on my office wall. A fucking werewolf in Brooklyn. No wonder everyone is so fucked up with Halloween and horror movies. All bullshit! Call

Marco and give him the address to the Fort Hamilton Parkway location. Only a few people know about it. No cops and no bullshit. After that, call our guy at One Police Plaza. I want to know why he didn't tell me about the raids earlier. Not that it would have made a difference one way or the other. But I am still the boss, Don Ginetti. After tonight, my wife will be home, Marco will be dead, and Nicky can leave me the fuck alone."

The associates looked at one another in confusion.

"Nicky?" asked one associate. "Sir, with all due respect, your nephew is dead."

Don Ginetti stood up and slammed his hands on the table. His face was red and his eyes wide open. "I know he is fucking dead, you asshole! All of you, get out and prepare for tonight. It all ends tonight."

*****

October 31, 12:30 p.m.

In a secure location, Danny Marco sat at a table with Josephine Ginetti, wife of the Untouchable Don, Salvatore Ginetti. He had given her food and water to keep her well. Danny Marco was exhausted. Wearing his dirty hoodie, jeans, and dark T-shirt, he stared at the disposable phone, waiting for information on where to make the exchange: the don's wife for his mother, his fiancée, and best friend Paul Corillo.

His world had been turned upside down ever since that night at the cabin when he met Lisa Jacobson. He was now part man and part animal. His father, Peter Marco, died at the hands of Nicky Ginetti. The pizzeria was gone. His dream to marry the love of his life was unsure. He father spoke to him in his mind, compelling him to destroy the Ginetti family and unleash the beast. He was once a proud NYPD detective, and now he was being hunted by the very people he had worked with to bring down all criminal elements. And he was being hunted by the Ginetti crew. He had terminated just about every member associated with Salvatore Ginetti, and now it all came down to this night, Halloween night. Will he survive after tonight? Will his family and Mrs. Ginetti survive after tonight? And his alter ego, the werewolf? Never in his dreams had he ever imagined that a werewolf was real. He watched it all on television. He was a fan of werewolf movies, but he never thought they actually existed until the night at the cabin. One way or the other, tonight he would put an end to the Ginetti family once and for all. And if it meant death to save his family, so be it.

"Penny for your thoughts," Josephine Ginetti said to him. "You look like you were far away."

Shaking his head, he smiled. "Mrs. Ginetti, if you only knew. I am tired, Mrs. Ginetti. I want this all to end, and hopefully today it will. I just want my family back, and then I will turn myself in."

"And say what? That you were behind all the killings?"

"Correction. I did what I had to do to get rid of your husband's criminal empire. Your husband hurt so many people and walks with a smile on his face, the Untouchable Don. How could you be married to a lowlife like him?"

"Now you hold it right there." Josephine Ginetti pointed her finger at him. "He was a wonderful, gentle, and caring man when I met him. He had nothing back then. His family struggled to support him and his sister. He worked very hard to support his family when I married him. Once, he was beaten up so badly coming home from work with food for our family. They beat him up because he was Italian. No one offered a hand to help him. After that, he became very bitter. He decided one day that no one would ever harm him, his family, or friends ever again simply for being Italian. After that, the life that he has now chose him, and he never looked back."

"Didn't it every bother you the amount of people he has hurt and all the corruption he has caused? Did you ever question him?"

"Question him? No, I could never do that. To question him would be like a betrayal to him and our family. I had to stay quiet and take care of the children. I was never allowed in his office with his friends. I just made sure they had coffee and food to eat. And when the meetings were over, they all went home, and he would come sit by me and watch TV. He would smile at me and ask about the children and grandchildren. He loves his family so much. They are his world."

"What about my world? I had a great life—a good job, a loving fiancée, and wonderful parents and sisters. My grandfather built Marco's Pizzeria from the ground up. He also struggled as a young boy in America. But he worked very hard and was ridiculed and made fun of because he could not speak the English language well. But he didn't let that bother him. He also worked hard all his life. And when he made enough money, he opened Marco's Pizzeria. He worked long hours with his wife, my grandmother, to bring something good to the community and live his American dream.

"My father, Peter Marco, worked with him, and my grandfather taught him the business until my grandfather retired and left the business to him. My father took over the family business and made it the best. Everything was going well until your nephew Nicky Ginetti decided to ruin everything my family built. In the end, my father was killed defending his business, his legacy, and his life from your nephew just because my father would not accept his business proposal. Your nephew took everything away from my family. My father, the pizzeria, and everything are gone because of your family.

"Tell me, Mrs. Ginetti, what gives your husband the right to take away my life while he lives like the asshole king he is and walks away with a fucking smile on his face while people like me have to suffer because of him?"

"I don't know. I wish I could take back what happened. I wish I had an answer for you, but I don't. I am sorry."

"Sorry is not good enough for my family, Mrs. Ginetti. My family has suffered enough. Nicky started this, and I will finish it for the memory of my father. Tonight, everything will end, and your husband will pay for it."

Suddenly the burner phone hummed. Danny quickly grabbed it and saw the message from Don Ginetti: Meeting place tonight on Fort Hamilton Parkway, Brooklyn. A warehouse distribution center on Sixty-Fifth Street. Exchange will be at midnight. Don't grow a brain and try to be a hero.

"It's finally here. Halloween night, I will get my family back." *Will I come out of this alive? God only knows*, he thought to himself. *But at midnight? Will there be a full moon out tonight?* He checked the weather on the Internet. *Cloudy skies till after midnight, clearing by two o'clock in the morning. Risky? Maybe. I have to take that chance. It must end tonight.*

He texted back and looked at Mrs. Ginetti. "Well, Mrs. Ginetti. Tonight could go well or badly, depending on how your husband wants to end it. I just want my family back, and then I will turn myself in."

"I will try to talk to him and tell him to walk away. I don't want any more people to die."

"We shall see, Mrs. Ginetti. We shall see. I'm sorry I have to do this, but I have to start getting ready."

CHAPTER 14

October 31, Halloween, 3:00 p.m.

Stepping out of the elevator at One Police Plaza, Lt. Robert Gabriel was angry and determined to get answers, but he was furious that no one had told him about the raids on the Ginetti locations. Why was he left in the dark? He wanted answers, and only one man could give it to him. Lieutenant Gabriel approached his office. "Lieutenant Mano, what the hell is going on?"

Lieutenant Mano was caught by surprise and told his secretary to please step out and close the door, and she did. "And a good morning to you, Lieutenant Gabriel."

"Don't give me that morning BS. I want to know why the hell I was left out on the raids. I have every right to know."

"First of all, Lieutenant Gabriel, how dare you come to my office with that tone? Sit your ass down and control yourself. Let's try to be more civilized."

Lieutenant Gabriel shook his head and cracked a smile. He sat down. Then Lieutenant Mano sat down.

"Now that we understand each other, let's try to have a normal conversation."

"A normal conversation?" asked Lieutenant Gabriel. "Fine. I want to know why. Why the fuck didn't anyone tell me of the raids today? Do you know how stupid I looked when I was asked about the raids and had no clue what the fuck my superior was talking about? What are you trying to pull, Mano? Headlines? Your face in the news as the man who took down the Ginetti crew!"

"Hold on," said Lieutenant Mano, raising hands. "This is not about headlines. This is about bringing down the Ginetti crew. We have been after them for years, and now we were able to round out just about every man in his crew and close down their illegal operations. This is huge, and we are not even done yet until we get the king himself, Don Ginetti. We had to move fast, and I'm sorry if I didn't include you in the party, but there were others who were left out in the dark. We had to get this done. How about this. When we get the next warrant, you can go out and arrest Salvatore Ginetti yourself so the whole world can see you?"

"You are a fucking wiseass, you know that? Tell me, how were you able to get any information on the Ginetti operations?"

"From a source."

"A source? Come on. Tell me something. Who is this source?"

"I don't know."

"You don't know? What the hell does that mean, you don't know?"

Reaching into his desk drawer, Lieutenant Mano took out the envelope with the letter in it and handed it to Lieutenant Gabriel.

"What's this?" asked Lieutenant Gabriel.

"This was found on the windshield of my SUV when I went to see the carnage from the last attack on the Ginetti crew this morning."

Lieutenant Gabriel took out the letter and began to read. "There is no name on this."

"Very good. You are a smart old man."

"Don't give me that shit. No one saw who left this?"

"No, not even my driver."

"Do you think it was Marco?"

"At this time, I cannot say."

"Fuck this. So you are telling me someone out of the blue left this on your ride, no one saw who, and this someone wrote all the places of operation by the Ginetti crew, and this huge bust was set on its way."

"That's just about right, Lieutenant Gabriel." Lieutenant Mano leaned back in his chair.

"You mind if I borrow this?" asked Lieutenant Gabriel.

"Yes, I do mind."

"Please?" Lieutenant Gabriel handed it over to Lieutenant Mano.

"You see, I was working with my secretary on a memo and to get copies of this letter to all the top brass, and you, but then you decided to come into my office storming like a white knight. You will get all the information and a copy of this by end of day."

"Fine." Lieutenant Gabriel stood up. "You know you will get a promotion for this."

"That's great. That means you will then be working for me."

"Don't bet on it," said Lieutenant Gabriel. He turned and started to leave but stopped and turned back. Pointing to the letter, he asked, "So tell me, are all those the addresses of all the Ginetti locations?"

"As of now, this is all we got, and it's huge."

"Are there more?"

"Maybe, but right now, I can't guess where. Why do you ask?"

Taking a deep breath, Lieutenant Gabriel said, "Nothing. I was wondering if there are more. I will be expecting your report later."

After leaving Lieutenant Mano's office, Lieutenant Gabriel walked out of the building, pulled out his cell phone, and made a call. "Yeah, it's me. We need to talk."

*****

October 31, Halloween, 5:00 p.m.

Watching the news from his office at One Police Plaza, Lieutenant Mano recapped the day's events.

A victory for the NYPD and federal agents as of now. The big fish has yet to be brought to justice. Salvatore "the Untouchable Don" Ginetti. How many people has this man executed? The list can go from here to Queens. Extortion, bribery, money laundering, illegal gambling, racketeering—these charges could never stick, but this time they will. The more evidence we get, and the more people talk, it's just a matter of time before Don Ginetti trades in his tailor-made suits for some nice colored overalls. I cannot wait for the day we slap the cuffs on him, Lieutenant Mano thought to himself as he leaned back in his chair.

There are still two other problems. Danny Marco and this so-called werewolf. I refuse to believe that the two are connected. Marco, a werewolf? That's just insane and irrational. In this day and age, who would ever believe that werewolves exist? And yet that night at the cabin, Lisa Jacobson and her father, and then Danny getting attacked by something unheard of. And the howling. What the hell attacked him that night? I could have sworn I saw a pair of glowing red eyes just looking at us.

He continued thinking to himself. *We get back to New York, and all hell breaks loose. Peter Marco is killed in a gun struggle defending himself in his pizzeria against Nicky Ginetti. Nicky Ginetti walks from the murder charge after the murder weapon and his bloody shirt just happen to disappear from the evidence room. A mole in the department? No proof has been found whether there is or there isn't. Then Nicky Ginetti and several of his boys are massacred by what people are saying was a hairy-looking beast with razor-sharp teeth and paws. And not just that night but several nights over and over. Each crime scene was worse than the other. And every crime scene had one name to it: Danny Marco.*

And that night at the hospital. The fake cop, and that werewolf just busted out of Danny's room. Danny was nowhere to be found. Now Paul Corillo is missing, along with Ellen Marco and Danny's fiancée, Marie. And now this tip I received from this morning. Everything points to Danny Marco. Danny, where are you? Please, for the love of God, turn yourself in. I cannot think about this no more. It's Halloween night. Before my wife kills me, I need to go home.

He turned off the TV and started getting ready to leave when his secretary entered his office.

"Lieutenant Mano, sir?"

He looked up at her with a smile. "What are you still doing here? You should be long gone already. It's Halloween. Time to get dressed up and go out for some fun."

She smiled back at him and said, "Oh, I know, sir. My husband is getting the kids ready before I get home. It should be a fun night. But, sir, this just came in for you as I was about to leave."

"No, the day is over. This can wait. It's been a long day."

"Sir, I do understand, but this came in urgently. And if it's something of importance, I would have felt guilty not giving it to you before I left for the night."

Smiling, he said, "Fine," and took the manila envelope from her. On the envelope was his name. *For Frank Mano.* But there was no sender's name. Looking up at her confused, he asked, "Who gave this to you?"

"It came from the mailroom. I questioned the mail carrier about that, and he said that was how he found it in his outbox."

Smiling, Lieutenant Mano said, "Hmm. Quite a mystery we have here. Okay then, I will look at this before I leave."

"Anything else, sir?"

"Happy Halloween. Enjoy your night and be safe."

"Thank you, and a happy Halloween to you, sir." She turned and left his office.

More bullshit? he thought. *I should retire now.* He took a deep breath, sat down in his chair, and proceeded to open the envelope. He took out a typed letter and began reading. Suddenly his eyes were open wide, and his expression turned white. *What the fuck is this?*

*****

Hours passed. It was now Halloween night. Young children were dressed up in their favorite Halloween costumes, while their parents escorted them from house to house, trick-or-treating. Meanwhile, the adults were preparing to go to Halloween parties to celebrate the night. But tonight would be a different Halloween for several people. Would anyone walk away alive or not?

CHAPTER 15

October 31, Halloween, 11:00 p.m.

The forecast was cloudy skies. But things could change for Danny Marco. If his alter ego should come out before the exchange or during the exchange, it could mean death for everyone involved.

A white van was parked not too close to the distribution warehouse on Fort Hamilton Parkway, Sixty-Fifth Street, Brooklyn, New York. Inside were Danny Marco and Josephine Ginetti. Her hands were tied up, and she had a gag over her mouth so she could not scream, for her own safety. Danny Marco was nervous, and he should be.

He was about to make an exchange: Ginetti's wife for Danny's family. So many things played out in his head. What if something went wrong? What if he was killed before the exchange? And what if the clouds cleared up and the moon was full? So many questions went around in his mind. He must clear his head for the hour was almost here. He turned to look at Josephine Ginetti.

"Okay, Mrs. Ginetti, the time is almost here. I'm going to remove the gag from your mouth and untie your hands, but you need to stay quiet, please. You make any attempt to scream, and my family is as good as dead. Please promise me." She understood and nodded her head.

He untied her hands and removed the gag from her mouth. She spat out the dust from the gag and rubbed her wrists. "Let's get this over with, please," she said. "I just want to go home."

"And I want to get my family home too," replied Danny.

"If you like, I can speak to my husband and tell him to just walk away from this."

Danny just looked at her. "You think he will just walk away? I don't think so. Your husband has a reputation to keep. He will not just walk unless I am dead."

"Trust me. I am his wife, and he will listen to me. He may be a stubborn old horse, but his heart will listen to me."

"Let's just see what happens if he does," said Danny. He stepped out the back door of the van and helped her out. He looked around. The neighborhood was quiet. He could hear music coming from Shore Parkway near the Verrazano Bridge. Then he remembered that he was going to take Marie here tonight. He shook it off. "Come on," he said to Josephine Ginetti.

Danny Marco was being very careful of any surprises that might pop up as they started to walk toward the distribution center, when suddenly he heard, "Freeze, Marco. Hands up and do not move. You too, ma'am."

They both raised their hands. They had been caught, but not by the Ginettis. He recognized the voice. Coming up from behind with his gun pointed at them was Lt. Frank Mano.

"Frank, you should not be here," said Danny.

"Shut up, Danny." Lieutenant Mano searched Danny for weapons. "Okay, turn around slowly, and you too, ma'am. Keep your hands up." They both turned around.

"Frank, you need to get out of here."

"I'm not going anywhere until I get some answers now. Please excuse me, ma'am." He took out his badge. "I am Lt. Frank Mano, NYPD."

"Thank God," she said. "This man is crazy. He kidnapped me."

"What?"

"Frank, listen to me. She is Josephine Ginetti," Danny explained.

"Ginetti?" said Lieutenant Mano.

"Yes, Salvatore's wife. They got my family and Paul. So I had to get her. I made a deal with Don Ginetti. My family for her. Tonight, in this warehouse at midnight. Things will go badly if I do not bring her to him. Please, Frank, leave now."

"I am not going anywhere. And where is your werewolf friend? Is he getting ready to make his big entrance?"

Danny Marco was getting nervous as he looked around. "Frank, you just do not know the trouble that can happen tonight. How did you even know I would be here?"

"Don't talk stupid to me, Danny. I got your message that you would be here and to come alone. So here I am, and now you are telling me to leave."

Confused, Danny Marco said, "What message? The only message I sent you was the other locations. I never said to come here."

"Danny, you sent me a message that you would be here tonight. You told me to come alone and that you would turn yourself over to me."

Suddenly Danny realized what was going on. "Oh, dear God, we have been set up. The mole in the department. Frank, please get the fuck out of here now."

But it was too late for all of them. Another voice and several men approached them, guns drawn. "Drop the gun now." Danny Marco was shaking his head. *Oh my God.*

Despite Lieutenant Mano's years of experience in the NYPD, he had been caught off guard. "Damn it," he said as he slowly put down his service revolver.

One man took his gun, and two other men came up to them. "Nice and slowly, guys. Let's all go in."

One man looked at Danny Marco. "Mr. Ginetti has been waiting for you a long time. Let's not keep him waiting."

Another went up to Mrs. Ginetti. "Are you all right? Did he harm you?"

"No, he didn't," answered Josephine Ginetti.

"Fine. I was told to take you home. My car is parked on the next block."

"I will not go anywhere," replied Josephine Ginetti. "I am coming in to confront my husband and ask him to let it go and let everyone go."

"I don't think that is wise, Mrs. Ginetti."

"I don't care what you think, and don't touch me. Take us inside."

"Fine," said the man. "Don Ginetti will not like this at all."

She started walking with the man who spoke to her while the others escorted Danny Marco and Lieutenant Mano. They raised their hands up as they walked inside the warehouse. Danny Marco started thinking to himself, *If the clouds clear tonight, all hell will break loose. If you are going to save me tonight, please, do not kill my family. It all ends here tonight.*

Inside the warehouse, the fluorescent light shone brightly from above. There was the smell of cardboard boxes stacked up along two walls, and the floor was hard cement. They continued walking down the corridor, hands still up, with one man in front and another in the back, guns drawn and aimed at Danny and Lieutenant Mano. Then they started hearing voices coming from another room. As they got closer, the voices grew louder until they all entered the next room.

The Untouchable Don sat at the table with his associates. The smell of cigarette smoke filled the room. Danny counted at least a dozen men with Don Ginetti. Counting the other men who had escorted them into the room, there were at least twenty men or more. Danny Marco was shocked to see his mother, Ellen; his fiancée, Marie; and his best friend, Paul Corillo, sitting in a makeshift jail cell just a few feet away from Don Ginetti. Don Ginetti looked up as they entered the room and then stood up.

"Well, now that everyone is here, we can start the party."

"Danny!" screamed his mother.

Danny tried to run to the cell but was stopped by men pointing their guns at him.

"Let's settle down, people," Don Ginetti announced. "The night is still young."

Paul Corillo and Marie stood up with Ellen Marco. "Danny, what the fuck is going on?" asked Marie.

Paul grabbed her away from the bars. "Marie, relax," said Paul as they looked at each other. Paul could not believe Lt. Frank Mano was standing with him.

Don Ginetti focused on his wife, Josephine. He was angry. "I thought I told you to take her home," he said to one of his men.

"I refused to leave," Josephine replied. She walked over to him. One man tried to stop her, but Don Ginetti put his hand up, and she went to him and hugged him. "Did he hurt you?" asked Don Ginetti.

"No, and I hope you didn't hurt his family."

"They were well taken care of."

"Good. Now please, Salvatore, let them all go and let's go home and put an end to this. Enough blood has been spilled. Please, no more."

"Yeah, Ginetti," announced Danny. "We made a deal. Now let my family go, you bastard." He started walking toward Don Ginetti, only to get hit in the stomach by one of the men, and Danny went down. Ellen Marco screamed.

Lieutenant Mano quickly went to help Danny. "That was stupid, Danny." He looked up at Don Ginetti. "Ginetti, I am Lt. Frank Mano of the NYPD. You have your wife. Let's get this over with and everyone goes home. Holding everyone, including me, will make things worse."

"No one is going anywhere!" shouted Don Ginetti.

"You son of a bitch!" Danny yelled at him.

Nervous and scared, Josephine made one last plea to her husband. "Salvatore, please, for the love of God, let them all go and let's go home. It doesn't have to end like this. Please, Salvatore."

Don Ginetti looked at his wife. "Josephine, you know who I am. You know I cannot let things go. He killed Nicky." The don pointed at Danny Marco. "And now his family will watch me kill him."

"No!" screamed Ellen Marco and Marie.

"You don't have to do this," said Paul Corillo.

"Shut up!" Don Ginetti demanded.

"What happened to the man I married? You were so sweet and gentle until all this came into your life. We have children and grandchildren. Let's go home to them now. Let everyone go."

"I am sorry, Josephine, but I cannot."

Josephine Ginetti looked at him with anger, and then she slapped his face. Everyone was stunned, including Don Ginetti. "I hate you."

Don Ginetti rubbed his face and then said to the man next to him. "Have her sit down."

"Don't you touch me," said Mrs. Ginetti.

"Ma'am, please sit down," said the armed man. She sat down with disgust and anger in her face.

Don Ginetti looked at Danny Marco. "Bring him to me." Both men grabbed Danny and brought him to Don Ginetti. Frank Mano could not do anything, and Danny's family could only watch.

"Please, don't hurt my son," pleaded Ellen Marco; tears fell from her eyes as Marie and Paul watched.

The don looked at Ellen Marco. "I am sorry, Mrs. Marco. But he killed my nephew Nicky Ginetti."

"Your fucking nephew was killed by that werewolf. And your nephew killed my husband, Peter."

He ignored her. He reached for his leather bag and pulled out a cattle prod. "You know what this is?" Don Ginetti asked Danny Marco.

"Yes. Don't you stick it up your ass every night when your wife says no?"

Don Ginetti quickly jammed it into Danny's stomach; the surge of electricity stunned him while his family watched, helpless.

"Stop!" screamed Ellen Marco.

"That's enough, Ginetti," said Paul Corillo.

"I will decide when it's enough. Now shut the fuck up!"

"You piece of shit," said Lt. Frank Mano. He was hit in the stomach by one of the men and went down.

Don Ginetti grabbed Danny by his hair and screamed in his face, "How does that feel? Does it hurt? It should hurt. That's from my sister, you fuck. You killed her son, and this is from me." He jammed the cattle prod again into Danny's stomach, and more bolts of electricity surged into Danny, leaving him convulsing on the floor.

His mother and Marie screamed in horror. "That's enough," demanded Paul Corillo.

"Salvatore, please stop this. Enough," said Josephine Ginetti. But Don Ginetti did not listen. He was angry and would make Danny Marco suffer. He stuck the cattle prod over and over again into Danny Marco's stomach. The screams from his family for Don Ginetti to stop fell on deaf ears.

He grabbed Danny by his hair again and lifted his head up. Danny's face was white, and his eyes were red. "Tell me, asshole, where is your friend the werewolf? It's almost midnight. Is your friend coming to save your ass from me?"

Danny spat in his face. Enraged, Don Ginetti prodded him again and again and let him go. "Put them all in the cage!" The men grabbed Danny from the floor and Lieutenant Mano and brought them to the cage. A man unlocked the cage, and they were thrown inside. Ellen Marco and Marie rushed to Danny, while Paul Corillo aided Lieutenant Mano.

Josephine Ginetti screamed to her husband, "Salvatore, what have you become!"

"Shut up!"

She was in shock at how he had just spoken to her.

"Come on, Marco. It's Halloween night. All the scary people are out doing their thing. Where is your buddy the werewolf? I want his head, and I want your head, you fuck. It's fucking midnight, Marco. Where is your buddy now?" said Don Ginetti.

Danny was unable to talk from the electric shock of the cattle prod.

"I guess we have to kill you all."

"No!" Josephine Ginetti stood up. "Salvatore, this is not you."

"I told you to shut up."

Suddenly, Danny Marco was able to speak. "Hey, Ginetti."

The don turned around and walked to the cage. "Last words of a dead man?" said the don.

Danny Marco pointed up to the skylight. Everyone looked at it and saw what Danny was hoping to see. The clouds were gone, and the moon was shining bright.

"Oh, dear God," Paul Corillo muttered.

"The moon? What the fuck? Is your friend the werewolf coming from above?" the don asked, pointing up.

Laughing, Danny Marco responded, "No, you old fuck. He is already here."

Danny Marco screamed as he felt the transformation about to take place in front of everyone.

"Get away from him!" Paul pulled Ellen and Marie behind him. "Open the door!"

Don Ginetti, his men, and Mrs. Ginetti, along with the others in the cage, could only watch in horror. Danny got up on his knees and lifted his head. Everyone was stunned. Don Ginetti could not believe what he was seeing. His men quickly drew their guns and stepped back. Danny's facial muscles were pulsing, and his eyes were turning red. Danny screamed louder, but this time, his screams sounded more animalistic. His hands were getting bigger, and his fingernails were growing sharper. Hair was forming on his face as he growled. His teeth were getting longer and sharper. Lieutenant Mano couldn't believe what he was seeing. Danny's body was now getting bigger as he ripped his clothes off. More hair grew on his body, and his feet, which were getting hairy and sharp, ripped through his sneakers.

Don Ginetti could not speak. He was white as a ghost as he and his men started to back up slowly. Josephine Ginetti was speechless. Danny's ears had grown bigger as he roared louder and louder. Paul was shielding Ellen Marco and Marie while he and Lt. Frank Mano watched in fear. Finally, the transformation was complete. Danny was gone for now. His alter ego, the werewolf, had taken his place inside the cage as it stood up taller and angrier. It grabbed the bars of the cage and roared more, shaking the bars as if demanding to be released.

"Holy fucking shit. Can you guys believe what we just saw?" the don asked the men, but they could not say a word. They were sacred, and they started backing away more with their guns aimed at the werewolf.

Josephine Ginetti stood behind one of the men, scared to death.

"You can't get out, right? You fuck. I still win, and you don't," the don said.

The werewolf roared louder at Don Ginetti.

"Sir, I don't think you should antagonize it," said one of his men.

Suddenly the werewolf turned his attention to the others inside the cage and roared at them.

"That's it. Kill them, and then I'll kill you, you fuck."

Paul Corillo and Lieutenant Frank Mano were shielding the women, but there was only so much they could do. Paul Corillo raised his hands to the werewolf. "Danny? If you can hear me, don't do this. They are your enemy, not us." He pointed to Don Ginetti. The werewolf looked at them and then at Don Ginetti.

"You really think he understands you?" asked Lieutenant Mano.

The werewolf grabbed the steel cage again and started to shake it and then looked back at the people with him with blood in its eyes. Suddenly there was a crash from the skylight. Glass fell everywhere, and everyone covered their heads. Something had come from above. Don Ginetti and his men looked in horror as their eyes cleared. Another werewolf!

Josephine Ginetti screamed in horror. "What the fuck is this?" asked Don Ginetti. "Kill it!" He went down as his men started firing at the second werewolf. The people in the cage also got down to dodge the bullets. The werewolf was still shaking the cage door and roaring loudly as if it wanted in on the fight. The second werewolf leaped and attacked at will, killing the first three men. With razor-sharp hands, it ripped their throats. There was more gunfire from the other men, but the second werewolf was quick and fast as it killed the other men.

Don Ginetti was screaming for his wife to stay down. "Josephine, stay down and don't move. I will come to you."

She screamed his name. "Salvatore, help me!" His men were all yelling as the werewolf continued to attack. Inside the cage, the werewolf was getting angrier as it continued to try and rip off the door from the cage so it could join the battle with the second werewolf. Paul Corillo and Lt. Frank Mano were doing their best to protect

Ellen Marco and Marie from the hail of bullets fired by the Ginetti crew.

"We have got to get out of here and fast," said Lieutenant Mano.

"I understand, sir. If Danny can rip off the cage door, we may have a chance!"

"Danny?" said Lieutenant Mano.

"You know what I mean." Paul stayed low with his arm up, trying to see the battle between the second werewolf and the Ginetti crew.

"Danny, my poor baby," screamed Ellen Marco. "What have they done to you?" she asked, crying.

Marie could not accept what was happening, but it was true. Her fiancée, the love of her life, was a werewolf.

The Ginetti men were all scared, firing as fast as they could see the second werewolf, only to die by its hands. Don Ginetti was able to crawl to his wife, Josephine, and grabbed her. "Salvatore, what is going on?" asked his wife.

"Stay down, Josephine." He covered her.

His men were screaming, and one by one, the second werewolf jumped and leaped and killed with a fury. One man reached for Don Ginetti while firing his gun at the second werewolf. "Sir, please let's go."

Don Ginetti grabbed his wife and got behind his man with the gun. The man fired at the second werewolf while Don Ginetti and his wife tried to escape.

Inside the cage, the werewolf was starting to loosen up the cage door with all the strength from his rage until he finally ripped off the door and tossed it aside. Now the werewolf joined the battle with the second werewolf as it leaped and attacked the remainder of the Ginetti crew, slashing their throats at will and roaring with hunger for blood. The last of the Ginetti crew were dead and torn apart.

Both werewolves looked at each other and then raised their heads and howled as if claiming a battle victory over their enemy.

Inside the cage, Paul Corillo and Lieutenant Mano got up slowly. Their faces and clothes were covered in dust and debris from the battle they had just witnessed. Ellen and Marie were still down, holding on to each other in fear.

"Paul, what are you doing?" asked Lieutenant Mano.

"It's okay, sir."

"Paul, if they turn on us, I will kill you myself!"

Paul Corillo was now standing by the entrance of the cage. He was watching both werewolves as they continued to look at each other, growling and looking around. The second werewolf started to walk closer to the first and growled at the other, almost as if trying to talk to it. Suddenly Paul noticed something different about the second werewolf. The shape and size of this werewolf did not match the other werewolf at all. *What am I missing?* he thought to himself, until it finally dawned on him. The second werewolf was female.

Just by looking at it, its shape, size, and nipples, this werewolf was female. There was no question about it. And one name came to his mind. *Oh, dear God, Lisa Jacobson.* It was the woman they met at the cabin on Danny's bachelor getaway weekend. *It's her. I know it's her without a doubt. She has come to help Danny, and now she wants him.* She walked closer to him, growling, but he growled back as if he saying, "Stay away from me." *What could they possibly be thinking?*

"What the fuck is going on?" asked Lieutenant Mano.

"Sir, the other werewolf, you are not going to believe this, but it's Lisa Jacobson."

"Are you out of your fucking mind?" said Lieutenant Mano.

"Lisa Jacobson?" asked Marie. "Stay away from him!" she screamed.

Both werewolves looked at her and then back at each other. Suddenly the werewolf looked at where the entrance was and growled louder. He had sensed something. The other werewolf growled at him, but he growled louder and leaped forward toward the entrance of the warehouse. He was not finished. He was now going after Don Ginetti. The second werewolf watched but did not move. It looked back at the people in the cage; it howled, leaped up, and escaped through the skylight.

Paul looked back. "Come on. Let's get out of here!"

"Where did Danny go?" asked Ellen Marco.

"It's not Danny anymore," said Paul. "It's a werewolf. Come on. Let's go." He took her hand, and Marie and Lieutenant Mano followed.

As they moved toward the front entrance, Lieutenant Mano stopped and knelt down to one of the dead men. He took his gun and checked it. It was still loaded. He checked the dead man and found a cell phone. He quickly called a number.

"This is Lt. Frank Mano of NYPD. I need police emergency services at my location immediately!"

Outside, Don Ginetti held on to his wife, Josephine, trying to make their way to a car while his last man kept looking back with his gun aimed at the entrance door.

"Mr. Ginetti, we have to keep moving and get out of here. This thing is going to kill us!" He looked back and saw the werewolf emerging from inside the warehouse, roaring and coming straight toward them. The man fired his gun and yelled to get down. Don Ginetti got on top of his wife to protect her. The gun stopped firing. There were no more bullets left. The werewolf was now face-to-face with the last man. He grabbed him by the neck and picked him up. The man gasped for air.

Don Ginetti and Josephine could only watch in fear as the werewolf took his other hand and thrust it into the man's chest and back out. The man went limp, dead. The werewolf dropped him on the ground and howled at the moon and then looked down at his last target, Don Ginetti.

The Untouchable Don. The most feared man in organized crime. The people he hurt, and the many he killed. Businesses that were built from the ground up, he destroyed if no one paid him. Briberies, extortion, and money laundering. He had beaten all the charges and walked away with a smile and a cigar. Now, he was the scared man, defeated by a werewolf. His nephew and crew were all dead. He had nothing left and no one to protect him from the fury of the werewolf. He would soon be joining the dead.

The werewolf looked at him and growled. Don Ginetti slowly got up with his wife on the ground.

"Salvatore, what are you doing?"

"It's okay, Josephine." He looked at her and then at the were-wolf with his hands up, face covered in sweat, his clothes dirty, and his face white. He looked into the eyes of the werewolf. Paul Corillo and the others came out of the warehouse, followed by Lieutenant Mano, who was aiming the gun straight at the werewolf and Don Ginetti.

"What the fuck is Don Ginetti up to now?" asked Paul.

"Kill him, Danny," said Ellen. "Kill him for your father!"

Don Ginetti slowly got up with his arms up, staring into the eyes of the werewolf. "So it was you all the time, Marco. Are you happy now? You got your revenge. What are you waiting for, Marco?"

"Salvatore, please don't upset him," pleaded his wife.

"How is this even fucking possible?" asked Don Ginetti. "But here you are, and you are real."

The werewolf growled louder at him. Don Ginetti shook his head and coughed. "Man, you have some bad breath issues. Marco, listen to me. I have a proposal for you. You come work for me. Let's all forget what happened tonight and with Nicky. It's all done. You took out my crew and my nephew. Nicky was nothing but trouble. He started all this. But you and me, we are smarter. Join me, and we will rebuild. We will be in charge. The other families will have no choice but to follow us. If any one of them tries any bullshit with us, you can then take them all out until they admit that Ginetti is the only family in charge. No one will fuck with us! We will have ulti-mate power over everyone."

The werewolf just looked at him, moving his head and releasing a light growl at Don Ginetti as if understanding what he was saying or was just maybe about to strike.

"I don't like where this is going," said Paul Corillo. The were-wolf looked back at them.

"Hey," said the don. The werewolf looked back at him. "Pay no attention to them. I am talking. So what do you say, Marco? You and me. Together, no one will fuck with us."

Suddenly they could hear sirens getting closer and closer. "What the fuck?" said Don Ginetti. The werewolf started to get angry and growled louder. The backup Lieutenant Mano had called for was heading their way.

The sirens grew louder and louder until they saw the flashing lights of police cars, emergency services, and the SWAT. The officers moved fast and drew their weapons at Don Ginetti and the werewolf.

"Let's step back," said Paul Corillo.

A voice from a loudspeaker came on. "You are surrounded by the NYPD. Stand down with your hands up and do not move."

"Fuck! You set me up, Marco!"

"Salvatore, please, that's enough," said his wife.

Lights were centered on the werewolf, which caused him to cover his eyes and growl louder.

"You set me up, you son of a bitch!" He reached into his pocket, looking for anything he could use as a weapon. He pulled out a pen. Angry and frustrated, he took the pen and stabbed the werewolf in his arm, screaming, "This is for Nicky!"

The werewolf howled and pushed Don Ginetti to the ground.

Paul Corillo knew what was about to happen. "Oh shit."

The police said again, "This is your last warning. Get on your knees and put your arms up!"

The werewolf pulled out the pen from his arm. Looking down at a defeated Don Ginetti, he grabbed him by his neck and picked him up. "No!" Josephine Ginetti screamed.

"Release him," said the police officer.

Don Ginetti was punching the werewolf's hands, trying to free himself. Gasping for air, the werewolf took the pen and drove it into the head of Don Ginetti. Don Ginetti stopped moving, and his arms went down, blood pouring from his forehead. Then in one quick motion, the werewolf rammed his razor-sharp paw into the chest of Don Ginetti and ripped out his heart. Don Ginetti, the Untouchable Don, was dead. The werewolf let him go, and his dead body fell to the ground.

"Salvatore!" screamed his wife as she crawled to her dead husband. "Oh, my Salvatore. Why?" She screamed and cried. The werewolf had claimed victory again. It looked up and howled to the moon.

Now the police aimed their weapons at the werewolf. "Oh no!" Paul started running ahead. "Don't shoot. Please, do not shoot him." Then the sound of a helicopter with a bright light came over them.

"Do not move," said the police. "Stand down!"

"Danny, get the fuck out of here. They will kill you," Paul warned.

The werewolf looked at Paul, looked back at the police, released another howl, and started to make his run. He quickly started running toward the police, and they opened fire. Paul ran to Josephine Ginetti and dropped on her to cover her from danger. The werewolf was quick and fast; he jumped over the police cars and onto Fort Hamilton Parkway, heading north. The police all got in their cars to pursue the werewolf.

Lieutenant Mano and the women ran toward Paul Corillo. He stood up. "Frank, they are going to kill Danny. You saw it. He is the werewolf. You have to call and order a no-kill. He is still Danny. We have to follow him, now!"

Police officers ran up to them. "Take these three with you, and follow that werewolf from the call-ins," said Lieutenant Mano. "I am going to take the helicopter and follow from above."

"And then what?" asked Paul.

"That's an order, Corillo." Lieutenant Mano ran to the landing helicopter and got in. Paul and the ladies got into the police car and joined the chase.

"Oh God, please don't let them kill my boy," Ellen Marco was crying as Marie tried to comfort her. The police car sped away with other police cars, sirens on. They heard communication on the police radio.

"All units in the vicinity of Fort Hamilton Parkway and Sixty-Fifth Street. Werewolf has been spotted and giving chase. All units are advised to assist in chase."

"Werewolf heading toward Bay Ridge Avenue."

"Fuck! Mano didn't give the order for no-kill."

The werewolf was running and jumping over cars. People dressed up in their Halloween costumes were taken by surprise at this hairy beast running past them, thinking it was someone dressed up for Halloween with several flashing police cars in hot pursuit. More information came over the police radio.

"Werewolf spotted heading past Fort Hamilton and Bay Ridge Parkway."

"Heading toward Shore Park."

"Shore Park?" asked Paul. "Why would it be going there? Marie, did you and Danny go there a lot?"

"Yes," answered Marie. "We would take a walk there every Sunday."

"It could be the werewolf remembering things from Danny's memories."

"Memories?" asked the police officer who was driving.

"Shut up and keep driving, officer."

The werewolf was now in Shore Park. Festivities were still going on for Halloween night. People were walking around in their costumes. Music was playing in the background, but all that was about to change. People heard police sirens and soon saw a big hairy thing running toward them. They screamed and scattered, not knowing what it was. From the police radio, more information came. "Panic at Shore Park. Werewolf spotted."

The chasing police cars sped to the scene as fast as they could, moving cars out of their way.

At Shore Park, an ice cream truck was parked on the side. The driver was selling ice cream while wearing a werewolf mask. He leaned out to give an ice cream cone when suddenly there was a thump on top of the ice cream truck. The people by the truck looked up and screamed in fear. They started running away.

"What the fuck is going on?" said the driver when a hairy hand reached down and took the ice cream cone from his hand. The werewolf jumped down from the ice cream truck and looked at the driver wearing a werewolf mask. The werewolf roared as the driver fell back. Then the werewolf turned and kept running. The driver stood up and took off his mask.

"What the fuck?" he screamed.

The police units finally made it to Shore Park, where dozens of people were running away. The werewolf turned around and saw more people all dressed up in their Halloween costumes. It roared at them, not knowing what they were, and continued to run away from them toward the Verrazano-Narrows Bridge. A news helicopter had now arrived at the scene.

> This is News One reporting live from Brooklyn, New York. Reports are coming in of the hairy beast, this so-called werewolf, that attacked and murdered members of the Ginetti crew. Now from what we see below, it is running away from dozens of police units that are closing in on it at Shore Park. Many people have gathered here to celebrate Halloween and its festivities, but now there is panic below as dozens of people are trying to get away.

The werewolf stopped and looked around again. Then it roared at everything and everyone. It saw the police and flashing lights coming closer to it. It looked up at the helicopters. It did not understand what was going on, but it needed to get away. People were now starting to take videos of the werewolf. Dozens of police units, EMS, and SWAT had arrived and were moving in.

The police unit escorting Paul Corillo, Ellen Marco, and Marie had arrived. They exited the car to witness hell all around them.

"My God, they are going to kill my Danny," Ellen muttered. "Paul, please, don't let them kill my boy. It's still Danny!"

Paul looked around. They were heading toward the bridge. "Mrs. Marco, please wait in the car."

"No! That's my boy trying to get away!"

"Fine. Follow me."

Marie grabbed Ellen's hand as they tried to make their way toward the end of the park. "I cannot believe what the hell is going on. Please, God, save him."

The werewolf was now moving toward the jogging lane, running as fast as it could with dozens of police following behind and police copters following its every move.

Communication from the police radio said, "Werewolf is running toward Verrazano Bridge. All units, move in. All units, move in, and proceed with caution."

On the police helicopter, the voice of Lt. Frank Mano came on. "This is Lieutenant Mano. Do not—I repeat, do not—fire on subject unless authorized by me." *Damn it, Danny. Don't make me do this.*

The werewolf had made it to the end of the park. Looking around and roaring, it needed to escape from the crowd of people coming toward it, away from the bright flashing lights and the noise of the helicopter above and the spotlight on it. It did not understand, but it needed to get away and be free. The werewolf quickly jumped over the railing onto the grass and made its way toward the highway. Traffic came to a screeching stop. Cars hit other cars, and the werewolf leaped over them as it continued to make its escape. Police units from Brooklyn were on the highway, and other units moved in from the Staten Island side.

Paul Corillo, with Ellen Marco and Marie, had made it to the end, where police were blocking people from going farther. They made it to the front, face-to-face with other police officers and dozens of people.

"Sorry. You cannot go any farther."

Paul took out his badge and ID. "Listen, officer, I'm Detective Paul Corillo. Stand down and let us pass now!"

"I am sorry, detective. Please let me call this in first."

"Damn it, there is no time. Let us pass now!" The officer hesitated but then let them pass. "I need your radio." The officer gave him his radio. They were now at the edge of the walkway looking at the bridge and the chaos below.

Paul quickly opened the channel. "This is Detective Paul Corillo calling Lt. Frank Mano. Please respond!"

On the helicopter, an officer looked over and informed Lieutenant Mano of the message coming in for him and who it was from.

"Transmit on secure line," said Lieutenant Mano.

"Frank, please, don't do it. It's still Danny, your friend. You saw what happened at the warehouse. If you kill the werewolf, you will also kill Danny. Please, for the love of God, don't do it," pleaded Paul.

"And what do you want me to do?" asked Lieutenant Mano. "Catch it and study it? How do you expect me to explain to the top brass all the events from the cabin till now? I know Danny is my friend, but as a lieutenant of the NYPD, I have a job to do to protect the citizens, and if it means using aggressive force, so be it. I have given the order not to fire until they hear from me. Now let me do my job! Mano out." He ended the transmission and ordered the pilot not to receive any more calls from Detective Paul Corillo.

"Frank? Frank? You son of a bitch!"

"What is going on?" asked Marie. "Is he going to kill him?"

The look on Paul's face said it all.

"No!" screamed Ellen Marco. "Please don't kill my son." Marie tried to comfort her. Paul Corillo made a promise to Danny that he would protect him. Now all he could do was watch as all hell was about to break loose.

On the highway leading toward the Verrazano-Narrows Bridge, the werewolf was leaping from car to car, desperately trying to get away from the lights flashing around him and shining from above. The werewolf noticed that ahead of him, police units from the Staten Island side had closed traffic and were moving in. It looked behind and saw more police moving in from the Brooklyn side. It was trapped. The werewolf looked to its right at the huge suspension cable that led up to the tower of the bridge. It quickly leaped onto the cable and started making its way up, without regard for its own life. It just wanted to escape and not be captured.

CHAPTER 16

People in their homes and at local bars were now drawn to their TVs as the news report came in.

This is News One reporting live over Shore Park in Brooklyn again. As you can see, there is chaos and confusion below on this Halloween night. Dozens of armed police units are hot on the trail of this so-called werewolf that has struck and killed all members of the Ginetti crew. For what reason, we do not know.

But at present, as you can see, dozens and dozens of people and members of law enforcement are on the ground as this werewolf, or someone wearing a wolf costume, has made its way to Shore Park with police officers on its trail. Where did it come from? No one knows, but for now... Hold on. Wait just one second.

Unbelievable! We just received confirmation that the werewolf is now climbing up the suspension cable that leads up to the first tower of the Verrazano Bridge. We are trying to get a live feed, and yes, here it is. It's climbing on the cable with rapid speed and no fear. How is it doing this?

Police from both sides have closed off the bridge and gathered in the middle of the bridge

with motorists watching. This is just insane. I
cannot believe what I am seeing!

It's climbing higher and higher to the tower
without stopping.

From the ground, Paul Corillo, Ellen, and Marie watched in
fear along with dozens of people who were trying to get closer to take
a video of what they were seeing.

"Oh God! Oh God in heaven," muttered Paul with fear in his
face.

"Please don't kill my son," Ellen Marco screamed, tears in her
eyes. Marie's eyes were also filled with tears. Both women watched
as the werewolf continued to make its way up the suspension cable.

From the police helicopter, the pilots, along with armed police
officers and Lt. Frank Mano, could not believe what they were seeing.

"Who or what is that fucking thing?" asked the pilot.

"Pay attention to your controls and shut up!" screamed
Lieutenant Mano.

Another police helicopter joined them, along with other armed
officers with high-powered automatic weapons.

"Open a channel," ordered Lieutenant Mano. "No one is to
fire unless I give the green light. I repeat, no firing unless I give the
command." He closed the channel.

Below, the werewolf continued to climb higher and higher. Its
huge paws grabbed the suspension cable for support as it made its
way to the top of the tower with everyone watching below, including
the media. At the local bars and homes, everyone was glued to their
TVs.

This is News One reporting with another
update on this werewolf at Shore Park. As you
can see from our live video feed, it is still climbing up the suspension cable of the bridge and is
almost near the top of the tower. How is it doing
this, and if it's just a man in costume, how in
God's name is he able to balance himself walking

on the cable with ease and no fear of falling? This
is a first for me and for everyone watching.

With every ounce of strength it had, the werewolf made it to
the top and then climbed on top of the first tower of the bridge. It
stood upright, looking around and then up at the dark sky at the full
brightness of the moon. The werewolf howled, its howls growing
stronger and stronger. Then it raised its arms up in the air, feeling the
energy from the moon making it stronger and stronger.

From the news chopper, the reporter continued.

Ladies and gentlemen, as you all can see, the
werewolf has made it to the top of the tower and
is howling. Not sure if people watching can hear
it. Newsroom, can you hear it? You can. Again,
here is the live feed on this Halloween night. This
werewolf has made its way up the suspension
cable of the Verrazano Bridge onto the tower and
is now howling at the moon. Now with no place
to go, it is trapped. There is a drop of 693 feet
if it falls to its death. Now, will the police take
action? All we can do is watch.

From below, nobody could believe what they were seeing.

The werewolf had made its way up to the tower of the bridge.

"Oh my God," exclaimed Marie as she held on to Ellen, who
was in tears.

Paul Corillo was trying again to contact Lieutenant Mano, but
no response. "Damn you, Mano!"

Above, Lieutenant Mano ordered the pilot to open the speaker.
He looked at the werewolf as they started to move in closer. "You on
the tower, this is Lt. Frank Mano of the NYPD. You have no other
place to go, and you are surrounded by dozens of NYPD officers. I
order you, stand down with your hands up and surrender."

The werewolf just growled at them and swung its paws, trying to get them to back away. The werewolf did not comply and was starting to get more aggressive. It roared.

"I repeat, stand down and surrender!"

As the second NYPD helicopter got closer to the werewolf, without hesitation, the werewolf leaped toward the second chopper. It clung to the windshield and started banging with its razor-sharp paws. From below, Ellen screamed, "No!" as she held on to Marie. His hands on his head, Paul could not say a word. Tears started falling from his eyes for his childhood friend, Danny Marco.

From the news chopper, the reported continued, "Oh, dear God, the werewolf just leaped onto the police helicopter, and now it's banging on the windshield as if trying to get in. I have never seen anything like this. The police chopper seems to be losing control."

Inside the other chopper, Lieutenant Mano was trying to contact the other chopper. They were in danger of crashing. "This is Lieutenant Mano, regain control. I repeat, regain control. You are too close to the tower!"

From below, everyone was watching in fear as the werewolf continued to cling on to the windshield of the helicopter and bang on it with its other paw. From the ground, Danny's fiancée screamed in fear. The werewolf roared as the pilot inside tried to regain control. The chopper moved to its left, which was too close to the tower, so the pilot pulled up in desperation, going over the tower. Just as it was about to pass the tower of the bridge, the werewolf released the windshield and landed back down on top of the tower as the helicopter moved away. The werewolf stood up and howled again as if victorious.

On the other chopper, Lieutenant Mano breathed and shook his head as he radioed the other chopper. "This is Lieutenant Mano. Change position to our side and await further orders."

Down below, everyone watched in fear as the werewolf leaped off the chopper. "My God," exclaimed Paul Corillo. "That was way too close!"

"Danny!" screamed Ellen Marco.

"Paul, what are they doing now?" asked Marie.

Paul looked up again as the second chopper came side to side with the first. Paul knew what was about to happen. He grabbed the police radio again and attempted to contact Lieutenant Mano. "This is Detective Paul Corillo, NYPD, calling Lieutenant Mano. Come in please." No response. "Damn it. This is Detective Corillo calling Lieutenant Mano." Still there was no response. Everyone was looking up at both choppers and the werewolf. "Damn it, Frank. I know you can hear me. Frank, please, for the love of God, no. This will haunt you the rest of your life. Danny is our friend, our brother. Do not kill him. Use a tranquilizer rifle. Stun him with a Taser. Please do not kill him."

There was no response as he watched both helicopters getting ready in position.

"Danny, I'm sorry I couldn't protect you," Paul muttered. Tears fell from his eyes.

In the chopper, Lieutenant Mano heard everything Paul Corillo said. Memories flashed into his mind from when they were going on the trip to Pennsylvania, the stop at the pizzeria, Danny's parents, the laughter in the car and in the cabin, the Jacobsons, Lisa Jacobson, and the attack on Danny that changed his life forever. Then at the warehouse when he saw Danny turn into the werewolf.

Danny, I am sorry, he thought to himself. *But I have a job to do.*

"Sir?" asked the officer next to him.

"What is it?" asked Lieutenant Mano.

"I'm sorry, sir, but you seemed to be in a daze."

"It's okay. Signal the other chopper to get ready." Both choppers lined up, and the shooters on both choppers prepared their weapons.

Meanwhile, on the ground, Paul looked at Ellen and Marie. "Oh, I am so sorry to you both. There is nothing more I can do."

"No!" said Ellen Marco. "No! Don't kill my son."

Both Marie and Paul tried hold her back. All three started to cry.

From above, the news chopper reported, "It looks like both police choppers are ready to make a move. We are being told to move farther away. We are now moving to a safer distance, and we will continue showing you this live feed as much as we can. Something is about to happen."

People at the bars and from home were still glued to their TVs.

Back at the tower, the werewolf was enraged. It was roaring loudly at the police choppers and swinging it arms at them. The crowd below and on the bridge were getting intense.

Lieutenant Mano had made his decision. "God forgive me." His chopper was now eye to eye with the werewolf. "This is Lieutenant Mano. Everyone on my command." The shooters were ready, their weapons aimed at the werewolf.

The werewolf saw the red dots aimed at its chest and tried to swat it from his body, not knowing what it was. The werewolf then looked directly at the chopper carrying Lt. Frank Mano as if it were making eye-to-eye contact with Lieutenant Mano. The lieutenant saw this and did not understand. Suddenly, in one gesture, the werewolf nodded his head to Lieutenant Mano, as if he were saying, "It's okay, Frank. I forgive you." Lieutenant Mano's eyes started to get watery.

Then the officer said to him, "Sir, your orders." From below, all they could do was watch in fear.

The news reporter said, "Looks like they are about to take action on the werewolf. Again, we will try to bring in as much live feed as we can. What we are witnessing is just complete insanity."

Meanwhile, sitting in his command chopper, Lt. Frank Mano, a decorated police officer of the NYPD, had never in his wildest dreams thought of facing a werewolf. But now a decision had been made to protect the public.

"This is Lieutenant Mano," he said on the police headset. "This is Lieutenant Mano. Fire at will. Fire at will!" The officers on board both choppers heard the order and unleashed a hail of bullets from their high-powered automatic weapons, striking the werewolf over and over as it swung its arms and stepped back.

On the ground, onlookers watched as both choppers fired their weapons at the werewolf and sparks flew from the choppers. Paul, Ellen, and Marie could do nothing but watch in horror.

"No!" screamed Ellen Marco. "Danny!" Hysterically crying, she was no longer able to stand up; she fell to the ground. Marie and Paul tried to shield her from what they were watching above.

"I love you, Danny!" shouted Marie, tears streaming down her face.

Paul was in shock and also crying. He did not see the werewolf getting shot. All he could see was his childhood friend Danny Marco being shot down by a barrage of bullets from the two choppers. The werewolf refused to go down as more bullets hit it. More missed the target. The force of the bullets had pushed the werewolf back; it was nearing the edge of the tower.

"This is News One. The police have begun firing at the werewolf. What a horrific scene we are witnessing. This werewolf is not going down but is getting too close to the edge of the tower."

"This is Lieutenant Mano. Cease fire. I repeat, cease fire!"

The shooting stopped. The werewolf was in a daze; blood oozed from the bullet wounds. Then it roared. But it was a roar of pain as it looked up at the moon. Everyone watching below and on TV started to feel a sadness for the werewolf. With blood pouring from its mouth, it looked up at the full moon and gave off one last howl. Leaning back from the edge of the tower, the werewolf fell backward, straight down, 228 feet, until it hit the dark waters under the bridge and sank into the water.

This is News One reporting live. To those who were watching, we have just seen an ordeal come to a horrible end. The werewolf was shot multiple times by the police with their high-powered weapons, and then it fell from the tower into the dark waters below the bridge. I cannot tell you what I am feeling inside. But I can tell you this. There is absolutely no way anything could have survived that fall. This is News One signing off on this Halloween night. Thank you.

The helicopter carrying Lieutenant Frank Mano landed on the field at Shore Park. Lieutenant Mano was on the police headphones as it landed. "I want all available divers in the water now! Don't give me that bullshit. I saw it fall off the tower, and now I want the body found. That's an order!" He took the headphones off and dropped it. He was playing over and over what he had to do. It hurt him inside, but he had no choice.

Stepping off the chopper, he could see dozens of reporters trying to pass through the police line to speak with him. He did not want to talk to anyone. He needed to step away and clear his mind.

As he was walking away, he heard someone call his name from behind. "Mano!" He turned around, only to get punched in the face. The man who hit him was Detective Paul Corillo.

"You son of a bitch. You killed Danny."

Other officers rushed in and restrained Paul from hitting Lieutenant Mano again. Lieutenant Mano rubbed his face and shook his head. He looked at Paul, who was being held and cuffed by the police.

"No, no cuffs," said Lieutenant Mano. "Release him."

"But, sir, he assaulted you," said one police officer.

"It's okay, son. He is Detective Paul Corillo. I will handle it from here. Now, release him."

They released him, and Paul shook off their hands from him.

"Come with me, Corillo."

"Why?" asked Paul. "So you could shoot me too?"

Lieutenant Mano looked at Paul Corillo with anger. "You struck a superior officer. I could have you locked up right now, and you will never go home. Now come with me."

They started walking toward a police van where other police officers stood. They saluted him, and he saluted back. "Please give us a moment inside the van."

"Yes, sir," said the officer.

The officer opened the door, and Lieutenant Mano stepped in. "Come inside, Paul." Paul stepped in, and the back door was closed. "Sit down." They both sat down. "What the hell is wrong with you, Corillo? Hitting me in front of other officers? I can have you fired, and you can say goodbye to your pension. You couldn't just come up to me, you had to make a scene."

"Fuck that. I don't give a shit about my pension, you fuck. I pleaded on the radio for you not to kill him, but you blew me off. Danny was my best friend. We grew up together. He was my brother. We always had each other's backs. You and the others, we had a brotherhood. We were always there for one another. Then that night at the cabin, I regret every day going there and meeting that bitch Lisa Jacobson. Danny's life was changed forever, and you guys just left him. Only Amato and I stood by Danny. I did everything I could to protect Danny, but it wasn't enough. You saw what happened hours ago at the warehouse. You saw Danny physically change into the werewolf. I know it's too incredible, but we all saw it, and you can't say you did not. But instead of helping Danny, you had to go ahead and take matters into your own hands. All that firepower from the choppers. We all saw it, Ellen and Marie. Everyone saw it. Ellen Marco is a mess. She will never be the same again. But you, this should advance you in your career."

"Enough!" exclaimed Lieutenant Mano. "I've heard enough. I've listened to you, and now you will listen to me. You don't think I have a heart? You don't think that I care? Well, detective, you are so wrong. What did you expect me to do? What we saw tonight was not Danny anymore. It was a fucking werewolf. My God! A werewolf in Brooklyn. How many other states can say that? I had no choice. It had to be done. Even if he had been captured, Danny would have probably changed back to himself, and then he would have been dissected. Is that what you wanted? You think Danny would have wanted that done to him?"

Paul tried to speak, but he was cut short.

"No! You listen to me. This is very tragic. It will haunt me for years to come even after I retire. But I had no choice. It had to be done, and it's over. Now the divers must find the body."

"What?" asked Paul Corillo. "You don't believe it survived that fall?"

"No, I am not saying that, Paul. But the last thing I need is for the body to wash up on Staten Island or, worse, the Jersey shores.

Christ. How am I going to fill out the report without being made a fool at One Police Plaza and higher-ups? This is going to be a long night."

They both took a deep breath.

"Paul," said Lieutenant Mano, "the other werewolf that came through the skylight."

"Lisa Jacobson," replied Paul.

"Well, that's fucking great. Another werewolf in Brooklyn."

"I don't think we will see her again," admitted Paul.

"Are you sure about that?"

"I am very sure. When I saw them together, it almost looked like she was trying to get him to leave with her, but from what I saw, he would not leave, so she got out of there."

"Well, I hope we never see her again," said Lieutenant Mano. "Hey, wait. How did you know it was her?"

"The shape and size," answered Paul. "Everything about that werewolf was female."

There was a knock on the back door. "Yes," said Lieutenant Mano.

The back door opened to more police. "Sir, the divers are in the water and conducting the search."

"Thank you." The lieutenant stood up with Paul. "Have you set up a command center?"

"Yes, sir. Please follow me."

"Paul, I will get back to you later." He stepped out of the van, and they led him to the command center.

Paul stepped out of the van. There were still more people and dozens of reporters waiting to speak to anyone. He walked over to a makeshift tent and stepped in. Ellen Marco was sitting down and being checked by medical, and next to her was Marie. After Ellen was checked, the medic asked them if they wanted any coffee or something to eat.

"Yes," said Paul. "Please. We could all use some hot coffee and food."

"Very well," replied the medic. "I will be right back."

Ellen looked at them both. She was very sad, and her eyes were red from crying after what she had just seen. Marie was the same. She looked at Paul. "What do you have to tell us? Did they find him?"

"The divers are now in the water looking for him. I doubt they will find him."

"You doubt?" asked Ellen.

"I am sorry, Mrs. Marco, but that fall from the top of the tower... We must be realistic. Nothing could have survived that fall."

"Well, until they find him, I am not leaving," she declared.

"It's best for you to go home and rest," Paul suggested. "I will inform you the minute I hear anything."

"No," Marie protested. "We are not going anywhere until his body is found."

Shaking his head, Paul said, "Fine. I will get some cots for you both to sleep on."

The medic returned with food and coffee. "Here you go. Anything else you need?"

"Yes," said Paul. "Please bring us cots and blankets."

"Yes, sir. I will be right back." Looking at his watch, the medic said, "This is going to be a long night."

As the long night hours turned to daylight, the divers started coming out of the water and reported back to a very tired Lt. Frank Mano.

"Report."

"Sir, we searched as far as we could. Divers in Staten Island found nothing."

"Unacceptable. Get a fresh team of divers ready to go in. We must find that werewolf."

"Cancel that order."

"What?" said Lieutenant Mano. He turned around to see the police commissioner.

"At ease, everyone."

"Sir, you cannot just stop the search. I am sure we will find it," Lieutenant Mano reasoned.

"Lieutenant Mano, these men are exhausted," the police commissioner said. "They have been at this all night with no results. My decision stands. The search is over. Send these men home and clear the area immediately."

"Yes, sir." *Damn it*, Lieutenant Mano thought to himself. He turned around and saw Paul coming closer to him. "You heard?"

"Yes. So that's it? His body is gone?"

"I think it's for the best," replied Lieutenant Mano. "I know it sounds cruel, but it's for the best, and you know I am right."

A tired Paul Corillo took a deep breath. Now he must tell Ellen Marco and Marie.

"I would like to come with you and offer my condolences," said Lieutenant Mano.

"Are you kidding me? You are the last person they want to see. Lieutenant Mano, please just give them some space and time."

"Fine."

As Paul started to walk away, another police officer stopped him. "Detective Corillo?"

"Yes," said Paul.

"I have a call for you. Your wife."

"Damn it." *I never got a chance to call her*, he thought. "Thank you." He took the phone while walking back to the tent and spoke with her. "Honey, I am so sorry. I have so much to tell you, and I will."

The news came on with a special report.

> This is News One coming to you live from Shore Park in Brooklyn, New York. For anyone who saw it last night, the NYPD chased this werewolf that attacked the Ginetti crew all the way to Shore Park. It climbed all the way to the top of the tower of the Verrazano Bridge. Police choppers were left with no choice but to shoot it down, and it plunged into the water. Divers searched all night and could not find it. But one question remains. Why did it go after the Ginetti crew?

Every known member of the crew was brutally slain by this so-called werewolf. And last night at a warehouse in Brooklyn, the Untouchable Don, Salvatore Ginetti, and members of his crew were found dead. All the bodies had a huge hole in their chests. The only survivor of this massacre was the wife of Don Ginetti, Josephine Ginetti. Now what she was doing there remains a mystery. We tried to contact her, but family members declined to comment, and they requested she be left alone to mourn the death of her husband.

The most dangerous and powerful man in the New York Mafia is gone. The neighborhoods that he controlled in Bensonhurst and Dyker Heights can now rest easy. For now.

And this now just coming in from One Police Plaza. The identity of the werewolf has been confirmed as former NYC detective, Daniel Marco. From the information we received, there was bad blood between Detective Marco and Nicky Ginetti, who was also killed by the werewolf. He was the nephew of the late Don Ginetti. We are gathering more information on what started this feud, and we will have it shortly.

But until then, Brooklyn owns a debt of gratitude to Detective Marco for putting an end to the Ginetti era. But why dress up as a werewolf? How was he able to run so quickly and leap over cars and people with such agility? One more question remains: How did Detective Marco withstand all that gunfire? Even with a bulletproof vest, it's amazing his body wasn't ripped apart. Our condolences to the Marco family. This will be a Halloween no one will ever forget. On a side note, is this a cover-up by the police, accusing one of their own as the werewolf? Could there really be a werewolf living in Brooklyn? From all the eyewitness reports and videos, you just have to wonder at the possibility. But then again, it was Halloween night.

One last thing to our viewers. If you should wake up in the middle of the night and hear howling in your neighborhood, take my advice and go back to sleep. We will have more coverage on this later in the day.

This is News One.

CHAPTER 17

November 1, 8:00 a.m.

A police car had just parked outside the home of Ellen Marco. Ellen and Marie stepped out of the car. They were both exhausted and tired from last night.

"Can I get you anything before I leave?" asked the police officer.

"No, thank you," answered Ellen Marco. "Thank you so much for driving us home."

"You both have a great day." The officer drove away as they both walked to the front door and opened it. They both stepped in, and Ellen closed the door. They walked over to the sofa, sat down, and leaned back.

"Ellen, I am so sorry for your loss," Marie said. "You didn't deserve this. None of us did. I just cannot get the image of Danny turning into a werewolf out of my mind. It's just so hard to believe what we saw."

"Marie, there are some things in this world that cannot be explained, and this is one of them. I am sorry too. You were going to get married and start a life together." Tears rolled down Ellen's cheeks. "Oh, Danny. May you be in peace, my son. He is now with his father."

"How will I live without him?" Marie wiped the tears from her eyes. "I loved him so much. There were times I just wanted to knock him out with all the jokes he played on me, wearing his werewolf mask when I was stepping out of the shower and scaring me to death.

He was just so much into horror movies, and I constantly told him to grow up. But that's what he liked."

"Yes, he was a child at heart and just wanted to have fun. Can you stay a little bit longer with me, dear? I just don't want to be alone right now."

"Of course, I will. We are still family."

Ellen looked at the phone and noticed the red blinking light. She had twenty unread messages. "Oh dear, I think my daughters might have been trying to reach me last night. I need to call them and let them know."

"Okay." Marie walked over to look outside the window. "Strange."

"What is it?" asked Ellen.

"There are no nosy reporters outside."

"No?"

"I thought there would be, but there is no one outside looking at the house. I find that very odd since the media told the world Danny was the werewolf."

"Well, those nosy reporters better leave me alone. They dare not mess with a hot-blooded Italian," Ellen declared. They both laughed.

Marie was still looking out the window when a car pulled next to the curb. "Oh boy, I think I spoke too soon."

"Who is it?" asked Ellen.

Paul Corillo stepped out of the car and opened the back passenger door, and a dog jumped out and ran to the front door of the house.

"It's Paul and your dog."

Happiness came to Ellen. "Oh, how could I forget my dog?" Marie opened the door, and the dog came running in toward Ellen and jumped on her. "Oh, my little pooch." She hugged and kissed him. She looked up and saw Paul walk in. "Paul, thank your wife for looking after him. It didn't dawn on me to look for him when we came home."

"You had a lot on your mind." Paul closed the door behind him.

"How did you know he was alone in the house?"

"I didn't. A few days ago, my wife was home when she heard the doorbell ring. She opened the door and found him tied to the post with a note on it asking her to take care of him."

"Danny," Ellen muttered.

"Yep, that's what I thought. With all that was going on, he made sure the dog was in good hands and well taken care of."

"Please sit down, and I will make us all tea or coffee."

"Sounds great," said Paul.

"We have a funeral to arrange," Ellen added. "And I need you both with me."

Ellen started to prepare beverages when the dog started barking at her. "I will feed you in one minute," she told the dog.

"He can't be hungry. We fed him an hour ago," Paul said.

"Why is he barking?" asked Marie. From there, the dog ran to the back door and started barking and jumping. "Does he have to go?"

"Strange," Ellen muttered. "The last time he acted like this was when…"

Suddenly they looked at one another and made their way to the back door. Ellen opened the door, and the dog ran quickly to some overgrown bushes. They followed until they saw, lying on the grass, a very dirty and naked man. Danny Marco.

"Danny!" screamed Ellen as she leaned down to pick him up.

Paul and Marie were ecstatic, tears streaming down their faces.

Danny Marco had come home. His werewolf instincts returned him home. He woke up, groggy and tired. "Mom," he muttered.

"Yes, it's me. Thank God you are alive."

They helped him into the house and sat him down on the couch. They quickly got clean rags to wipe the dirt from his face and clean his arms and hands.

"Danny, how are you still alive?" asked Marie.

"Marie," said Ellen.

"No, it's okay," assured Danny. "I should not be alive."

"Jesus Christ!" exclaimed Paul. "Danny, do you have any recollection of last night?"

"Paul, all I remember was getting prodded by Ginetti. After that, everything went blank. What happened to Don Ginetti?"

"He's dead. Your alter ego killed him," Paul answered.

"What?"

"We all saw you change into the werewolf," Paul added.

"Oh, dear God." He buried his face in his hands and then looked at his mother. "Mom, I am so sorry you had to see that. And you too, Marie."

Paul told Danny about the events at the warehouse until the final showdown at the Verrazano Bridge, and how the sharpshooters kept shooting the werewolf until it fell off the tower into the dark waters. Danny was in shock at what he was hearing.

"Danny, I just do not understand. You survived an onslaught of bullets and the fall from the top of the tower. I am sorry, Ellen. But, Danny, there is no way to explain how you are still alive."

"It was the werewolf. He saved my life. That crazy animal saved me," answered Danny.

"Danny, did you know that second werewolf was coming?" asked Marie. "Please tell me the truth. Was she Lisa Jacobson?"

"Yes, she was."

"So you contacted her?"

"No, it didn't happen like that."

"Please, Marie, not now," interrupted Ellen.

"It's okay, Mom. No secrets," assured Danny. "When I was surveying another Ginetti hot spot, I was walking away when I heard someone say my name. I turned around, and it was her. We spoke, and it turns out she was watching every move I made but never made any contact until that day. She knew I was outnumbered and offered to help me."

"In exchange for what?" asked Marie.

Danny looked at Marie. "In exchange that I go back with her to Pennsylvania."

"And you said yes?"

"I did, but I did not mean it." Marie looked away. "Marie, I would never hurt you, and you know it. But I had to say yes so she would help."

"And she did," added Paul. "But after you both took out the Ginetti crew, it looked like her werewolf was trying to get you to leave with her, but your werewolf didn't, if that makes any sense at all."

"It does, Paul."

"And then she was gone," Paul continued.

Danny looked at Marie. "Honey, I still love you. We should get married right away."

Marie looked at him in confusion. "Get married? Are you kidding me?"

"Why not?" asked Ellen. "Don't you still love him?"

"I do," answered Marie. "But there is just one problem that is stopping us from getting married."

From the front door, there was a hard knock. "Attention inside. This is Lieutenant Frank Mano of the NYPD. Danny, we know you are in there. We had the house under surveillance. Please open the door."

"No! I am not losing you again." Ellen stood up.

Danny grabbed her hand. "Mom, it's okay. I am tired of running. The Ginettis are gone. It's over." He looked at Paul. "Buddy, please open the door." He then stood up.

"Danny." Ellen was crying.

"It's okay, Mom."

Marie walked over to Ellen, while Paul went to the front door and opened it. NYPD officers walked in, guns drawn.

"Lower your weapons," Lieutenant Mano ordered. The officers complied.

"I should have known you would not give up," said Paul.

"Stand down, detective," Lieutenant Mano ordered. He walked toward a very tired-looking Danny Marco. He smiled at Danny. "I am happy you are alive, Marco."

"Are you?" asked Ellen.

"Mom!" Danny said.

"It's okay, Marco. I deserved that. But I am happy you are alive. I knew you weren't dead. All that firepower, and here you are. Danny, I am sorry, but I still have a job to do. Officer, please place Mr. Marco in custody."

The officer handcuffed Danny and arrested him.

"We will get you out, Danny," said his mother. Danny was escorted outside, followed by Lieutenant Mano and other police officers into a waiting police car. Then they drove away with Paul, Ellen, and Marie watching.

CHAPTER 18

Taking a deep breath and looking at his interrogators, Danny Marco was totally exhausted. He told them everything, and now he just wanted to sleep. But it was not over yet.

"Well, I told you guys everything. What else is there to tell? I know it sounds fantastic and insane to believe, but it's all the truth. I have no reason to lie."

"No reason to lie? Are you insane?" said the man interrogating Danny Marco, Lt. Robert Gabriel of Manhattan's Internal Affairs.

Lieutenant Gabriel turned to his assistant. "Please turn off the video." And he did. The lieutenant looked back at Danny Marco. His face was turning red. He leaned forward from the table. "Marco, listen to me very carefully. I gave the NYPD 100 percent of blood, sweat, and tears. I made it my mission to put away as many bad guys as I could. I busted my tail every day and night, and I moved up in rank to where I am now. We have been after the Ginetti crew for years. Every time we thought we had them, they would slip through our fingers. Every time we thought we had Don Ginetti, there was another setback, and he would walk out of the courthouse smiling for the cameras. Witness tampering, bribes, and threats—he used everything he had at his disposal to change the outcome of the trial. That's how he got his nickname, the Untouchable Don."

He leaned back and scratched his thinning gray hair and sat back up. "But now, you tell me that after all the police investigations and years of hard work just trying to put away Don Ginetti, it all ended last night. And how? Simple. Danny Marco turned into a werewolf, killed Salvatore Ginetti and his crew, and saved the day. We should pin a medal on your chest!"

"It's not like that," Danny reasoned.

"Stop! I am not done. I don't want to hear this bullshit about a werewolf in Brooklyn. Jesus Christ, Marco. You put me and even the NYPD in a bad way. You are an NYPD detective."

"Former detective," added the assistant.

"Shut up!" screamed Lieutenant Gabriel. He looked back at Danny. "A former detective of the NYPD and now a werewolf with a stupid story about going to Pennsylvania for the weekend, getting bit by something, and becoming a werewolf because you met"—he looked at his notes—"a Lisa Jacobson. And she told you it was your destiny. Are you fucking me? Why don't you just admit you both shacked up?"

"Sir, may I?" interrupted Danny.

"No, you may not! Marco, listen to me. Do you honestly expect me to take this video confession to the higher-ups at One Police Plaza? If I show this to them, I will be laughed at and made a fool of. The commissioner will send me back to patrol, all because you are a werewolf. Tell me, Marco, how stupid do you think I am?"

After taking a deep breath, Danny Marco responded, "Well, sir, with all due respect, you are Internal Affairs."

"Very funny, Marco. So now you are a damn comedian. Very funny. Everyone, laugh. And you guys behind the mirror, laugh. Marco said something funny." He stood up and pointed his finger at Danny Marco. "How is this for a good laugh, Marco? You are done! Charges against you are as follows: public endangerment, avoiding arrest, and murder. You cannot take the law into your own hands, Marco. We have a legal system for that. Yes, the Ginetti crew were bad, but we do need justice to serve our city."

Danny looked at Lieutenant Gabriel. "Justice? You say justice? Tell me, where was the justice for my father when Nicky Ginetti killed him? Did my father get any justice? No! The murder weapon Nicky Ginetti used and my father's blood on Nicky's shirt just vanished from the evidence room. No evidence and then no trial, and Nicky walked out of the courthouse smiling like the prick he was. No justice for my father, and the family business was gone. I have said this over and over—there is a mole in the department. Whoever they are, they have been very slick not to get caught. You need to find this mole and put a final nail in the Ginetti coffin once and for all. My family needs closure."

"Marco, I am sorry for your loss. I never met Peter Marco, but I heard from everyone he was a good man. But as far as a mole in the department, there is no proof that there is one."

"Well, that is why you need to do an investigation," replied Danny.

"And we will. But for now, you will be sent to a holding cell until your trial date. Guard." A police officer came in. "Uncuff him and bring him downstairs to lock up."

As they walked down the corridor, Paul Corillo and Lieutenant Mano came out of the next room. Danny did not say a word to them as they walked past one another.

Lieutenant Gabriel came out of the room with his assistant, and they were confronted by Paul and Lieutenant Mano. Lieutenant Gabriel told his assistant to wait for him by the front desk, and he left, holding his cell phone.

"Are you kidding me? The other guys in there will be all over him," said Paul.

"He will be in a separate cell," the lieutenant assured him.

"Well, that is reassuring," replied Paul.

"What else can I do?" asked Lieutenant Gabriel.

"Take it easy, guys," said Lieutenant Mano. "We are all on the same team."

"Really, Frank?" asked Paul. "Maybe we are, but not him." He pointed at Lieutenant Gabriel. "Remember, he is the rat squad!"

"Paul!" said Lieutenant Frank Mano as Paul walked away.

"Let him go," replied Lieutenant Gabriel. "Why are you still here?"

"Excuse me, lieutenant, but this is still my case," answered Frank Mano.

"*Was* your case, lieutenant."

"What?"

"You are no longer on this case. I have been given full authority by the commissioner. I expect to receive everything you have from the beginning till now on my desk first thing Monday morning. Good night, lieutenant." Lieutenant Gabriel started to walk away.

Lieutenant Mano just looked at him, face turning red, and saying under his breath, "I would love to see that werewolf take a bite out of your ass, you fat fuck!"

As Lieutenant Gabriel walked away, he pulled out his phone. "It's me. Where are you?"

Paul went downstairs to the holding cells. He walked past some cells holding arrested people, and they all gazed at him. He paid them no mind. He kept walking and made a right and continued down the end to a lone jail cell. Inside was a very tired Danny Marco, and outside the cell was his mother, Ellen Marco. She was sad and exhausted. She still could not believe what she had witnessed. Her son Danny was a werewolf. How was this even possible? But it was true. And when she saw him turn into the beast, it was an image she prayed she would never see again. But now, her poor son, a former proud NYPD detective who gave 100 percent to arrest the bad guys, now found himself in the very jail cell he put them in, all because of one very bad guy, Salvatore Ginetti.

May God forgive him for his terror in the neighborhood, but I don't, she thought to herself.

Paul arrived and looked at them. "Are they going to put him away in some nuthouse and experiment on him?" asked Ellen Marco, looking at Paul.

"I don't think they will," answered Paul.

"Right now, only we know who killed Don Ginetti. But the truth will come out soon," muttered Danny. "How much longer do you think it will be before the moon is full again? My alter ego will be on the loose again. It's better to just put me away in a sealed environment so I won't hurt anyone again."

"Danny, please don't say that," pleaded his mother. "There must be a cure for this."

Danny looked at his mother. "Mom, you need to be realistic. What kind of life could I have always worrying I would change into a werewolf during the night? What kind of life would that be for Marie, who would always be scared? Wait a second. Where is Marie? Why isn't she here?" Danny stood up and looked at Paul and his mother. They looked at each other, not knowing what to say to him. "What is going on? Did she get hurt?"

"No, Danny, she didn't," said Paul. "But you need to sit down."

"Fuck that! I have been sitting down long enough. Now, where is she?"

His mother slowly reached into her purse and took out an envelope. "Marie could not be here tonight. Danny, I am so sorry. But she wrote you this letter and asked me to give it to you." She held it out. Danny reached for the envelope. He opened it and took out the folded letter, and something fell to the floor. It was the engagement ring he had given Marie. Tears started to flow from his mother's eyes as he began reading the letter. He heard Marie's voice in his mind.

Dear Danny,

I don't know where to start. So many things are going through my mind. I love you so much. I wanted us to start a life together and raise children and watch them grow up as we got older. But, Danny, all the dreams we planned vanished the night you went to the cabin.

How do you expect us to have a life, knowing deep inside you are a werewolf? I would not be able to embrace you at night while we sleep, kiss you good night, and make love to you. We would not be together on holidays, and if we had children, there is no way of knowing if they would inherit your werewolf DNA. Even if you were given some new drug to help you sleep, the chances of that not working will be a nightmare for both of us. And the thought of locking you up in chains somewhere every night? That would be so wrong and unfair to us.

As you are reading this letter, I am about to board a plane for Dallas, Texas. I accepted a position at a hospital in Fort Worth. I just cannot live in Brooklyn anymore. There are too many bad memories. But I will always cherish what we shared. Please don't try to find me.

I hope and pray someday medical science will find a way to cure you. I will always love you. Please take care of yourself and your mom.

Goodbye, Danny

He looked up after reading the letter, his eyes red. Tears were streaming down his face.

"Brother, I am so sorry," said Paul.

"Danny, she should have stood by you regardless. Running away does not solve anything," his mother reasoned.

"Mom, it's best like this. What kind of life could I give her? It's not fair to her. She did the right thing, and I forgive her," Danny answered.

Ellen's phone beeped. She took it out and saw it was her daughter. She was outside waiting for her. "Why won't she come in to see you?" Ellen asked.

"Mom, please, it's okay." Danny stood up and returned the letter and ring to her. "Please, Mom, take this home." She put them in her purse. "Go, Mom. Get some rest. You need it."

"I will come see you tomorrow, and I will bring your sister with me, or I will drag her out of the house," said Ellen.

"Mom, please just go."

Paul turned and motioned for the night guard. He came and escorted Ellen out as she said, "I love you, son."

"I love you too, Mom," Danny replied.

After they left, Danny walked closer to the bars to talk to Paul without anyone hearing. "Any news from upstairs?"

"Yes. Lieutenant Gabriel is taking over your case."

"What? I thought Lieutenant Mano was in full charge."

"He was, until the commissioner gave full charge to Gabriel. I don't know what will happen next," Paul admitted.

"You must find out where they will move me."

"Don't worry. Right now, you need to get a good night's sleep. And don't worry about the moon. The chart shows no full moon for the next couple of days."

"And then what?"

"We can't know for sure. Danny, I wish I had an answer for you. I will speak with the medic and see if they can give you something strong to help you rest."

"Fuck that! We are running out of time."

"Danny, I can't just bust you out of here, and you know that. My hands are tied. We will get bail for you and bring you home. Danny, you have to see that GoFundMe. Everyone, even people you never met, are sending money to get you out of jail. You are a hero."

"I am not a hero. The NYPD are the real heroes. I just did... No, my alter ego did what he had to do and got rid of the Ginetti crew. By the way, what's going on now since Sal Ginetti was killed?"

"Not much," answered Paul. "His wife had a funeral for him, and he was laid to rest. She had the nerve to say he was a good man. What bullshit! No one will ever know how he died. They have been quiet since his passing."

"So I guess she will not say what she saw at the warehouse?" asked Danny.

"Are you kidding? If she does, she will end up in Bellevue Hospital for sure. The Ginettis are history. Let's all move on. You want some coffee or something?"

"Yes, I could go for some fresh coffee," answered Danny.

"Good. I will be right back."

Paul started to walk away when Danny got up and said, "Wait, Paul!"

"What is it?" Paul came back.

"Paul, I just realized. We never searched the evidence room for the gun and bloody shirt after Nicky was arrested."

"The room was searched. Nothing was found. It's probably long gone. Whoever the mole was, they covered their tracks very well."

"No, Paul. The evidence room must be searched again. Something may have been missed. Paul, please go and search it again and take your time. If you can't find anything, then fine."

"Danny," said Paul.

"Damn it, Paul. Please do it for my family. For my dad. Please, Paul."

Paul took a deep breath. "Okay. I will go there now. I cannot promise you anything."

"I know, Paul."

"Fine. I will be back within an hour." He started walking away.

"Make it two hours," Danny said. "I have no plans tonight." Paul smiled as he walked away.

CHAPTER 19

Walking down the corridor past the jail cells, Paul Corillo left the secure room and went to the elevator. He pressed up. The doors opened, and he got inside. He pressed the button for the third floor, which would take him to the evidence room. As the elevator door closed, the one next to it opened. Lieutenant Gabriel stepped out and walked to the holding cells. He was holding paperwork.

The officer on duty stood up. "How may I help you, sir?"

"I am here to take Danny Marco to a secured location. You will find all the paperwork has been approved."

Confused, the officer said, "Sir, I don't see Lieutenant Mano's approval."

"Lieutenant Mano is no longer in charge. I am. Now, release him to me."

Upstairs, the elevator stopped on the third floor. Paul Corillo stepped out and headed toward the evidence room. He approached the officer on duty and presented his badge and ID. "I'm Detective Paul Corillo. I need to get into the evidence room."

The officer looked at him. "I'm sorry, Detective Corillo, but I can't let you in right now."

Confused, he asked, "Why not?"

"There is one person in there now. He was given private authorization to the evidence room. No one is to enter until he leaves."

"That doesn't make sense," said Paul. "Who is in there?"

The officer gave him the sign-in sheet and pointed to the last name below. He was confused as to why this person was in the evidence room. He put down the sheet, walked away, and took out his cell phone to make a call.

"Lieutenant Mano speaking."

"Frank, it's Paul. Are you still here?"

"Yes. What is it?"

"Can't say on the phone, but can you get to the evidence room as soon as you can? I will explain when you get here."

Back downstairs in the holding cells, Danny Marco had been cuffed and was prepared to leave with Lieutenant Gabriel. "I don't get it," said Danny. "Why are we leaving now?"

"Because, Marco, if we don't, tomorrow the whole area will be flooded with people and media. Plus, we don't know if there is anyone else from the Ginetti crew who is looking to put a bullet in your head. It's best we go now. I am taking you to a secure location until you are released on bail."

Danny was confused. His police instincts started to kick in.

Something was not right.

"Does Paul know?"

"Not yet. But he will be contacted, and he will meet us at the location. Now please shut up and let's go."

They headed out the back entrance to a waiting car. The officer escorting them helped Danny get in the back seat. He then looked at Lieutenant Gabriel. "Sir, are you going to drive him yourself?"

"Son," said Lieutenant Gabriel, "when I was a rookie officer, you were just an itch in your father. I am perfectly capable of driving the prisoner, if that is okay with you?"

"I am sorry, sir," said the police officer.

Lieutenant Gabriel walked around the car, got in, started the ignition, and drove away. Danny was convinced something was wrong, but he did not know why.

Back inside the evidence room, a lone man had convinced the guard on duty that no one else should enter the room. He went to the far end of the evidence room and pulled back a metal shelf. Behind the metal shelf was a wall that looked like a wall to the naked eye but wasn't. He started to scratch off old paint to reveal a keyhole to an old safe that had been forgotten.

He inserted the key, and the lock opened. He opened the door, and brittle paint fell off. Inside the safe was a lone box. He took out the box, but before he could open it, he heard a gun click from behind him. His eyes widened as he heard, "Very slowly, turn around and don't try anything foolish." He turned around.

Paul Corillo and Lieutenant Frank Mano both had their guns aimed at him. "Guys, just let me explain."

"Shut up!" said Paul. "And don't move." He walked over to him and handcuffed him, while Lieutenant Mano still aimed his gun at Lieutenant Gabriel's assistant. He then holstered his gun while Paul opened the box and, to his surprise, found the missing murder weapon that had killed Peter Marco and the bloody shirt of Nicky Ginetti. "You son of a bitch," said Paul. "You were the mole. All these years, we tried to get Salvatore Ginetti, and all the evidence disappeared because of you. And now, Danny Marco is in jail because of you. You are a disgrace to the NYPD." Paul got in his face.

Lieutenant Mano stepped in to pull Paul away and looked at Lieutenant Gabriel's assistant. "I should leave you two alone and let him deal with you. How much did Ginetti pay you? Was it worth it? You betrayed your NYPD brothers. Just wait till Lieutenant Gabriel hears about this. You are finished. Who else is in on this? Tell us now, and maybe we can work a deal. When Lieutenant Gabriel finds out he had a mole right under his nose, he will never show his face anywhere again."

Laughing, the assistant looked at both Lieutenant Mano and Paul Corillo. He knew it was over, and he told them. "Boy, he sure had you guys fooled. After all this time, until now."

They looked at the assistant with confusion. "He?" Paul asked. "Who is it?"

Running out of the evidence room, Paul Corillo made a call to the front desk while Lieutenant Mano escorted the cuffed man to the officer on duty. "Lock this man up," he said, still holding the box with the missing gun and bloody shirt. "He is the mole that has been feeding information to the Ginetti crew."

Looking back at Lieutenant Mano, Paul said, "Gabriel left about half an hour ago with Danny."

"He left?" He quickly called from his police radio. "This is Lieutenant Mano. I am issuing an all-points emergency bulletin for the arrest of Lt. Robert Gabriel!"

*****

Driving away from the police precinct, Danny Marco sat in the back seat of the unmarked police car while Lt. Robert Gabriel drove. Danny's head was down, not looking up. Lieutenant Gabriel looked at the rearview mirror at him.

"Don't worry, kid. Everything will soon be all right. Once we get to the secure location, I will explain everything to you."

"And then what?" asked Danny.

"You let me worry about that. I will take care of this. Do you understand, Danny?"

"Yes." Danny shook his head.

"Good. I like it when people understand. Let's all move on and be happy."

*****

Running out of the police precinct, Detective Paul Corillo and Lt. Frank Mano got into a police car, started the sirens, and sped out. "We are locked on to his GPS," said Lieutenant Mano. "He is heading toward Shore Parkway. Where the hell is he going?"

*****

In the unmarked car, Danny thought about what Lieutenant Gabriel had just said. *I like it when people understand. Let's all move on and be happy.* He had heard this before, but where? He closed his eyes and started to think back. His mind went back to his childhood. He saw himself and Paul when they were kids. He remembered when they walked into Mr. Chin's store, and there was no one there. Then he remembered hearing one man talking, and when they came to the front, he saw Mr. Chin and two other men. He started to remember what the man had said to him and Paul. "Forget what you saw and forget us. Let's all move on, and everyone can be happy." And then the final frame flashed in his mind.

As he and Paul were leaving the store, he never took his eyes off the man who spoke to him. Their eyes were locked on as a young Danny walked past the store window. Now the picture in his mind stopped for that one second, staring at the man inside the store. Those eyes looked back at him, and he remembered those words. He suddenly realized who that man was—the man driving the car, Lt. Robert Gabriel.

Looking up with anger, Danny said, "You son of a bitch! It was you. In Mr. Chin's store, it was you who beat him up and gave me and Paul twenty dollars to not say a word. You are the mole!"

"Ahhh," said Lieutenant Gabriel. "You finally remember. After all these years, you remembered. I have aged somewhat and gained some weight, but I never thought you would remember me. Danny, I watched you grow up to become the man you are. And when I heard you enlisted with the police academy, I honestly didn't think you would make it. But look at you. You made it. From patrol to detective, you made it. I have to say I am disappointed. Why, twenty dollars was not enough? I would have given you more if you asked. But no, you had to become a cop."

"Tell me, how much?"

"How much?"

"Yes, how much did that fuck Don Ginetti pay you to be his mole? You are a disgrace to the NYPD and to everyone! Do you really think you will get away with this?"

"Come on, Danny. I got away with it all this time, and no one ever knew, and no one will ever know. And one more thing, Danny. How much I was paid to be the mole? Not one cent!"

"What?"

"You see, Danny, my name is not Robert Gabriel. My real name is Angelo LaRusso. Salvatore Ginetti was my brother-in-law."

Danny was at a loss for words. The man driving the car, a decorated officer in the NYPD and Internal Affairs, was a Ginetti. How was he able to fool everyone?

"Please, Danny, don't look at me like a bad soap opera. My brother was able to pay off a lot of people to look away and falsify my records. Everyone thought Don Ginetti only had two sisters. We had to change everything. And it worked very well within the department. As far as everyone was concerned, I am Lt. Robert Gabriel."

Danny shook his head. "So you are not taking me to a secure location, then. You think killing me will make things go away, lieutenant? Or should I say Angelo LaRusso? So this is the order from the Ginetti crew, to kill me."

Laughing, Lieutenant Gabriel answered, "You dumb fuck. You just don't get it. There is no one left in the crew. It's just me, and this is personal!"

"What?"

"Danny, I promised my wife I would make this right for the family, and I have to."

"What the fuck are you talking about?"

"Marco, Nicky was my son."

*****

In the police car, Paul Corillo was trying to contact Lieutenant Gabriel on the police radio, but he was not picking up. "Damn it. He has probably gone dark. I just cannot believe it. He's Angelo LaRusso. Our records didn't show Sal Ginetti had a brother-in-law."

"I know," replied Lieutenant Mano. "They kept it quiet all these years. And now we know how Don Ginetti was able to beat the system and walk away free. I can't believe he used NYPD. That's how he was able to hide the murder weapon that killed Peter Marco. That fuck Nicky Ginetti. I can still see that smirk as he walked out of the courtroom. But why now? Why take Danny now? Doesn't he realize that once we catch up with him, he is done? GPS tracker shows he is heading toward the Verrazano Bridge."

A call then came on the police radio. "This is central dispatch calling Lieutenant Mano."

Paul picked up the call. "This is Detective Paul Corillo. Lieutenant Mano is driving, but we can hear you. What do you have?"

"Officers were interrogating Lieutenant Gabriel's assistant. He left out one piece of information that he didn't tell you."

"What is it?" asked Lieutenant Mano.

"Lt. Robert Gabriel is not who he says he is. His real name is Angelo LaRusso, brother-in-law of the late Salvatore Ginetti."

"We know that," said Lieutenant Mano.

"That explains a lot."

"Is there more?"

"There is more, sir. His son was Nicky Ginetti."

"Holy shit!" remarked Paul. "Now it all makes sense. That's why he took Danny tonight. It's revenge for Nicky's murder. He is going to kill Danny tonight!"

"Dispatch, this is Lieutenant Mano. I want choppers in the air tracking the GPS on his car!"

*****

"Nicky was your son," said Danny.

"Yes," replied Lieutenant Gabriel. "And you killed him. You must be punished. I promised my wife. She needs peace."

"Peace? What about my mother? She hasn't had peace since Nicky killed my father. Where is the justice in that? Your son thought he was God!"

"Shut up. I know Nicky was trouble. He always got into fights in school and got suspensions until he was kicked out. Lord knows we tried everything we could to change him. He just would not listen to me! He would tell me his Uncle Sal was a real man and that I was second. I slapped him so hard I knocked his tooth out. And when I heard what happened at the pizzeria and your father, that was it. I was going to ship him out to another state. I was going to take care of it, but my brother-in-law insisted that we wait until things got quiet. But then you had to go to the warehouse that night. You and Corillo and your friend, this so-called werewolf. When we got the news, we were told Nicky had a big hole in his chest, like something had ripped his heart out. He was no angel by a long shot, but he was still my son, my only son. His mother will never be the same again."

"So by killing me, you think this will bring closure to your wife? Gabriel or Ginetti or whatever the fuck your name is, killing me will not bring him back. Turn yourself in now before it's too late." Danny looked from his window. They were driving onto the Verrazano Bridge. "And where the fuck are we going?"

*****

Lieutenant Mano was driving with the police sirens on so the other motorists would move out of his way. They got to the bridge, tracking the GPS signal.

"He's moving fast," said Paul.

"He could be going to Staten Island," replied Lieutenant Mano. "That doesn't make sense."

Paul grabbed the police radio. "This is Detective Paul Corillo. Contact Staten Island Command. Let them know of the situation at hand. Lieutenant Gabriel is to be apprehended. He has a hostage, Detective Danny Marco."

"Confirmed," said Command. "This is central command. Lieutenant Gabriel has crossed the Verrazano Bridge onto the Staten Island Expressway. Eyes in the sky confirm. Other units are moving in, but traffic is heavy."

"So he is not going to Staten Island," muttered Paul.

"Shit!" said Lieutenant Mano. "He is going to Jersey. Once he crosses the state line, we can't pursue anymore! Get in contact with Jersey Command!"

*****

"Jersey, Danny," answered Lieutenant Gabriel. "We will soon be in New Jersey. Oh, and by the way, do you really think I will turn myself in now? Really, Danny. No. Once I get you to Jersey, I will take you to a nice spot I found just for you. And once you are gone, you are looking at the new head of the Ginetti family."

Danny was shocked at what Lieutenant Gabriel had just said. "You? The new man in charge of the Ginetti crew? Are you crazy? How will you even get away with that?"

"Simple, Danny. You see, no one knows of me, so here I am, Lieutenant Robert Gabriel of NY Internal Affairs. And Don Angelo LaRusso, head of the Ginetti crew. Do you understand, Danny? I will play two roles, and no one will know. I will rebuild the gang from the ashes and make us stronger and more fearful. No one will fuck with the Ginettis. And as long Lieutenant Gabriel is in command, the NYPD will always be ten steps behind. Accept it, Danny, you lost, and I won. The Ginettis always win. Damn traffic!"

Danny shook his head. He could not let Lieutenant Gabriel do this to the NYPD. He must do something and fast.

*****

Following with other NYPD cars, Lieutenant Mano was doing his best to catch up and not cause an accident.

"This is dispatch. I have New Jersey Command."

"Acknowledge," replied Lieutenant Mano.

"This is Capt. John Marks of New Jersey Police Command. How may we assist?"

"Captain, this is Lt. Frank Mano, NYPD, and Detective Paul Corillo. We are in pursuit of a black SUV. The individual driving is one of ours, Lt. Robert Gabriel. He has a hostage, former NY Detective Danny Marco."

"Marco?" said Captain Marks.

"Yes, he is the same man. We need your assistance. They are about to cross the state line and must be stopped."

"For what reason?" asked the captain.

"Lt. Robert Gabriel is not who he says he is. His real name is Angelo LaRusso, brother-in-law of the late Salvatore Ginetti."

"Ginetti? How did this happen?"

Shaking his head, Lieutenant Mano responded, "Captain, when this chase is over and Lieutenant Gabriel is in custody, I will send you a full report. I will bring the report myself. But for now, we need your assistance!"

"Understood."

"We will send you the GPS coordinates. And one more thing, I need permission to cross the state line and join the pursuit."

"Not going to happen. We can handle this. We do not need your assistance," replied the captain.

"I did not say you can't handle this, but Marco is an NYPD detective, and he is my responsibility. I would do the same for you."

"Give me a minute," said the captain.

"Fuck," remarked Paul.

"He will get back to us," assured Lieutenant Mano. "We need to get ahold of Gabriel now!"

*****

From behind him, Danny could hear sirens. *They know,* he thought. *The NYPD knows.* "Do you hear that?" Danny asked. "The NYPD is hot on your trail. It's over."

"Shut up!" said Lieutenant Gabriel. "I've come this far and will not be stopped." He continued driving fast, weaving through traffic. The state line was getting closer.

Paul, Danny thought, *if that is you behind us, don't let me down.*

*****

"This is Capt. John Marks, New Jersey Police Command. Authorization to cross state line is confirmed, but only you, no others."

"Understood. And thank you," said Lieutenant Mano. "Paul, call Command. Inform them to call off the pursuit and let them know we have been granted authorization to cross the state line. I just hope we are not too late."

*****

"Garden State Parkway coming up," announced Lieutenant Gabriel. "You see, Danny, I am two steps ahead. No one can catch me. No one! We are home free."

Danny continued to look back as they crossed the state line. Lieutenant Gabriel got off the first exit, driving past other cars. Danny could only pray. Lieutenant Gabriel was driving recklessly.

*****

Driving past the state lines, Lieutenant Mano and Detective Corillo were still on the chase, while other NYPD cars got the order to stop behind the line. From there, Lieutenant Mano was joined by New Jersey State Police as they followed the GPS.

Lieutenant Gabriel was speeding, and all Danny could do was hang on. Gabriel quickly made a right turn down a street to a closed mechanic shop and came to a full stop. With police sirens in the distance, Lieutenant Gabriel jumped out with a gun in hand and opened the back door.

"Get out, Danny," Lieutenant Gabriel ordered. He grabbed Danny with his gun to his head and moved fast to another car. He opened the back door and forced Danny in. Then he got in the driver's side, started the car, and sped out just as the Jersey State Police were racing to where the GPS signal stopped. Lieutenant Gabriel drove down several blocks and then stopped the car in a dark construction area.

Lieutenant Mano arrived with Paul to where the chase ended. Jersey State Police were already there. An officer turned and walked up to them as they got out of their car.

"Lieutenant Mano, I am Captain Marks. The trail ended here. But no one is in the car."

"What?" asked Paul.

"Gabriel must have switched cars and got away," said Lieutenant Mano.

"So we lost them," replied Paul Corillo.

"Take it easy," said the captain. "We have ordered all state police to check all vehicles from this area and farther out."

"Danny will be dead by then," replied Paul.

"I am sorry," offered the captain. "We are doing the best we can."

"It's okay," assured Lieutenant Mano. "Please keep us informed."

"I will." The captain headed back to the other officers.

"I cannot believe this," remarked Paul. "That fuck Gabriel or LaRusso or whatever his name is, he's going to kill Danny. How the hell are we going to find him now?"

"Paul, I have a feeling Lieutenant Gabriel is in for a big surprise, and it should be coming up now," said Lieutenant Mano.

Paul turned and looked at him. "What are you talking about?"

"Look up at the night sky."

They both looked up.

"A full moon. Jesus," exclaimed Paul. "There was not going to be a full moon tonight." They both looked at each other and smiled. Paul looked up again and shouted, "Danny, he is the last one! Finish this, Danny. Finish this tonight! Rip his fucking face off."

*****

Back inside the car, Lieutenant Gabriel said, "You see, Marco, I win again. The Ginettis never lose. You fucked with the wrong people, Marco."

Danny had his head down until he saw a brightness coming from the windshield. At first, he thought it was a sensor light at the construction site, but then he took a good look. "The moon, it's out. But my charts said no moon."

"Yeah, your charts," said Lieutenant Gabriel. "I did some editing on your charts to confuse you. So what's next? The werewolf is coming to save your life? Let him come. I will blow his brains out!"

Danny started to laugh as he put his head down and closed his eyes.

"What are you laughing at, Marco?" Suddenly Lieutenant Gabriel's mobile phone rang. "Who the fuck is this? Mano! keep your mouth shut, Marco." He answered the phone. "Lieutenant Gabriel speaking."

"Gabriel, or should I say LaRusso, it's Lieutenant Mano."

While they were speaking, the power of the full moon started to fuel Danny's body. He was shaking, and sweat ran down his forehead. He started breathing heavily. The change was coming, and this time, Danny welcomed it. Lieutenant Gabriel did not even see what was happening to Danny. His head was down as he talked to Lieutenant Mano, but when he looked up, it would be the very last thing he would ever see again.

"Gabriel, or should I say Angelo LaRusso," said Lieutenant Mano, "your ass is about to get bit."

"What the fuck are you talking about?"

Suddenly he heard a deep growl. He dropped his mobile phone and looked up at the rearview mirror. His eyes were wide open and his mouth quivering. He was not seeing Danny Marco anymore. What he was seeing was the face of the werewolf.

He turned to look in the back. The werewolf's red eyes opened, and it lunged for Lieutenant Gabriel. He screamed, and a howling followed.

EPILOGUE

A lone man was driving a Jeep, making his way to a familiar place. It was early in the morning. The sun was up, and the sky was blue. The lone man was getting closer and closer to his destination.

As much as he did not want to come here since that one night, he felt a calling to be here—to be at the cabin where his life had changed forever. Never did he think he would come back, but Danny Marco came back.

He stepped out of the Jeep and walked to the cabin, but he did not go in. He looked around until he heard sounds from the bushes next to the trees. He looked toward the bushes and saw Sebastian Jacobson and his daughter, Lisa, come out. Danny was not surprised to see them at all. Following them were several other people. Danny just looked at them. They made their way to the Jeep and stopped.

But Lisa Jacobson walked closer to Danny and then stopped. They just looked at each other, not saying a word. Then Lisa Jacobson smiled at him. "Danny, my love, welcome home."

The End?

ALTERNATE ENDING

Newark Liberty International Airport

A man was waiting to board a plane. He checked in, went to his seat, sat down, and put on his seat belt. The plane prepared to depart. The captain spoke on the intercom, informing the passengers that the plane was ready for takeoff. Within minutes, the plane was in the air.

After two hours in the air, the captain said, "Thank you for flying American Airlines. We hope you had a comfortable flight. Please fasten your seat belts. We will soon be landing at DFW Airport in Dallas, Texas."

The plane landed. After several minutes, the man went to claim his baggage. After retrieving his suitcase, he walked out of the security gates. He saw his ride. The driver was holding a sign with his name on it. He walked to the driver, showed his ID, and then got in the car. The driver got in and drove them away.

Thirty minutes later, the man arrived at his hotel and checked in, and then went back to the car that had driven him to the hotel. He was driven to a house for sale in Grapevine, Texas. He stepped out and told the driver to come back in an hour. He went up to the house, stood at the front door, and rang the bell.

The door was opened by a beautiful lady with a real estate office badge on her dress. She smiled and said, "Welcome to Texas, Mr. Marco. Hope you had a great flight."

"I did," Danny Marco replied as he entered the house.

The agent showed him the entire house. He said, "Yes, I will buy this."

"Excellent. Let me get the paperwork in my car."

As the agent was about to walk out, Danny stopped her. "Excuse me. Out of curiosity, are there any wolves that come by at night?"

"Wolves? There haven't been any reports of wolves here in over fifty years. Why do you ask? I would be terrified."

"Terrified? You shouldn't be. Wolves are misunderstood and highly intelligent creatures. They could be your protector and best friend." Danny Marco smiled at the agent standing by the doorway.

"I see." She smiled back at him. "Please give me a minute to get the paperwork." She turned and walked out the door to her car.

Danny Marco was standing by the door, watching her walk away. Smiling, he kept watching her walk to her car. Then, he looked up, and his eyes were glowing red.

The End

ABOUT THE AUTHOR

Luciano Di Giallonardo was raised in Brooklyn, New York. His family came from the Province of L'Aquila, Italy, in the Abruzzo region and is very proud of his Italian heritage. His favorite dish is marinara sauce over angel hair pasta. He loves Italian cannoli and gelato, and he is a fan of classic horror and gangster movies.

Printed in the USA
CPSIA information can be obtained
at www.ICGtesting.com
LVHW092158300124
770443LV00034B/373